T0158783

MYSTERY OF
THE STURBRIDGE KEYS

MYSTERY OF THE STURBRIDGE KEYS

CHRISTMAS UNLOCKED

LINDA HOURIHAN, HHCP

MYSTERY OF THE STURBRIDGE KEYS
CHRISTMAS UNLOCKED

This is a work of fiction. All of the characters, names, incidents, organizations, and dialogue in this novel are either the products of the author's imagination or are used fictitiously.

iUniverse books may be ordered through booksellers or by contacting:

iUniverse
1663 Liberty Drive
Bloomington, IN 47403
www.iuniverse.com
1-800-Authors (1-800-288-4677)

Because of the dynamic nature of the Internet, any web addresses or links contained in this book may have changed since publication and may no longer be valid. The views expressed in this work are solely those of the author and do not necessarily reflect the views of the publisher, and the publisher hereby disclaims any responsibility for them.

Any people depicted in stock imagery provided by Thinkstock are models, and such images are being used for illustrative purposes only. Certain stock imagery © Thinkstock.

ISBN: 978-1-5320-0761-3 (sc)
ISBN: 978-1-5320-0762-0 (e)

Library of Congress Control Number: 2016915515

Print information available on the last page.

iUniverse rev. date: 04/29/2017

"To be ignorant of the lives of the most celebrated men of antiquity is to continue in a state of childhood all our days."

Plutarch

"There is only one race, the human race."

Author Unknown

"God is closer to you than your next breath."

Linda Hourihan, HHCP

CONTENTS

DEDICATION

This book is dedicated to my grandchildren, Kevo and Liam Kearsley, Chris and Alex Eppley, and Rory and River Bibeau. You are the impetus for this book.

My love surrounds you everywhere you go. It is my joy to be with you and share life with you. The best thing I can share with you is my life journey. The journey of my life has a very strong spiritual and religious side. That has been my path, the way I learned and applied what I learned through this life. For me, having God in my life is the only reason for everything in life. God is the filter, the lens through which I see all things, measure all things, and make sense of all things. Without God, nothing makes any sense.

My experiences in life demonstrate to me that there is God, the Creator of science and first impetus of all seen and unseen things. Jesus is a real historical person, the first Creation of God's love before he came to earth. God and his active force, which we know as the holy spirit of God, is available to you and to me when we live our lives in the way God originally intended for all Creation. God and Jesus are worth getting to know.

This book is also dedicated to my children, Keith Kearsley, Marie (and Anthony) Paturzo, Kevin (and Nikki) Kearsley and Katie (and Steven) Bibeau; and my grown step-children, Mandy (and John) Eppley, and Mike (and Chrysanthi) Hourihan.

No matter where you go in this life, my love will find you there also, sharing moments and pleasures whenever life allows it.

I hope you enjoy this book, which took me over a year to research and a lifetime to experience. You can take from that what you will.

There are more in my family who have requested not to be mentioned. If you ever change your minds, let me know, and I will write and dedicate a book to you too, based on love. Love is the only thing that matters, and the measure of how well we live this one life we get.

FOREWORD

This book is inspired by a set of large keys handed down to me from my grandfather, F. Louis Tetreault. I am sure these keys went to the farm on Blackstone Street, Mendon, Massachusetts, either to the barn, locked chests, equipment, or to the house both he and my grandmother, Maria (Benoit) Tetreault lived in. My mother is number thirteen of fourteen children. Mom, aunts, uncles and cousins, my extended family, I love you all. I am so glad my Canadian French grandparents had so many children, or else I would not be here, or have had so many cousins to make my childhood so happy.

Or the keys might have belonged to my grandparents' Vermont cottage or the shed on Sheldon Hill Road, with the Wardsboro Brook directly behind it, where my sister, cousins and I would brave the icy waters flowing into our tiny, dammed up swimming spot. When I was young, I would often spend weeks and months living with them in their home away from home, while my mother, as a single parent, worked full time painting radon on watch hands so they would glow in the dark. Both my beloved grandparents have since passed away, and were very dear to me. I treasured them and everything about them, even these keys.

I am married to the most wonderful husband in the world, John T. Hourihan, Jr. As a published author of three books himself, he is an award winning newspaper columnist in northeast USA, and former copy editor for local newspapers. He has taken me on countless trips to my childhood Vermont retreat cottage of my grandparents.

Just seeing this place brings a smile to my heart, remembering the wintery days when it was so cold that the snow froze hard enough for me to ice skate on, and the smell of the huge cast iron, wood burning cooking and heating stove.

If I close my eyes, I can see the round wooden kitchen table with aunts, uncles and cousins seated around it, playing a game of Canasta. I remember when I was three years old, as if it were yesterday, when unknown to me, Pepere would place a real egg under my wooden pull toy chicken, in the summertime. Memere would have me check to see if the chicken laid an egg each morning, just outside the front door of the house. It was always there. I remember wondering why the egg was so cold on warm mornings!

There were swings in the two-seater, wooden swing with Memere, always saying the rosary, and walks with Pepere up the once dirt road after dinner to see deer in the meadow. I remember seeing Pepere fishing on the river's edge, and Memere frying fish up for his breakfast.

There were cousins just across the Wardsboro River in the back yard, narrow at this point, which we crossed by walking across the larger stones in the river. There were more sets of cousins further down the river where we occasionally had cookouts. Depending on the attitude of the river, we would spend time walking around on the larger stones elevated above the rushing river, now more expansive and challenging.

Cousins without cabins, from Massachusetts to Mississippi, also escaped to Memere and Pepere's Vermont getaway.

All of these treasured memories my husband helps keep alive by visits to my home away from home, still in the exact same beautiful condition as I remember it, with the apple tree out front and the icy Wardsboro River flowing in the back yard. My single-board seat, homemade swing used to hang from the old forest pine tree near the river. Now this seat is a welcome sign on my front porch.

I wish to thank my husband for his loving patience, encouragement and editing skills, transforming my dream to write this book into reality.

My husband is the author of *PLAY FAIR AND WIN, BEYOND THE FENCE CONVERGING MEMOIRS*, co-authored with Amanda Eppley; and his latest novel, *THE MUSTARD SEED: 2095.*

Now that I am a grandmother myself, I find myself on the flip side of life, now enjoying my grandchildren, taking them to Old Sturbridge Village in Sturbridge, Massachusetts, sharing rides with them in the Hartford–Worcester Stagecoach, or the horse drawn trolley, which to this day is drawn by the Belgian horse team of Jim and Jerry. The animals at Old Sturbridge Village are the only names I retained for this work of fiction. All other names have been changed.

The book's timely publication covers the April 20, 2016 announcement by the United States Treasury planning to put Harriet Tubman's picture on the front of the $20 bill, moving President Andrew Jackson to the back by the year 2020. Fascinating information between President Abraham Lincoln and Charles Darwin is also included in this work of fiction.

The names of Old Sturbridge Village including all of the buildings at this location, and the Christmas by Candlelight celebration are real. However, I have never attended the Christmas by Candlelight celebration, and the adventures in this book are pure exciting fiction.

Also real names in this area are: Thai Place, Annie's Country Kitchen, The Bird Store and More, Southwick's Zoo, McLean Hospital, Harrington Hospital, B.T.'s Smokehouse, and the Sturbridge Tourist Center.

PREFACE

Grammy Rose takes her four grandchildren and two daughters to celebrate the 70ᵗʰ Anniversary of Old Sturbridge Village of the 1830s. They attend the annual Christmas by Candlelight celebration. Time Travel is the way they all learn history, ancient history, pre-history and Bible prophecy, by using antique keys to unlock antique books, and their minds.

The family lives on Grammy Rose's beloved shores of Lake Nipmuc in Mendon, Massachusetts. While Southwick's Zoo is a major tourist attraction in Mendon, the cultural exchange program between Old Sturbridge Village and Southwick's Zoo mentioned in the context of this book is fictional.

The over-all theme of this book is based on a famous quote from Plutarch, "To be ignorant of the lives of the most celebrated men of antiquity is to continue in a state of childhood all our days." This theme echoed in todays' more modern, popular quote by an unknown author today also applies, "There is one race of people, the human race."

Brie is the female, thirteen-year-old protagonist of the story, who struggles with belief in God. Her grandmother has a strong belief in God, while her Aunt Cher does not. She discusses her thoughts and feelings with her cousin and best friend, Abby. Brie's crisis of faith reaches its climax when she discovers firsthand how Christmas begins in the days of Nimrod and Ishtar, while she attends the Christmas by Candlelight celebration at Old Sturbridge Village in current time. Brie and Abby share their thoughts, ideas, feelings and suspicions as they each come to their own conclusions as they time travel through history, pre-history and ancient history.

The family gets split up in the workshops at Old Sturbridge Village. While some of them time travel to the past, the others go into the conference and welcome centers, houses, bank, farm house, barns, taverns, parsonage, Quaker and Center Meetinghouse pottery and blacksmith shops, via horse drawn sleigh and stagecoach. History comes alive as they learn little known facts about the Underground Railroad, connections between Abraham Lincoln and Charles Darwin, Charles Dickens, the Panic of 1837, the Rev. Adin Ballou, the Flood and ice ages, angels, Nephilim, Noah, Nimrod and Ishtar, and how the Babylonian, Mede-Persian, Greek and Roman Empires came to be. Everything they learn reveals the secret Old Sturbridge Village in the 1830s has discovered.

CHAPTER 1

CHRISTMAS BY CANDLELIGHT

As the first rays of sun greet Brie through the window, she bounces out of bed, and shakes Abby to see if she is awake. Abby's sleepy eyes are suddenly wide open, with the promise of Grammy Rose's surprise to take them, their brothers and mothers to Old Sturbridge Village today. Thirteen year-old Brie and her nine year-old brother, Greg, slept over their cousin's house last night, adding to the excitement. Abby heads directly to her eleven-year-old twin brother, Abe's room to make sure everyone is awake. Greg's hyperactive sleep kept jostling him since it was dark, with the promise of the day that lies ahead of them. Today is the day they had been waiting for. Grammy Rose is taking them to Old Sturbridge Village, celebrating its 70th Anniversary this year. They love this yester-year village, complete with its horse-drawn carriage ride, homemade candy and candles, and neat buildings where the millers, bakers, bankers, and artisans work. They enjoy going from the farming fields, filled with oxen plowing deep furrows, and people planting in the springtime, to the shooting range where the would-be 1830's soldiers fire their muskets at practice targets in the autumn. The Village, as they call it, is fun, but being with Grammy Rose is more so. Everything with Grammy Rose is an exciting adventure.

This is the first time they are going to Old Sturbridge Village for the Christmas by Candlelight celebration. Grammy Rose discovered the Village is having a special holiday turkey dinner with cranberry sauce made from the very cranberries all four grandchildren personally picked from the Village cranberry bog last month. The dinner is to be lit by the homemade beeswax candles they helped make at their last visit, when they dipped their strings into melted beeswax over and over until the long, slender candles were judged perfect. The beeswax is also from the beekeeping area in the Village, next to the large herb garden and behind the hands-on crafts center they love so much.

The meal is to conclude with a Gingerbread House Contest and storytelling about how Christmas came to be around a huge fireplace in the most prosperous family's home, Salem Towne House, the largest house in the Village. Grammy Rose doesn't know who likes Christmas more, her grandchildren, or herself.

"Hey Abby! What are you doing?" Abe yells, as his sister jumps up and down on his bed. Abe trampolines half-way to the ceiling with every bounce.

Brie copies the antics of her cousin, landing on the feet of her once airborne brother.

"Wake up! Wake up! Today's the day!" Abby squeals, unable to contain her delight, finally landing her butt on the foot of the bed.

Abner Thomas and Abigail Rose Le Beau have more than one thing in common, but perhaps the most obvious is their brilliant and beautiful red hair, a hand-me-down from Grammy Rose. Grammy Rose is proud of her full name, Danielle Rose Rousseau, and proud to say she is all French. Her genealogy traces back to Quebec, Canada and before that to Bretagne, France. The whole family is all French. Grammy Rose used to speak Canadian French, but she has no one to speak it with now. But that red hair dubbed her Rose from childhood on, so Grammy Rose it is.

Somehow, the red hair gene missed their mother, Cher Marie Le Beau, who was born with dark brown hair, and a touch of her mother's natural curls. Both the twins are blessed with the red hair ending in curls, which warms Grammy Rose's heart. Oddly enough, Grammy Rose, Abe and Abby's hair matches their personalities to a "T," determined and stubborn, yet somehow carefree and generous, with a magnanimous spirit, and an inquisitive curiosity that knows no bounds. Cher's personality is much more mellow, protective and cautious.

Brie and Greg cannot be more different from each other. Brie's long blonde tresses topping her long and lanky, graceful body are quite a standout to Greg's curly dark hair on his stout body with its hyperactive, attention deficit mind.

"It's funny how some things seem to skip a generation, like Brie, Abe, Abby and my fascination for all things old, mysterious puzzles, and how things work. Cher likes the modern and innovative, like Greg, quick to decisions and novel approaches. Our family is so close, yet so different. I am very religious, always seeking what the Bible really teaches. But Sarah and especially Cher don't seem to have the quite the same interest," Grammy Rose thinks.

This past August, Cher had greeted her mother, "What a beautiful sunny morning," as her Mom made her way up the three wide cement stairs, bordered by a prolific herb and flower garden on each side.

"This morning I made us some mint and chamomile tea from the herb garden," Cher welcomed.

"Thanks for the early morning invitation. The mint and chamomile smell so fragrant," her Mom said, taking a refreshing sip in the cool morning before the heat of the day set in.

"You asked me the other day if I minded you speaking to the kids about God. I've been thinking about that. I figure this is a good opportunity, and we can have breakfast in the process," Cher said, bringing up the subject and taking hot cinnamon buns out of the oven.

"Sounds delicious to me." Her Mom smiled.

"Well, about God, I figure when it comes to religion, Abby and Abe can make up their own minds. You know I do not believe in God. I've already spoken to them about my beliefs. They will observe my life, and they'll observe yours. Since Andre died, I don't believe in God anymore. God certainly did not listen to my prayers. It doesn't matter to me. They will figure it out. And I do like that you share your life with them. It keeps it all real." Cher took a long drink from her tea and her thoughts.

"I personally don't want to get stuck in arcane and organized religion, except for Christmas and the holidays. I do love making homemade fudge, Christmas cookie trays for the neighbors, and decorating with festive lights, evergreens, and yule logs for every table in the house. I try to keep our family tradition alive since Andre's passing, of getting the

Christmas tree from Kelly's Tree Farm. That's a family tradition as far back as Abby and Abe can remember," Cher added.

"I remember the year I went with all of you to pick out a tree. The kids had so much fun. But they were hard to keep up with," Rose chuckled.

"Yes. Abe and Abby pick out a half a dozen Scotch pine and Blue Spruce trees on the lot. Then I choose the best tree among them for the house. I like to choose the tallest and widest, and most fragrant tree possible, which usually means the Scotch pine since they are the most fragrant," Cher reminisced, a melancholy smile gracing her lips.

Before his untimely death, Andre Pierre Le Beau used to carry out the time honored tradition of hand sawing the tree, and carrying it out on his shoulder, or pulling it on a blanket. Tying it to the roof of the car and getting it to stay there was another fiasco they fondly remembered.

To this day, once at home Abe and Abby begin stringing popcorn and cranberries together for authentic decorative strands of garland, fingers sticking together and their T- shirts dyed red from seeping cranberry juice. They like alternating these strands on the tree with their famous green and red construction paper circle garland, and homemade ornaments created from last year's Christmas cards featuring glue and glitter galore.

Not even the death of the twin's father four years ago draws Cher into any kind of formal religion, as much as Grammy Rose prays. Cher remains insulated from religion, seemingly as a kind of self–preservation, in order to be firmly grounded in reality.

"Let's pack a picnic lunch and hike up to Mount Wachusett today," Cher had said on that fateful day.

"I'll get the backpacks and gear out of the shed," Andre responded, smiling on his way out the door.

"I'll make sandwiches," Abby said, as her brother raced for the bread.

After the two-hour drive on some slippery roads on the way, the Le Beau family, with Grammy Rose in tow, parked at the lower parking lot at the base of the mountain.

"It still looks slippery from that early frost that snuck in last night," Grammy Rose said.

"Yes, I bet the trail might still be slippery too," Cher said, "until it warms up and melts."

"I want to take the extreme hike, the one along Outer Rim Trail," Andre announced. "Why don't you and your Mom and the twins take the meandering trail up the easy side of the mountain? I'll meet you at the Crag Ridge Lookout picnic tables. I have my cleats on. It's not much longer in time. You will have longer to hike, and I'll take my time at the cliffs. We ought to meet each other around the same time. Just be careful everyone."

All agreed it was a good plan.

Sirens blared as Grammy Rose, Cher, Abe and Abby were halfway up the other side of the mountain. Grammy Rose got an eerie feeling in the pit in her stomach and glanced at Cher, who froze in her spot. Their feelings were not the only things that froze. The ground below their feet had become a frozen nightmare. If the cliffs on Outer Rim Trail were as slippery as this terrain, then Andre could be in serious trouble.

Eight pairs of trembling legs slid, jostled and somehow made it back down the mountain. Hikers they came across where the two trails met said there was a mountain lion that had come upon a hiker on Outer Rim, who had gone off the trail. They saw the hiker fall off the cliffs, which had become shear ice. They also said they saw the mountain lion get scared off into the tree line.

By the time they got to the bottom of the trail, ambulances, police and fire personnel were all around the crumpled body. Grammy Rose grabbed the twins and held them close, while Cher pushed past the onlookers to see her lifeless husband. She collapsed. EMT's rushed to her, and brought her, her children and her mother to McLean Hospital for treatment for shock. Like Mount Wachusett, it is also in the town of Princeton. They all benefitted from McLean's attention to trauma and separation anxiety, and Cher's soon to be panic attacks.

Life was never quite the same after Andre's death, but Rose took it upon herself, these past four years, to help Cher and her grandchildren out as much as possible. Today's visit to the Old Sturbridge Village Christmas by Candlelight celebration is just the thing to brighten their moods.

"The twins are going to love today and so will their cousins," Grammy Rose thinks. *"They love Old Sturbridge Village, and they love Christmas, so this will be a grand adventure."*

"Surprise!" Grammy Rose greets as she arrives at her older daughter, Sarah Anne Benoit's house. Not only did her two daughters live in Mendon like she did, Sarah and Cher had also chosen to live on the shores of her beloved Lake Nipmuc. The sisters and their families had settled on either end of Taft Avenue, making a short walk from house to house, with the Mendon Town Beach smack in the middle of them. Grammy Rose lived in the red house on the hill overlooking the lake on Uxbridge Road, closer to Lakeview Park, but still within walking distance to both her daughters and their families. Beautiful breezes blew all summer long through Grammy Rose's sunroom windows, cooling the entire house where the girls grew up.

"Are you ready for a real Old Sturbridge Village adventure?" Grammy Rose asks Sarah, as her daughter opens the front door of her quaint Cape home on the soothing shores of Lake Nipmuc.

"Yes. The kids are also so excited about this. None of us have ever been to the Christmas by Candlelight celebration before. The kids slept over at Cher's house last night. You know how they love that. Renee is off on a business trip, but I'm still free," Sarah responds.

Although Sarah does not like how her husband always has to take trips for work, she does enjoy these times with her sister and mother that allow them to stay close, especially these days near the holidays.

Renee Sebastian Benoit is the king of the world to Brie. She is Daddy's girl. Everyone knows it. Brie observes her father feeling the weight of the world on his shoulders since Uncle Andre died. She does all she can to make him happy, which is pretty easy since he is a jovial, positive, forward thinker. She notices he is hardworking with a larger than life, compassionate spirit. She admires that. Her Dad never complains. Uncle Andre was her Dad's closest friend. Brie watches her Dad lend a helping hand in any way he can, with groceries, clothing shopping sprees, trips, and money. She admires him for being such a good role model.

In her heart, Grammy Rose knows how much Abby looks up to Brie, who is already in junior high school. Brie loves history almost as much as she loves reading books about time travel. Brie and Abby are very close. They love to share secrets, especially from their brothers. Though there is only one and one-half years between their ages, they seem as alike as the twins themselves. When they aren't giggling over the antics of their brothers, they can be found reading books together in the hammock hanging between the two towering Eastern Hemlock trees in Grammy Rose's back yard in warm weather days.

This past summer Grammy Rose was watering her garden in the sunny spot on the side of her house which sits high above Lake Nipmuc across the street, when she overheard Brie and Abby talking.

"What are you reading today?" Brie asked Abby. They both had one leg over each side of the large hammock, like ragdolls.

"I'm reading *Time Travelling with a Hamster*, by Ross Welford. Al has a hamster who travels back in time with him. What I like about it is that even though Al's father died, he left Al a time machine that he built in a bathtub. Al wants to go back in time to try to change the future so his father doesn't die, but he's afraid of what might happen if he changes the future. You know. What's your book about?" Abby asked.

"I picked up a time travel book too. That's my favorite kind of book. Mine is, *A Traveller in Time*, by Alison Uttley. I love it. Penelope visits a hidden library and goes back in time to England, during the reign of Queen Elizabeth I. Penelope is torn between freedom and fate. She has to decide whether or not to help free Mary, Queen of Scot from prison. You know how I love hidden library stories," Brie said that day.

Toot. Toot. Toot, honks Grammy Rose's Honda Pilot SUV coming up the Le Beau's driveway, complementing the choir of crows breaking the silence of the dawn. In no time, the SUV is loaded with its passengers. Brie and Abby get in quickly so they can sit together. Greg, not wanting to be outdone by his older sister races to beat her.

"Calm down Greg. Get in your seatbelt," Brie's Mom cautions. "You are in charge of your energy. You have to tell it to listen to you today, so we can all have a good time. You don't want your energy to get you into trouble."

Greg knows how his energy gets him into trouble all the time. He is going to try harder today, and prove to his Mom that he is just as grown up as his sister, or at least as grown up as his twin cousins.

"This Honda Pilot is the best investment I made since I retired," Grammy Rose thinks. She spent her working life a holistic health counselor/ practitioner.

The next thing Brie knows, Grammy Rose's eight seat SUV is filled with Abe, Greg, her Mom, Aunt Cher, herself, Abby and Grammy Rose as the driver. The extra seat is always available in the unexpected event that her Dad might possibly come along one day.

The first traditional stop of the day's adventure is an early morning breakfast at Annie's Country Kitchen on Main Street in Sturbridge, their favorite breakfast place on their way to the Village. They have a whole day for adventures before the Christmas by Candlelight celebration tonight. Their favorite store in the area is The Bird Store and More on Cedar Street.

"Hey Mom," Brie's Mom says excitedly. "I'm getting you this bear proof galvanized bird feeder pole. Remember you told me last year the black bears destroyed all four of your bird feeders?"

"Yes I do. I miss feeding the birds. I'm afraid I will be enticing the black bear to come around again," Grammy Rose responds.

"Grammy Rose, look at this." Brie points to a computer set up near the bear proof bird feeder. "It shows black bear trying to get at the feeders on this pole, but it has no luck."

"It says the black bear come around less often, now that they know they cannot successfully get at the black oiled sunflower seed," Abby adds.

"Can we go to that big building where I got some used books last year?" Brie asks once back in the Pilot.

"That's a good idea. There are many antique shops, a little further down Route 20," Grammy Rose says, pointing the Pilot in that direction.

Brie and Abby head straight for the book section, deciding on which books would make for great summer time reading in the hammock. Brie hits the jackpot with an ancient history book filled with pictures. Abby picks up another time travel book. Grammy Rose manages to find a cast iron skillet to add to her collection. Aunt Cher and her mother successfully bargain with a dealer who is willing to let books go for a quarter each. Abe and Greg are in their glory with a worn in baseball glove, and not so worn board games. The day draws on with rays of sun glistening on blankets of new fallen snow, slowly transmuting into dark shadows peeking out behind tall trees etching the road as the day wears on.

The Pilot winds its way past the old forests of Sturbridge, turning off Route 20 onto Stallion Hill Road towards the Museum Main Entrance across from the Sturbridge Tourist Center, BT'S Smokehouse on one corner and Thai Place with the best Pad Thai in the world around on the other. Although Pad Thai is Brie's favorite, her brother is deathly allergic to peanuts. Grammy Rose drives past her favorite restaurant straight to the Christmas by Candlelight celebration, just a stone's throw from there.

Once at Old Sturbridge Village, today's light dusting of snow atop yesterdays' unexpected snowfall sets a perfect backdrop to the evergreen garland and red bows lining the path to the spacious parking lot. The heavy scent of pine lingers in the air.

"Follow the greeters with the oil lamps to the Oliver Wight Tavern," Sadie directs, part of the Village staff awaiting this evening's guests on the sidewalk entrance. She hands them each a map of the grounds and continues her instructions for the night.

"There are a lot of fun adventures in each of the buildings in the Village this evening. There is no particular order to the workshops tonight. After your meal, you can stop in the Fuller Conference Center for an educational talk, or you can walk through the exhibits and displays at the Visitors Center, next to the Clock Gallery. You are all invited to go outside onto the dirt roads packed with snow into the Village. Stay straight, and you will walk past the Friends Meetinghouse on the right. That is where our Quaker friends hold their Sunday meetings. You can learn about the Underground Railroad program taking place at the Friends Meetinghouse. A lot of history is explained in each of the buildings tonight," Sadie welcomes with a big smile, sweeping her arm toward the tavern.

Each window in the Oliver Wight Tavern glows with a beeswax candle securely set in a tin candle holder Brie remembers being made in the Tin Shop earlier in the year. As she walks towards the warm flickering candles, Brie observes the Victorian carolers singing outside as they line the walkway and complement this picturesque scene. She and Abby join their voices in Christmas carols as they enter the Tavern. Grammy Rose hands the Mrs. Cratchit's Christmas Dinner Invitation to Brie to present to one of the Cratchit children dressed in traditional, colonial 18th century garb.

"Tiny Tim is so cute!" Brie whispers into Abby's ear. They giggle and watch Greg and Abe go over to talk to Tiny Tim, seated on a stool by the fire, his crutch leaning against the bricks.

"The fireplace is so nice and warm," Abby notices.

"Sure is," Brie agrees, drawing in a big breath of the aroma of hot apple cider, cloves, nutmeg and cinnamon hanging in the entryway of the tavern, almost in a competition with the turkey and stuffing dinner, and the scent of evergreen boughs and yule logs on the large fireplace mantel and tables.

"Christmas is my favorite time of the year," Brie says, loving the warm holiday glow she feels inside her heart.

The evening's festivities include horse drawn sleigh rides, now that the snow is freshly fallen again, a gingerbread house contest in another fire-placed room in the Oliver Wight Tavern, and apple cider mulling demonstration at the Cider Mill, inviting guests to escape the frenzy of modern day Christmas chaos.

"I am interested in the history of the holiday traditions. Grammy Rose said that is taking place in the Fuller Conference Center across the walkway," Brie says.

"Me too," Abby says. "I like decorating with Christmas trees and evergreens."

"I like the mistletoe." Brie gives Abby a wink. Both girls chuckle.

Brie investigates history with the enthusiasm that Harry Potter, Encyclopedia Brown and Nancy Drew solve mysteries.

The tallest Cratchit daughter takes their coats. She has braids and is wearing a white bonnet, full sleeved gray blouse and a full navy linen skirt covering a petticoat. A homemade navy crocheted shawl covers her shoulders.

Brie and Abby love the dresses on the women scurrying to help the guest find their seats. The women are wearing homemade dresses with full sleeves to the wrists and full-flowing, long skirts gathered around the waist, without a bustle in keeping with the 1800 era. White, ruffled bonnets are tied under their chins, while aprons are tied in big bows behind their backs.

The wooden, unpainted floorboards creak occasionally as they walk to their table. Brie is fascinated by the huge fire crackling on the other side of the room, spreading light, warmth and cheer, and the smell of wafting smoke escaping on occasional downdrafts.

"I wonder if any loose bricks are hiding spots for old recipes or other interesting surprises," Brie whispers to Abby so their brothers do not hear. Brie loves a good mystery.

"OK, everyone, please find your seats. Our servers will be by shortly to serve you hot cider from the pitchers crafted here at the Village," Mr. Cratchit directs.

Brie and Abby, lead Abe and Greg to the long, candle-lit table where their Moms, and Grammy Rose are sitting. Cider is now served in the tins cups made earlier in the fall at the Village Tin Shop near the Town Common, a keepsake tonight's guests get to take home with them in honor of the 70th Anniversary Celebration. The Christmas feast begins with platters of turkey, stuffing, cranberry sauce, carrots, mashed yellow turnips and potatoes, homemade rolls, and apple and pumpkin pies.

In no time, the dinner is finished and the dishes whisked away. Clyde Jennings, a scruffy man in a long black coat and a tall, wide brimmed hat appears in the door, ringing a leather strap of bells.

"Horse-drawn sleigh rides are taking passengers on the outer Village loop, from the Bullard Tavern to the Freeman Farm House. They are taking place from now to closing. Belle from Charles Dickenson's *A Christmas Carol*, has hot chocolate for all guests this evening at the Freeman Farmhouse. No rush. We are taking small groups, because our two horse team of Jerry and Jim, our two Belgian draft horses are pulling a sleigh. They will be making stops at the School House for an interesting history class on the Mede-Persian Empire, and the Blacksmith Shop for a history class on the Grecian Empire. Both of those stops have fireplaces." Clyde chuckles, adding, "of course there is a stop at the Potter's Shop and hot-fired kiln."

"We will continue unveiling the secret behind the mysterious history and the effects of the Old World Empires on Sturbridge Village in 1830 at the Center Meetinghouse, on your way to the farm, or on your way back, by way of the Dummerston Bridge, and conclude at Bullard's Tavern. The Hartford-Worcester Stagecoach is the second horse-drawn passenger vehicle, taking passengers around the center of the Village. It can also drop you off at the Center Meetinghouse for those who need a ride." Clyde smiles kindly.

"Bullard's Tavern is a good place to visit this evening, if you want to get some of the roasted chestnuts. Father Christmas is in there sitting by the fireplace, roasting them for all the guests. He is also telling the history of his coming into being, and about his many names like, Saint Nick, Santa Claus, and jolly old elf." Clyde winks.

"The Gingerbread House Contest is in this building where you are right now, in another room with a fireplace, here in the Oliver Wight Tavern. Just follow the signs," Clyde adds.

"If you prefer to ride in the horse-drawn Hartford-Worcester Stagecoach around the center of town to see our living Little Town of Bethlehem scene in the Town Common, our beautiful Morgan horses will be glad to make your wish come true. The Stagecoach will be loading at the Fenno Barn, and can also make a stop at the history class on the Babylonian Empire being held near the fireplace in the Salem Towne House. This ride can also take you to any stop around the Town Common," Clyde says, pointing out his route.

"The history of all the programs tonight, and how they relate to Old Sturbridge Village, will be demonstrated in the Visitor Welcome Center, with a bright blue star pinpointing Old Sturbridge Village on the timeline at the year 1830. The timeline takes us from the historical empires mentioned, through the 1830's, with a focus on slavery and emancipation. Old Sturbridge Village's time period is the same time period of President Lincoln. It's a fascinating historical timeline. We hope you enjoy it," Clyde announces, proudly tipping his big, black hat.

"Please stay calm around the horses, and keep in mind not to run in the Village tonight. Sudden loud noises they do not expect in the dark spook them. We do not want any run away sleigh or stagecoach rides tonight," Clyde chuckles.

"We're still looking for last year's guests who took that fateful sleigh ride when the horses got scared, reared up and took off. The horses came back with the sleigh, of course, but no one knows what happened to the guests!" Clyde winks again, with a gleam in his eye.

Brie, Abby, Abe and Greg shoot each other wide-eyed glances.

"Is he for real?" Greg asks.

"No, I don't think so," Sarah says, "but better behave like he says, just in case."

"Mom, Abby and I want to be together tonight on the rides and workshops," Brie pleads.

"Yes, and I want to go with Abe in the first stagecoach ride tonight," Greg eagerly agrees.

Sarah, Aunt Cher and Grammy Rose nod approvingly to each other.

"OK. But everyone must be on their best behavior tonight. Greg and Abe, you boys are with me." Brie's Mom says, offering to take the tougher assignment of the night, or so she thinks.

Brie's Mom, brother and Abe take advantage of the first horse drawn stagecoach ride around the Little Town of Bethlehem living manger scene. The crisp, cold, night air makes them snuggle deeper into the scarfs, crocheted by Grammy Rose. The scent of Grammy Rose's favorite perfume, Emeraude by Coty, still lingers in the yarn.

"Let me introduce you to Manitou, our eight year old Morgan stallion. The Algonquian bands of Indians in this area became known as the Nipmuc Indians. Their territory was known as Nipnet, which extended as far north as Vermont and New Hampshire borders, and south into Rhode Island and northeastern Connecticut. The Native Americans believed in the Great Spirit called Gitche Manitou. Meet Manitou," Clyde says gesturing to the horse on the right.

"You should call the horse on the left Gitche," Abe chuckles.

"You guessed it. Gitche is a mare, a female horse. Manitou is a stallion, a male horse," Clyde teaches.

"When Gitche and Manitou came to Old Sturbridge Village four years ago, it seemed like these black beauties chose us more than we chose them. Both of them seem to embody the generous Great Spirit of the native people of this land. Their names fit them. They are a perfect fit for Old Sturbridge Village, both in their loving natures, their strength and their willingness to work. Originally, Morgan horses came to America with the early colonists from England," Clyde informs.

"They are beautiful! How much do they weigh?" Abe asks excitedly, admiring their brushed manes, braided and decorated with tiny red bows.

"They each weigh about 1,200 pounds, and are 15 hands," Clyde responds.

"Hands?" Greg asks looking at his own hands.

"Yes. That is how tall they are. Each hand is about four inches, making them 60 inches, or five feet tall. That is, five feet from the back hoof up to their withers," Clyde says pointing to the horse's rumps.

The boys laugh.

Sarah stands in front of Manitou, captivated by his distinctive head and large, expressive eyes.

"He likes you. He has a very sweet disposition. You can pat him if you want to," Clyde suggests.

"His neck is so strong. His muzzle is so soft and his mane is so long and thick," she notices.

Manitou nuzzles her cheek, melting her heart.

"Morgans are known for their charisma and companionableness. They seek a relationship with everyone they meet. I think you are one of his favorites. Climb aboard," Clyde welcomes.

Clyde takes the giant step to the driver's seat aboard the nine passenger New England Concord-style stagecoach. He turns around to face his guests.

"By the year 1830, Morgan horses were known as popular working horses, and were also respected for their shining coats, and tall, regal stature. Did you know that the first Morgan horse comes from a man by the name of Justin Morgan who lived in Springfield, Massachusetts, just down the road a ways? Originally he was a teacher, composer and horseman. He acquired a bay colt in 1789, and named him Figure. Since the practice in those days was to call the horse by the owner's name, Figure became known as the Justin Morgan horse. His colt is the founding sire of the Morgan breed."

"These are beautiful horses," Abe says.

"And their coats are so shiny," Greg adds.

Clyde smiles and continues.

"Justin Morgan moved from Springfield to Randolph, Vermont. Figure's ability to out walk, out run and out pull other horses was legendary. His stud services were offered throughout the Connecticut River Valley and in Vermont over his lifetime. Gitche and Manitou are in his line. Figure moved on to other owners after Justin Morgan's death. From that time on Figure worked on farms, hauling freight, and even served as a parade mount at militia trainings. Figure died in 1821, which is a little before the time in history that we are sharing with you tonight," Clyde says, as he gently addresses the reigns, making a clicking sound with his mouth to get his horse team moving for the first ride of the night. The Morgan's hooves are muffled against the packed snow.

"Did you know that the town of Sturbridge was a major stopping point in the stagecoach transportation system? The line ran directly past the entrance to Old Sturbridge Village. You came in to Old Sturbridge Village tonight by way of Stallion Hill Road, but this road used to be called the Worcester – Stafford Turnpike," Clyde says.

"But this stagecoach says it is the Hartford – Worcester Stagecoach. Why is that different?" Abe asks puzzled by the difference in the names.

"I see you are very observant," Clyde says. "The stagecoach stop here was a major rest and destination stop. There were many different stagecoach names for the cities and towns they transported people to and from. Many travelers also stopped here on the way from Boston to New York, and from Providence to Worcester. Every ten miles the stagecoach would stop to change horses," Clyde explains.

"Now we refuel at gas stations," Sarah comments.

"Did any famous people ride this stagecoach?" Abe asks.

"Certainly. President John Quincy Adams rode this stagecoach system on his way home to Boston. You might also like to know the Freeman Farm was an actual working farm here in Sturbridge Village back in the day. Silas Freeman was one of the young sons of Pliny and Delia Freeman. Silas changed careers, his work as a farmer for driving the stagecoach," Clyde says.

The large and small animals that are part of the manger scene to their right in the Town Common do not seem to mind the snow beneath their hooves. The breath from their noses encircle their heads like wreaths of fog in the cold of the evening. The manger scene is magnificently displayed, with ample bales of hay serving both as food and warmth for the sheep, cows and deer. The Bactrian camel set up to the far left of the stable, however, appears to be stealing the show. Some of the Victorian dressed carolers are making their way to the front of the living display and stand between the three wise men and the drummer boy, while other carolers holding kerosene lanterns line the walkway from the Visitor's Center to the Town Common. It is a heart-warming, carol filled stop in time.

The first stagecoach ride around the Town Common is off from the Fenno Textile Mill, passing the Fitch house and barn, bank and bake shop on their left. Gitche and Manitou follow the road to the right as Clyde ever so gently coaxes the reigns in that direction. Clyde points out the Salem Towne House with the history of the Babylonian Empire awaiting them and its effect on Old Sturbridge Village. But the boys wish to continue the stagecoach ride around the Town Common, now transformed into the Little Town of Bethlehem.

Another right turn in the road brings them to Bullard's Tavern with roasted chestnuts and Father Christmas. Still they press on.

"The Parsonage is to your left. It is the home of the minister in the year 1830. You will find the minister inside the Parsonage tonight, with an interesting presentation on angels," Clyde points out.

"The minister preaches at the Center Meetinghouse. Of course, church meetings are held in the Meetinghouse, but this is also where we hold our town government meetings, elections, political events and lectures. Tonight you might like to go there to listen to the interesting history class on the Roman Empire and its effect on this 1830 community," Clyde invites.

Obviously Gitche and Manitou know the road around the Town Common and take another right before the Center Meetinghouse and the horse sheds. Clyde describes the second religious building to their left, saying, "One thing not to miss tonight is the presentation in the Friends Meetinghouse. Our Quaker population is hosting an educational workshop on the Underground Railroad which was flourishing in the 1800's. That is a very enlightening presentation," Clyde gestures to the building they had walked past on their way to the stagecoach ride.

"Also waiting you inside the Religious Society of Friend's Meetinghouse are relatives of Levi and Catherine Coffin, two famous Quakers who are believed to have helped over three thousand slaves to escape during this time. Levi is often referred to as the president of the Underground Railroad. He lived in Indiana before he moved to Cincinnati, where his home is now a National Historical Landmark. Tonight we have characters portraying members of his family, Gabe and Lily Coffin, as they might have been in 1830 helping the cause of freedom for all people.

"Their presentation includes pictures of actual moving walls and hidden passage ways in homes and town buildings which helped all people get to freedom. I know my skin looks white, but my own genealogy includes black men and women, who bravely escaped in this way. I am honored to be among the people who have transformed racial prejudice into the melting pot of humanity. The Quakers foster forgiveness as a means for both sides of bigotry to move past their prejudices. The way I see it, there is only one race, the human race," Clyde says, hoping his words fall on understanding ears.

"That's exactly how we feel. We've been talking about this after watching the news on TV. The inner cities have so much trouble. People are getting shot and killed. Not everyone is prejudiced. I'm not." Abe responds.

"Tommy is my friend, and he is black. We're on the same hockey team," Greg adds to the conversation.

Sarah smiles, proud of the boys.

"Among the slaves who hid in the home of Levi and Catherine Coffin was "Eliza," whose story formed the basis for the character of the same name in the abolitionist novel *Uncle Tom's Cabin*," Clyde continues.

"My sister, Brie, read that book last summer," Greg says.

"It's a good book. Over in the Quaker Meetinghouse, you will also learn who first made up the concept of evolution, and what President Abraham Lincoln thought about this new, unproven concept. Little known connections between President Abraham Lincoln and Charles Darwin can be learned there tonight. Did you know they were both born on February 12, 1809?"

They all shake their heads no.

Then turning his attention back to the beginning at the Fenno Barn, with the Town Common to his right, Clyde highlights their newest attraction, the Bactrian camel, presently chewing on a mouthful of hay while striking a pose and looking directly at them.

"Southwick's Zoo in Mendon and Old Sturbridge Village have an educational exchange program these days. Tonight we are benefitting from a guest appearance from Camille the camel. That's definitely another attraction to check out tonight," Clyde suggests.

"How about a ride to the Salem Towne House for your next historical adventure?" Clyde asks.

"That's a good idea," Sarah agrees, noticing that house has a nice, warm fire in the fireplace going inside. She also notices that in the entire time they circled the Town Common, she did not see her daughter, her sister, her niece, nor her mother anywhere. Maybe it was not such a good idea to separate after all.

CHAPTER 2

GET THAT DONKEY!

A wall of warm air welcomes Sarah, Greg and Abe to the North Parlor of the Salem Towne House. Greg races to the crackling fire and saves the closest three seats nearest the fireplace. More guests gather round the fireplace and fill in the empty spaces in the room and hallway.

Horace Abrams finishes a hot cup of apple cider and puts his tin cup on a tray offered by a young servant dressed as an angel. Like the assorted angels at dinner and at the outdoor living manger scene, this angel was topped with silver garland halo and decorated angel wings.

"The angels look so pretty. I like the angels. This is the part of the religious holiday I like," Abe says to Greg.

"But," Horace says peering over his wire rimmed glasses, "did you know that Christmas is not really a religious holiday?"

"But that's when we celebrate Jesus' birthday!" Abe exclaims. Abe listens to his mother say there is no God, but at Christmas, he's a believer.

"Let's begin at the beginning," Horace states. "Welcome to the history of Babylon, and how it relates to Old Sturbridge Village in 1830. We will see if the modern Christmas is indeed celebrating the birth of Jesus, as you say. The Center Meetinghouse parishioners here in 1830 think they have discovered the secret of King Nebuchadnezzar's dream, from the book of Daniel in the Bible. The discovery of this secret is so exciting that they have shared this secret down through the ages, to this very day. It relates to the Babylonian Empire, which we will cover now."

Horace leans back in his chair, and begins his oration.

"Let's go back in time, after the great flood destroys the people of the earth. Life begins anew. People begin again to flourish, and settle in the Fertile Crescent, between the Tigris, which used to be called the Hiddekel, and Euphrates rivers. It is the beginning of the great city of Babylon, built upon the remains of the pre-flood city of Babel. It is where most of Iraq, Syria, Lebanon and Israel are today, stretching from Bagdad to the Persian Gulf and the Mediterranean Sea. At that time, it was built as mostly Sumerian city-states."

All of a sudden, Horace is talking about places they keep hearing about on the news. As they warm up, they listen for clues that connect the Babylonian time to 1830 in Old Sturbridge Village.

Horace continues.

"There was much building going on in Babylon with roads, an extensive canal system, and of course, one of the Seven Wonders of the World, the Hanging Gardens, which no longer exists. The city had towering walls and a Processional Way, including the Hanging Gardens and nearly 50 temples honoring Babylonian, manmade gods. They even built a replica of the tallest temple tower ever built by human hands, the Tower of Babel, two hundred, ninety-five feet high. It was built to a local god, Marduk, some say Mithras, the most popular god in the Babylonian pantheon. Just for point of reference, the Statue of Liberty you are familiar with in New York, is three hundred and five feet tall. This ziggurat was a pyramid-shaped temple which began approximately 2100-1100 BCE. It was made of baked bricks with brilliant blue enamel, which needed constant maintenance so the bricks would not erode away. Why do you think that might be?" Horace asks.

"Because it is a desert," the tall boy next to Abe says enthusiastically.

"You are correct," Horace says.

"Over at the school house tonight, you will learn how the Medes and the Persians conquered Babylon in 539 BCE, including all these buildings we are talking about here in this workshop. The replica temple tower I am telling you about is recorded to never have been finished.

"However, before that, thousands of years were devoted to the customs and traditions of Nimrod and his wife, Ishtar, in the capital city of Babylon. The Bible is sometimes used for historical and geographical reference. Genesis 10:10 tells that Nimrod began his kingdom in the land of Shinar, founding the cities of Babel, Erech, Accad and Calneth. Any questions?" Horace asks.

"An interesting note is that Nimrod also goes into Assyria and builds the towns of Nineveh, Rehoboth-Ir, Calah and Resen. He then calls the whole region Babylon," the tall, thin man in the long black coat says.

"That is correct. What is your life's work, sir?" Horace asks.

"I am a retired professor of Antediluvian history, that is, ancient and pre-history," the man smiles back.

"So happy you can be with us this evening," Horace welcomes. "Let's continue from the point in history following the flood, at the time of the Babylonian Empire. Nimrod is now king of the Babylonian Empire. Nimrod and Ishtar began to honor themselves as god and goddess. As a matter of fact, all other gods and goddesses in every culture in the world, in every religion, are an off-shoot of these manmade and mythical gods and goddesses," Horace pauses for a moment to see if he has captured the attention of his younger audience.

"There are a lot of religions in the world today. Some of them have hundreds of gods and goddesses, like the Hindu religion. Are you saying they all started at this time in history?" Sarah asks.

"Yes, that's right," Horace affirms. "Once the concept of creating gods and goddesses to explain human life, and what is beyond human understanding, started with Nimrod and Ishtar, other cultures simply adopted this idea. For example, Ishtar called herself, 'Semiramis, Night Goddess of the Moon,'" Horace teaches.

"Nimrod and Ishtar are also the ones who began the concept of reincarnation and the notion that the soul does not die after death," the tall, thin man adds.

"Yes. As a matter of fact, because Nimrod and Ishtar wanted to deny that death would ever overtake them, they said that Nimrod would be reborn. Later history shows that in order to keep this belief alive, it was rumored that King Nebuchadnezzar was the reincarnation of Nimrod. Nimrod set himself up in opposition to God, and even declared himself a god, Marduk, to be worshipped by the people."

"So Nimrod has the tower built to glorify himself, and says he is the god Marduk?" the lady with the white fuzzy hat asks in a surprising voice.

"Yes. In keeping with his reincarnation theory which he promotes, he begins cutting down evergreen trees from the forest, nailing them to the beams in the houses and decorating them with silver and gold. Sound familiar?" Horace glances around the room.

"Yes! That's just like our Christmas trees," Greg declares.

"More preciously, your Christmas trees are exactly like Nimrod's pagan trees. Remember, Nimrod was upset with God because God sent a flood to wipe out life on earth. So Nimrod and Ishtar made up their own traditions and man-made gods, beginning with themselves, as substitutes for the God of Nimrod's great-grandfather, Noah," Horace recaps.

"I didn't know that. This is Babylonian history?" Abe asks full of wonder.

"Yes indeed. The Babylonian history begins with Nimrod and Ishtar. Nimrod comes from the land of the Canaanites, named after Canaan, son of Ham, Nimrod's uncle," Horace says.

"Ham, what a funny name," Greg laughs.

"Did you know that Ham is one of the three sons of Noah? Nimrod's father is Cush, Ham's brother. After the Great Flood, Canaan, Ham's son, gets sent away, and settles along the southeastern border of the Great Sea, now known as which sea?" Horace quizzes.

"The Mediterranean Sea," the man next to Sarah answers.

"Correct. This becomes known as the Land of Canaan. It is where Nimrod's promotion of nature gods, and all other kinds of man-made gods were created. Nimrod's creation of the god of sowing is with us to this very day, the god of Saturn. Does anyone know what it was called?" Horace asks.

"Saturnalia was the feast day devoted to Saturn," the tall, thin man answers.

"That's correct. It was celebrated on what we now know as December 17 each year. Nimrod figured if he could start a reason to appease the god of the sowing then people would keep promoting it, because they certainly would want good crops to grow next year at this time. It would be a grand celebration, a time of gift giving, eating and drinking, and merriment of all kinds without limit. He even decreed work holidays to make his proclamations more popular. It worked," Horace says.

"Sounds like fun. It's nice to get a holiday off from work." The guests agree with Sarah.

"Nimrod figured if there could be a god of sowing, why not have a god of the sun itself? So Mithra, some say Mithras, the god of the sun, was born. Does anyone know the feast day of Mithra?" Horace asks.

The room of guests ponder for a moment.

"The shortest day of the year?" Sarah guesses.

"You are correct. Nimrod, and no one else, chooses what we now know as December 25 for the feast day of the return of the sun god Mithra. The people in this 1830 Village really do believe in the God of Creation, but not these manmade gods. The inhabitants of the Village also believe in Satan, the devil, and really do see an evil hand at work, trying to get them to celebrate anything on December 25, especially anything having to do with God. This is more like a bad joke to them," Horace says, taking a sip of cider.

"Really?" Greg asks, listening more intently now.

"You can imagine how the settlers here in 1830, Christian or not, wanted nothing to do with this tyrannical leader and his wife, promoting false gods and false worship as if they were real. The same thing goes for the manmade gods and goddess of the stars of the night sky, immortality of the soul and astrology, which began with Ishtar. She promoted herself as the "Semiramis, Night Goddess of the Moon," Horace explains.

"What is your name son?" Horace asks, gesturing to Abe.

"I'm Abe."

"Earlier you said something about Christmas celebrating the birth of Jesus. Are you aware that nowhere in the Scriptures, is any good person ever recorded to have kept a celebration, feast or banquet on the day of their birth? There are only two instances in the Bible writings that refer to birthday parties. Do you know what they are?" Horace asks carefully eyeing his audience.

"The daughter of Herodias dances for Herod for his birthday. At the end of the dance he says he will give her anything, up to half of his kingdom. She asks her mother what to ask for, and Herodias tells her to ask for the head of John the Baptist," Sarah remembers, with the ghost of CCD lessons gone by rushing through her mind.

"That's right. That account is from the New Testament," Horace agrees. "Anyone remember the first birthday instance mentioned in the Old Testament?"

The guests do not remember.

"It is when the Pharaoh in Egypt has a birthday, and hangs the chief baker. Those are the only two references for birthdays in the Bible," Horace explains.

"Really?" the woman in the fuzzy white hat sitting next to Sarah asks.

"Only pagans who worshipped the gods and goddesses of the sun, moon, and astrology celebrated the days of their births. Neither the Jewish people, nor Jesus, nor any of his followers ever celebrated the birth of people either. They celebrated people's whole lives, and all they did, at their deaths. You will notice at the time of the birth of someone as important as Jesus is, we don't even have the exact date of the birth of Jesus on record, not even the year of his birth." Horace notices all of his guests have a very surprised look on their faces.

"They did not celebrate Jesus' birthday? We sing Happy Birthday to Jesus every Christmas morning," a young quizzical voice erupts from the little blonde in pigtails.

"No, they did not celebrate it. Most scripture scholars discern that Jesus was most likely born around September or October, not December. Also, there is no tradition in Judaism of celebrating birthdays, otherwise we would have a list of birthdays from Noah, Abraham to Moses, King David and many others, but no such thing exists. There are no birthdays within Judaism, including the Torah, nor within Christianity down through the ages," Horace teaches.

"But I like birthdays, and birthday parties. I like the cake and ice cream," Greg interjects.

"And I like the presents and celebrating with my friends," Abe adds.

"This is why, most of the 1830 villagers chose not to celebrate Christmas. They didn't want to celebrate the false gods, nor celebrate the day of Jesus' birth." Horace says, trying to get his audience back on track, and scans his audience for the upheaval that usually follows this part of history of which they would rather be ignorant.

Guests peer into the eyes of the people next to them, eager to know more. Horace continues.

"Few, if any, inhabitants in 1830 here celebrate Christmas. In our workshops tonight we are educating our guests of the original feast and celebration rituals that were first celebrated two thousand years earlier than the era of Jesus, and exactly why many of the people of 1830 chose not to celebrate them," Horace informs.

"Is Old Sturbridge Village typical of all towns in 1830 who think this way?" Abe asks curiously.

"Yes. Christian villagers here in 1830 simply thought this was outright ridiculous nonsense. Christians believe that Jesus came to set the record straight about believing God, the Creator of all. They do not believe in magic ceremonies, folklore, myths, nor immoral revelry. They believe that Jesus came to free people from the lore and addiction of false gods along with false religions that humans invented," Horace says.

"You are right about that," the tall, thin man says. "Did you know the original "sun log" came to be called the yule log? The word "yule" means "wheel," which has long been a pagan representation of the sun and astrology."

Horace smiles at his educated, participating guest in this workshop, appreciating his confirmation on these little known facts.

"Yes. You will notice people today still refer to the Christmas season as the sacred yule-tide season. The holly, evergreens, wreaths, yule logs and mistletoe are relics of pre-Christian times, part of Teutonic nature worship. The early Christians here in Old Sturbridge Village wanted to worship the God who created nature, not the nature itself, a mere creation of God." Horace pauses to let his words sink in.

"For the Christians of 1830 Sturbridge Village, who believe in Jesus, a real historical person, celebrating the fairytales of fairies, is too ridiculous to entertain," Horace says, pausing for a sip of cider brought by another angel. Hot apple cider is also offered to the guests in all of the workshops on this special night.

"History also shows us that people are not always kind to one another. The reason having different religious beliefs was such a dangerous thing then and now, is because people were sometimes put to death for not believing the right things," Horace sighs.

"You mean they killed people for believing in the wrong things?" Greg asks in disbelief.

Abe groans at the thought.

"Yes. History is full of examples, whether it is called ethnic cleansing, a holocaust, or the crusades, no human group of people is without their examples, even today. Then, rather than go by God's Word in the Bible, different groups began to inter-weave their beliefs, and include pagan popular human traditions," Horace says.

"Don't forget, it was just two hundred and twelve years prior to 1830 that the new word, "syncretism," was added to the Oxford English Dictionary. When you study about Plutarch in first century AD in your history class, you will discover he wrote about the history of different groups and what he did so they did not stay at war with one another," Horace says slowly, unsure how much history his young audience could absorb.

"Plutarch wrote *Plutarch's Lives*," Sarah says, explaining that Brie discussed this at dinner one night after she studied it in her ancient history class.

"Very good. He also wrote an essay *Fraternal Love* in his *Moralia*. Here is where Plutarch cites the example of the Cretans, where they compromised and reconciled their differences. They came together in alliance when they faced external dangers. They agree to disagree, rather than kill each other over their different belief systems." Horace lets this knowledge ferment in the minds of his quests.

"That's a good thing, right?" Greg asks.

"Very observant question. The word we are talking about here is syncretism. It means to combine not only different, but also contradictory beliefs, blending various schools of thought, especially theology and mythology of religion. The idea is to allow for unity for an inclusive approach to other faiths." Horace pauses again for his guests to arrive at his deeper point before he explains.

"Brie said they also did this in the arts and culture, and in politics," Greg says, bragging about his sister.

"When syncretism occurs in the expression of the arts and culture, it is known as eclecticism. When it occurs in politics, it is known as syncretic politics," Horace confirms.

"In spiritual circles, that's what we call interfaith today," Sarah adds.

"Correct," Horace acknowledges.

"What does this have to do with Christmas in Sturbridge Village in 1830?" Abe asks.

"So I haven't worn you out yet." Horace chuckles. "Why do you think there are two different houses of worship here at Sturbridge Village?"

The entire audience looks at each other, searching for the missing answer.

"When it comes to religion in 1830, not everyone wants to compromise their personal beliefs in God, as if all different beliefs are all the same. It is clear in 1830, the Saturnalia revelries and those practicing true Christianity do not mix. One has many gods and goddesses, and the other has the one God of Creation. It is like mixing oil and vinegar, shake as you might, it still separates. The Christians in 1830 call Saturnalia and all its human customs and traditions that honor other gods and goddesses, a false religion, which they believed is not the same thing as giving worship to their sovereign God. Christians believed then and now, that Jesus taught God's love and forgiveness, and that there is one true God," Horace says.

Now everyone is nodding their heads, appreciating this fact.

"At the beginning you said Christmas is not really a religious holiday," Greg says, his brain braiding.

"Does anyone have any answers for this?" Horace poses this question to his audience.

"I remember reading a newspaper article around 1990, about a school in Ohio, near Cleveland, I think, that had a court case about this. The school board had banned all nativity and other Christmas scenes on any school property because they felt it violated the separation of church and state," Sarah answers, brushing away twenty-five years of cobwebs from her mind.

"I remember that!" the woman in the white fuzzy hat recalls. "They were challenged in court by outraged parents who felt that Christmas was being stolen from their children and their community."

"But the board lost the case, because the people argued that Christmas was a worldwide tradition that was not part of, and transcended religion, since it was virtually part of all cultures worldwide," the tall, thin man answers.

"Correct again. The town was Solon, Ohio. The court decided that Christmas had no Christian roots. Even the Catholic Encyclopedia of 1911, which hasn't been published yet," Horace winks in his 1830 persona, "admits that Christmas was not among the earliest festivals of the Church. It says the first evidence of the feast is from Egypt, and pagan customs centering round the January calendar which gravitated to Christmas."

"Let's go outside to see the living display of the Little Town of Bethlehem and manger scene in the Town Common. They were just setting up when the sleigh pulled up," Greg says to Abe, sprinting from his spot. "Thank you Horace," Greg says over his shoulder on the way out.

"Can't keep that one still for long," Sarah says to Horace, bounding after her son and his cousin.

"Catch hold of the donkey!" the shepherd beckons, waving his arms in an attempt to corral the frisky beast back into his pen. The high-spirited donkey, fueled by flurries and invigorating cold air, has other ideas. Children run after him, with Greg and Abe in the lead.

"Oh no, not again!" Sarah laments, with haunting flashbacks from when the monkeys escaped at Southwick's Zoo in Mendon last year. That was a fiasco, but Greg was able to coax one of them back with a banana.

The faster the children run, the faster the donkey runs, around the Town Common, and straight into the Cider Mill, where piles of apple cores appeal to the eyes of the warm-blooded beast of burden escapee. Distracted by the scent and taste of his new found food source, the donkey ignores everything else for a few moments of delectable bliss.

"Here you are Pokey. Tonight I think I will change your name to Flash!" the shepherd chuckles as he put him back into his pen, which is also staged with sheep and a couple of the Sturbridge Village cows from the farm.

The smell of hot apple cider and cinnamon sticks also beckon Abe, Greg and Sarah to the Cider Mill, enticing them to stay for a moment. A minister topped by a black hat nods to each of them and smiles as he hands them cups of warm merriment in the cold night. The taste is sweet, reminding them of apple picking with Grammy Rose and the rest of the family a couple months ago. As they sip the hot cider, they gaze at the living manger scene before them on the Town Common.

The most popular animal attraction this year is the domesticated Bactrian camel featuring two humps and a surly attitude. He is kept in a separate enclosure, filled with hay. But tonight the camel prefers to eat the snow and small shrubs provided for his evening meal.

"The domesticated Bactrian camel is known to be the largest mammal in its native range, even rivaling the dromedary as the largest living camel," Southwick's Zoo animal specialist Ned Worthington says.

Southwick's Zoo is sponsoring the rare, pack animal guest this evening in the mutually benefitting education exchange program with Old Sturbridge Village.

"His shoulders are over six feet high, his head-and-body length is over eleven feet, and the tail is about twenty-two inches long. At the top of the humps, the average height is almost seven feet. His body mass can range from six hundred and sixty to two thousand, two hundred pounds, with males often being much larger and heavier than females," Ned adds.

"Wow, that's a heavy camel!" Greg exclaims.

"I heard camels shed their hair. Is that true?" Abe asks.

"Yes. This domesticated Bactrian camel's mane and beard of long hair grows on his neck and throat, as you can see, with hairs measuring nearly ten inches long. The shaggy winter coat is shed extremely rapidly, with huge sections peeling off at once, appearing as if sloppily shorn off. It's quite a sight. The two humps on the back are made up of fat, not water as some people think." Ned informs the growing crowd.

The Bactrian camel poses as if it is aware it is the center of attention. Unbeknownst to Sturbridge Village guests, village hunters with tranquilizer guns and humane wild animal trappers keep a vigilant watch over the animal and human guests. Gray wolves which have been seen in the greater Quabbin Reservoir area where Old Sturbridge Village is nestled, are predators of both.

The Old Sturbridge Village Town Common is staged as The Little Town of Bethlehem, with living cast of characters and traditional nativity scene animals. The manger scene is complete with a Mary and Joseph, a shepherd, and three wise men. Since it is not Christmas yet, there is no baby Jesus in the manger, and Mary is looking very pregnant. A choir of heavenly angels is singing, "Angels We Have Heard on High," in a semi-circle around the manger, while the little drummer boy completes the live, musical drama scene. The carols are catchy with outside guests singing along in the invigorating evening.

CHAPTER 3

SECRET OF THE HIDDEN LIBRARY

Meanwhile, as Santa's little green elves clear away every plate, cup and morsel from the Christmas by Candlelight Dinner, Brie and Abby brave the night air for a short walk over to the Fuller Conference Center, where the Origin of Christmas Traditions presentation begins. They beat Aunt Cher and Grammy Rose out the door.

Orator, Joshua Appleby, sits in period costume on a tall stool on the stage of the three hundred seat theater. The seats are ample and comfortable.

"Welcome, to the Fuller Conference Center," Joshua begins as many guests find seats. "This is one of the original buildings on the David Wight Farm. Then it served as a barn. Now we hold conferences and lectures in here. This Village reflects what this time of year was like in the 1790-1840 era. Specifically, we mostly depict the year 1830 AD. You won't find in our authentic setting anything not authentic."

"I love the history of this place, and Christmas!" Brie shares with Abby. Abby hugs her shoulder right back.

Brie has never come to this Christmas by Candlelight celebration before. She is so glad Grammy Rose brought her and Abby, and the rest of the family too. It has been a whirlwind day. They relax with twilight transforming into the night.

Joshua continues.

"People came to this new country, and to Sturbridge Village, for religious freedom, among other things. They came to this country to escape religious persecution from across the Atlantic Ocean, as well as in this new land. We are depicting the Little Town of Bethlehem, because Jesus was in fact born, a real historical person. But we are also explaining the beliefs of the people in our Village in 1830 because it was so central to how they lived their lives. You will learn that it was the pagans who celebrated with lit candles, wreaths, mistletoe, and garland, yule logs, decorated evergreen trees, and Saturnalia presents. You will also see some of these traditions in some houses, but the Christians in the 1830's did not believe in these superstitions. For this reason, you will not find any pagan Christmas tree in neither the Center Meetinghouse, nor the Religious Society of Friends at the Quaker Meetinghouse. Tonight we are educating our guests how these customs came into being. Does anyone have any questions?" Joshua asks.

"I do. I do," Brie says, waving her hand in the air. "You said these celebrations are pagan, but we celebrate them as religious. We celebrate Jesus birth. When did this change?"

"This is a very good question young lady. Think of your history books. Some things happen in the time we call AD, after the birth of Jesus, while other historical events happen in the time known as BC, or before the birth of Jesus. In the times before the common era, what we now refer to either as BC, or sometimes BCE," answers Joshua, "everyone from kings to the common people celebrated the day now known as December 25 as the feast day of the pagan god, Mithra, as the Divinity of the Sun, around 1400-1200 BCE, which is *before* the birth of Jesus." Joshua says with his blue eyes sparkling, having an affinity for lighting the fire of learning in young and not so young minds alike.

"Why do we now see a change from BC and BCE, to CE and AD? Doesn't the BC stand for "before Christ," and the AD mean "after death?"" Aunt Cher asks.

"That's a very good question, and also a common misconception. The truth is that your answer is only half correct. Let me ask you this. How could the year 1 BC have been 'before Christ' and 1 AD been 'after death?' Remember, Jesus was thirty-three years old at his death."

Joshua pauses for dramatic effect, then continues.

"BC does stand for "before Christ." But the reality is, AD stands for the Latin phrase *anno domini* which means "in the year of our Lord." The terms BC and AD are a dating system not taught in the Bible. This terminology was not fully used and accepted until several centuries after Jesus' death."

Joshua makes eye contact with his captive audience, realizing that he has just come upon a point that is making an impression on his adult guests.

"In the year 1830, we do use this terminology. It is interesting to note that the purpose for the BC/AD dating system was to make the birth of Jesus Christ the dividing point of world history. However, when the BC/AD system was being calculated, a mistake was made in pinpointing the year of Jesus' birth. Scholars later discovered that Jesus was actually born around 6-4 BC, not 1 AD. The funny part is, the birth, life, ministry, death and resurrection of Christ are the 'turning points' in world history, no matter what your personal belief is on religious matters. It was decided that Jesus Christ is the separation of 'old' and 'new.' BC was 'before Christ.' Ever since his birth, we have been living 'in the year of our Lord,'" Joshua explains, while checking his audiences' attention span.

"In recent times, there has been a push to replace the BC and AD labels with BCE and CE, meaning 'before common era' and 'common era,' respectively. Don't get caught up with semantics. What I mean is, 100 AD is the same as 100 CE; all that changes is the label. The funny thing to me is that the advocates of the switch from BC/AD to BCE/CE say that the newer designations are better in that they are devoid of religious connotation and thus prevent offending other cultures and religions who may not see Jesus as 'Lord.' The irony, of course, is that what distinguishes BCE from CE is still the life and times of Jesus Christ."

Satisfied with his explanation, Joshua looks around. "Any more questions?"

"Yes. Why was it such a big deal in 1830 not to celebrate Christmas, or the birth of Jesus on god Mithra's feast day? Isn't it our personal intention that makes our own celebration what it is?" Brie asks.

"I see you have an inquisitive mind. Well then, let me tell you more about this god Saturn and the celebrations of Saturnalia." Joshua takes a deep breath and says a silent prayer that his next words come out right.

"Every group in civilization had their version of a sun/fire god. The Egyptians and sometimes the Romans called him Vulcan. The Greeks and the Phoenicians called him Kronos, but they also called him Saturn, confusing the sowing god with the sun god, the god for which the Saturnalia was celebrated. It's not the first time the Gods, or the deities we call gods get confused. The Babylonians called the sun-fire god Marduk in the person of Nimrod, resurrected in the person of his son, Molech and the Druids called him Baal. However, there are no history books showing that Nimrod had a son, nor any children born to him. Nimrod is considered the father of all the Babylonian gods. I am explaining the earliest history on this subject. The people living in 1830 here in Old Sturbridge Village cared very much about this information." Joshua's audience is still riveted to his every word.

"Manmade celebrations to this god of the sun and of the fire included child sacrifice by fire to please the gods. Nimrod decided innocent infants made the most acceptable offerings. They also thought that burning their own children purified the parents from original sin. This is where the pagan doctrine of purgatory to purge the soul from sin comes from. The concept of purgatory is a pagan belief, not a Christian belief. Some modern day people think purgatory is a Catholic belief, but that is not correct. History teaches it is a pagan belief. Catholics adopted it. You can ask the minister about this when you visit the Parsonage tonight. Inhabitants of 1830 Sturbridge Village, both the Quakers and the more liberal thinkers attending the Center Meetinghouse, wanted to stay as far away from this terrible human tradition as possible. Not even replacing the birth of the Christ on Saturn and Mithra's feast days could entice them to celebrate it. They did not want to honor the false gods in any way, not even copying their most popular and fun holiday traditions."

The audience gasps in horror, followed by stunned silence, not expecting to hear that.

"I know this is shocking, but not all history is pleasant. Nations to this very day continue to do horrible things to one another. If we only take in the good things of history, and not what actually happened, we get a skewed view of reality. History has a history of repeating itself. We promote education so that we do not repeat the worst humanity has to offer. Everyone has to make their own decisions regarding this information. But everyone also has a right to know accurate history. This is exactly why the people of 1830 did not want to celebrate anything on any date honoring what they considered to be false gods, or would in any way keep remembrances of such tragic history," Joshua concludes.

"That's true," Brie says. "Most of the history I've studied has a lot of war in it, even with the Revolutionary and Civil Wars in the United States of America, and with the Native Americans who lived here."

"I was expecting to hear about St. Nicholas, like at the La Salette Shrine down in Attleboro," Aunt Cher says in a low heartache whisper to her mother. She might not believe in God, but to learn that babies used to be sacrificed for a manmade reason just made her sick.

"Yes, the Fatima Shrine in Holliston celebrates Christmas with lots of lights too," Grammy Rose remembers. "I never knew exactly what the awful traditions were that the pagans celebrated. I only knew that the celebration of Jesus' birth was placed on pagan celebrations, to Christianize it, if there really is such a thing."

"Let's go to the Gingerbread House Contest," Aunt Cher says, changing the subject, and not knowing how to deal with this new-found knowledge. The cruelty behind this holiday only made her opposition to a supposedly loving God more concrete.

"That's a good idea, Cher," Grammy Rose agrees.

"I was surprised to hear about the true origin of mistletoe," giggles Abby, who is making kissing faces to the boy next to Brie.

Brie blushes.

"I think I do like the partying parts of Saturnalia. I like the merry-making customs, the decorating and the good food," Aunt Cher confides quietly to her Mom. Aunt Cher gets up to see the beautiful miniature display of Sturbridge Village in the alcove, complete with a lit manger scene with Jesus, Mary, Joseph, shepherds, and three wise men carrying gifts. A miniature cow and a few sheep are also included. There is a bed of cotton for snow.

With that, Joshua tips his hat. The evening is well underway. But it is not like any other telling of Christmas they have ever heard.

For some unexplained reason, Brie and Abby race to the Gingerbread Contest, retracing their steps back to the Oliver Wight Tavern. Their mother and grandmother strive to keep up in a brisk walk.

With adrenaline pumping and rosy red cheeks glowing, Brie and Abby bound inside the Oliver Wight Tavern. Their feet forget to stop running.

"Stop!"

A stern Mr. Scrooge peers over his gold-rimmed glassed resting on his red, flaring nose.

They freeze like still, stone statues, only moving their eyes to each other.

"You see those candles?" Scrooge says, pointing his crooked cane to the beeswax candles resting in their holders, on the window sills.

"Oops!" they say in unison.

"We're sorry," Brie quickly says, forgetting to act her age.

"No more running. Do you understand?" Scrooge asks as he bends down to look at them nose to nose.

"Any trouble here?" Grammy Rose asks directly upon entering the familiar Tavern, followed by Aunt Cher.

"No trouble. No trouble at all," Scrooge smiles as he stands up. "Have a nice night." Scrooge tips his hat to Grammy Rose and moseys on.

"That was a close one," Brie whispers into Abby's ear. They giggle their way into the Gingerbread House Contest room.

"The gingerbread smells wonderful," Grammy Rose says to Aunt Cher, taking in a deep breath of sugary fragrance. She is secretly hoping she might win this contest, even though she knows it is for the kids.

"I'm a kid at heart," she thinks.

A warm crackling fire makes the fireplace come alive. Many tables are specially prepared with large, homemade gingerbread squares, assorted into cardboard bottomed kits. This Gingerbread House Contest room is permeated with the sweet smells of gingerbread, vanilla frosting, orange gummy half circle slices, and all sorts of candies, soon to be the windows, doors, and shingles attaching to their gingerbread square houses, with the white frosting as glue and snow.

There are so many people participating, making the room tight to work in. Brie, Abby, Grammy Rose and Aunt Cher keep looking for a space so they can all be next to each other. More and more people continue entering for the contest.

"Brie, Abby, let's go over to the side table near that fireplace mantle over there," Grammy Rose says quietly, motioning to the opposite side of the room where no one seemed to be.

"OK, we're not running," Brie says. "We're just moving fast."

Two sets of elbows and knees move both sets of gingerbread house kits at lightning speed, followed by a flash of Grammy Rose on their heels.

Maybe it is the chaos of movement, or maybe it is their different sizes, but whatever it is, Grammy Rose trips on Abby's right heel, forcing her head long into Brie's back, leaving her no chance except to catch herself on the mantle. But Brie's judgment is off, grabbing the metal statue on top of the mantle instead. As she falls, she keeps holding the statue, hoping not to crush her kit on the ground. She does not fall. Instead, all three of them hold onto each other for balance, and for a split second, all is still. Seeing all this, Aunt Cher suddenly appears, trying to stop them all from falling head first.

Then they are moving. The whole mantle wall is moving. They catch glimpses of the gingerbread room, everyone busy creating their own masterpieces. No one seems to be noticing anything unusual. They hear the leather strap bells of the horse drawn sleigh returning to take another tour around the Village. Perhaps Abe, Greg and her Mom would be heading for the holiday traditions talk with Joshua. But where are they heading?

Brie is so scared that no voice come out of her open mouth. Grammy Rose gasps. Abby and Aunt Cher look as if they are in shock. By the time they recover their senses, nothing makes any sense at all.

They look at each other, then look around the room. Brie feels for a door, to no avail.

"Brie, try to move that statue again on the mantle," Abby says frantically, knocking on the thick wooden wall, and yelling for help.

Nothing happens.

"They can't hear us because the wall is too thick, and that room is so noisy with so many people," Grammy Rose says. She doesn't want to say everything she is thinking so as not to scare the girls any further.

"What if we are locked in here and can't get out. No one knows we are in here," Grammy Rose thinks.

"This is Sturbridge Village. There is sure to be another way out of this room," Aunt Cher observes, trying to be sensible rather than her natural inclination to panic.

A wonderful aroma fills the room. Roasted turkeys and all the fixings line tables on the left side of the room, while an even more enticing row of apple and pumpkin pies that had not yet even been cut into fill tables on the right side of the room. There are no obvious doors, and no people or staff to be seen.

"We are in part of the kitchen, or the pantry," Aunt Cher notices, with a bit of color now returning to her cheeks.

"Remember, no need to panic. No forecasting panic. We are physically alright at this exact moment. So, breathe. Breathe in the peace. Breathe out stress. Breathe in balance. Breathe out what no longer serves me. Breathe in serenity," Cher remembers from her time at McLean. Her time there helped her so much, even more than she lets on to the others.

The flicker of such huge beeswax candles in glass globes shine a soft glow throughout the room, in every window, and on small tables leading down a narrow hallway they had not noticed before. At the worst case scenario, they could send Brie or Abby out through a window, but they are all locked, and are unable to be opened. They could break through the glass of the windows, but that seems to be a drastic measure they are not willing to take at this moment. After all, this is Old Sturbridge Village. There must be another way.

Brie is the first to venture down the hall, past a single bathroom with similar globe covered lit candles, and vanishes around a corner. The room she discovers is a secret hidden library lined with antique bookcases filled with old books.

"Hey guys, come here! Look what I found!" Brie exclaims excitedly.

Before her very eyes, lining all four walls, are bookcases filled with history. Brie is in heaven. A reading nook nestles in the corner. Several extra-large candles, also in glass globes and copper holders, are placed on heavy-beamed wooden shelves built into the walls, providing adequate reading light. Several huge volumes lay on antique tables before them in the center of the room: *Heaven Helps Earth; Noah, the Flood and the Ark; The Revenge of Nimrod – Sumerian King Enmerkar; Slave Away; The Creation of Creation; Jeremiah in Egypt; World Powers Foretold by*

Daniel; Living in Jesus' Time; Revelation of the Greek Myths; and lastly *Constantine and The Roman Empire.*

Abby is right on Brie's heels. Grammy Rose, not tripping this time, joins her growing grandchildren.

"Right up your ally," Aunt Cher says to Grammy Rose. "You love this stuff."

Each leather bound book is locked shut with a huge lock in the center front. It appears that these history books were not meant to be read by just anyone. The books are heavy and worn. It is a good thing that the tables they are on are made of very thick, hard wood.

Brie notices a ring of large antique keys as she investigates a drawer at the side of the heavy table on which the books are placed.

"Where did you get these?" Aunt Cher looks stunned.

"Right here in this drawer. Joshua was telling the real story of how Christmas began. I think he used these history books to share Christmas history with us. Check this out!"

Brie inserts the first big, two pronged key into the first book, *Heaven Helps Earth.* The key turns.

Click.

CHAPTER 4

Egypt Escape

The night sky is filled with twinkling stars. Brie looks up to see if the constellations look familiar. They do not. The air is pleasantly warm and gentle breezes caress them. Brie finds herself carrying a tin of figs; Abby has a plugged up jug of water under her arm; Grammy Rose is carrying a crocheted blue, baby blanket; while Aunt Cher has a basket of homemade muffins wrapped in cloth.

There is no snow, no Sturbridge Village, and no one else around, except for the shepherds watching their flocks in the field to their right. They observe the shepherds, all dressed in tunics and head coverings. Oddly enough, so were they. Brie and Abby exchange looks with Aunt Cher and Grammy Rose. Before they say one word, two of the sheep meander over to them as the family stands in the middle of the dirt road. Brie, reaches down to pat one of the gentle creatures.

"They are just curious," the younger shepherd says, making his way to his little lambs. "They love being outside, before it gets too cold."

"They are so soft," Brie notices. "Their wool is so thick."

"It gets thicker. They were shorn in the month of Ziv, but that was after Passover five months ago." He chuckles at his new-found understanding taught to him by the older shepherd. He is proud to share his knowledge with his new friends.

"Ziv was also called Iyyar from the Oral Torah." The younger shepherd beams at Brie.

This young shepherd has just received special instruction from the older shepherd, who learned these lessons well from going to the Temple. Occasionally when his shepherding duties allow, the younger shepherd goes to the Temple to hear the Rabbi recite the Oral Torah also.

"As you know, it is the month of Ethanim. It is almost the end of the summer. The Torah calls this month Tishri. In ten more days it will be Bul, which the Torah calls Heshvan. Then the light rains come, and the following winter months bring more rain, frost and snow. That's when they really need their wool to stay warm. The warm summer nights now are lingering into our next season. But when the cold, rainy and snowy nights come, it is too cold for me to be out in the fields by night, and too cold for my little lambs to be outside, too, even with their thickest coat of wool," the shepherd explains, with a confident smile.

Brie notices that it is not winter here. The evening air is still warm and comfortable. The family joins the other shepherd on the hill with the little lambs behind them so the entire flock stays together.

"Did you see the new star in the sky?" The younger shepherd points to the eastern sky horizon.

"I see it. It shines bigger and brighter than all the others," Abby replies.

"Yes. The star was just born," the shepherd boy continues. "I watch the sky every night. Many say a messiah, a savior is to be born around this time. The Rabbi reads to us from the scroll of Micah. It says, "And you, O Bethlehem Ephrathah, who are little to be among the clans of Judah, from you will come forth for me one who is to be ruler in Israel, whose origin is from old, from ancient days.""

"I never heard of Ephrathah. What is that?" Brie asks.

"You have not studied this? It was thought that Bethlehem Ephrathah was too insignificant a place for the expected messiah to be born. There is another town by the name of Bethlehem, in the land to the north along the Great Sea belonging to the people of Asher, west of Zebulun. But the scroll of Micah points out that although many think that the clans of Bethlehem Ephrathah are too small, that is exactly where Micah predicts the messiah will come from," the older shepherd shares, excited to be able to pass on this timely prophecy.

The conversation peaks Grammy Rose's curiosity. They are walking in the footsteps of history, yet in the present moment of it.

Before their next breath, the fields outside the village where they are standing with the shepherds and the sheep, shine ever so brightly, far more dazzling than the light of the moon, and brighter than the light of the blazing sun in mid-day. An angel of God appears before the shepherds, and God's glory is shining all around them. The shepherds and the family are very fearful. Brie and Abby hold onto one another behind Aunt Cher and Grammy Rose, all with trembling knees.

But the angel reassures the shepherds, "Do not be afraid! Behold, I bring you good news of great joy, the most joyful news ever proclaimed. This news is for all people everywhere! For to you is born this day in the city of David a Savior, who is Christ the Lord. How will we recognize him? You will find a baby wrapped in a blanket, lying in a manger!" the angel announces.

Suddenly, the angel was joined by a vast host of others, the armies of heaven, praising God singing; "Glory to God in the highest heaven and peace among men of goodwill on earth with whom he is pleased!"

"There are so many angels!" Brie exclaims.

"I can't count them all!" Abby agrees in a state of awe.

"They are shinning so brightly. It is mesmerizing," Aunt Cher says incredulously, noticing that her usual panic at such a strange happening is replaced by the deepest sense of peace and reverence she has ever known.

Grammy Rose is speechless, her emotions rising to heights of joy she has never experienced before.

All their hearts are lifted, soaring with the praise and adulation of Hallelujah, which means "Praise Ye Jehovah," Grammy Rose remembers, from her many years of Bible studies.

The singing and harmonies are incredibly beautiful and impossible to describe. They bask in the overwhelming joy of the moment.

When the great army of angels return again to heaven, the older shepherd says to the younger shepherd, "Let us go to Bethlehem Ephrathah!"

"Do you want to come with us to see this wonderful thing that has happened, which Jehovah has told us?" he asks the newcomers.

"Obviously we are in the time before Bible scribes take out God's name, Jehovah, from the Sacred Scriptures over seven thousand, two hundred

times, in a misguided attempt to not misuse it. The Lord's Prayer taught by Jesus, says to keep God's name holy, not erase it from memory," Grammy Rose thinks.

She smiles to herself, knowing that in her present time, God's holy name, Jehovah, is being put back where it was first written. Here they are in the time before his name has been removed. The shepherds are using God's name. In her own time, even Catholic and King James Bibles are putting Jehovah's name back in the Bible. This information was so striking when she learned it, that it burned into her memory.

"We want to come too!" Brie and Abby exclaim together, capturing Grammy Rose's attention back to their antiquated present day.

"Cher, let's follow these shepherds. We can stay close together. I would love to see this!" Grammy Rose agrees.

"This must be a dream. This cannot be happening," Aunt Cher says, shaking her head.

The immediate transition to this poignant time is both new, yet familiar. History is unfolding right before their eyes and ears. Grammy Rose has read the nativity story countless times in her life, but never before had she heard the awe-inspiring sound of the host of angels praising God as she just did, nor had she ever seen the glory of God shine so brightly. The shepherds had never experienced anything like this either, and could not deny it happening before their eyes. Little do the shepherds know how famous this moment in history is, immortalized forever.

They waste no time, with the shepherds and Brie in the lead, and the flock obediently following them along the uneven foot path. Abby's two new furry, woolen friends follow her too. Aunt Cher and Grammy Rose keep up amid the flock of sheep, careful not to trip on the happy little creatures.

They are not alone on this journey. Others are traveling ahead of them and behind them on their way to David's city.

"This is a busy time. It is the first registration of people of the earth of its kind. Caesar Augustus sent out a decree for all the inhabited earth to be registered. Even Syrian Governor Quirinius is interested in the outcome. Everyone belonging to the house of David is registering in Bethlehem. You might not find room to stay since it is so crowded. If that happens, there might still be some room at the stable where I plan to keep the flock overnight. The hay will keep you comfortable and the stable will keep you dry if the rains start," the older shepherd invites.

Bethlehem lies before them. They follow the bright light of the new star shining over the stable. They find Mary and Joseph resting, and the babe lying in the manger, just as the angel had said. Instinctively, the sheep lie down in the hay of the stable. When the shepherds see this, they make known the message that they had been told concerning this young child. And all who heard were astonished at what the shepherds told them. Mary reflects on all these sayings, pondering them in her heart.

Brie gazes in awe at the live manger scene before them. There is a small group of curious visitors who have come to see the new born baby, under the brilliantly shining star.

"Can you believe this Abby? This is the very first Christmas!" Brie excitedly says to Abby.

"Look how tiny baby Jesus is!" Abby answers.

"This looks like the Christmas manger scene alright, but there are no decorated Christmas trees, or wreaths," Aunt Cher notices.

"You must be speaking about the decorated evergreen trees and wreaths at Saturnalia festival honoring the god Saturn coming up in a few months. We celebrate Saturnalia for eight straight days until the feast of the Sun of Righteousness honoring the Babylonian god Mithra. So much merriment. We really enjoy these wild parties after the year of sowing, harvesting, and so much work. Do you celebrate this too?" asks the woman to Cher's left.

In her studies, Grammy Rose learned that in her current time, this Babylonian god Mithra is the same Mithra celebrated as an Iranian god in her time. December 25 celebrates his holiday.

"Yes," Aunt Cher answers.

"Aren't Christmas trees about celebrating Christmas? Joshua told everyone at Sturbridge Village about this earlier, but wasn't that just for dramatic effect?" Aunt Cher pauses to think to herself.

Grammy Rose gets a flash of her last Bible Study on Jeremiah, an Old Testament book written nearly six hundred years before the birth of Jesus. She shares the pagan custom of cutting down evergreen trees, bringing them into the house, and decorating them.

There is a waiting line before them so see the newborn babe. Grammy Rose chats with the locals, while they wait their turn.

"Jeremiah told the people not to cut down trees, nor decorate them with silver and gold, nor to tie them up so they didn't fall over. He told people not to do these and other popular human customs, like astrology that were very popular. Decorating trees for the celebration of Saturnalia was one of the most popular Babylonian traditions. When the Babylonians overtook the land, they made a great show of indoctrinating pagan celebrations hoping to replace traditions of God. The new trend of that day was to denounce God and believe in false gods," Grammy Rose says.

"We cut down Saturnalia trees, and decorate them with the Oscilla, you know, those little baby angels. They help us to remember our first-born children who we make walk through the fire, in order that we can reach enlightenment. It makes us feel close to our children who have passed over into eternal life. The famous Babylonia King Nimrod said to do this," the woman says.

"Jeremiah said not to do the things people have been doing as traditions like this, because they do not honor God. He said not to bow down to these manmade idols because the ways of the people are futile, foolish and vain," Grammy Rose says.

"It really is foolish when you stop to think of it. We cut down living trees in the forest, only to put them in buckets of water, hoping they live longer," the woman laughed. "I must admit there are a lot of idols around here that people worship. I think worshipping that golden calf was stupid. It never was real. I also think some people make idols out of other things too, like how they idolize other things in their life," the woman adds quietly, making sure that no one else hears her private conversation.

"It sounds like people also used to worship the evergreen trees they brought in their houses," Brie recalls from her ancient history class.

"Yes. The Druids did, along with some not so pleasant human ceremonial traditions like this woman mentioned. God never said to do that either," Grammy Rose says, nodding to the woman.

"I never realized we do that very thing God asks us not to do. Imagine us trying not to have a Christmas tree at Christmas?" Grammy Rose poses to Aunt Cher.

"I don't understand what you are saying. We have always celebrated Christmas with a decorated tree. What do you mean?" Aunt Cher is getting more upset with each passing second.

"Mom gets angry when she feels she has to live by religious rules, especially at the holidays," Abby whispers to Brie.

"I understand. I prayed so hard for your Dad too, for God to help him. It didn't work," Brie whispers in Abby's ear, with her heart breaking again. The cousins hug. "God did not listen to me either."

Instead, it is the woman to her left who answers.

"I know," says the woman. "I have heard the writings of Jeremiah, too. We don't really put faith in Saturn, or Mithra. We just enjoy the festivals of food and fun. These celebrations have taken place for almost two thousand years. Who is going to change that now?"

Two thousand years? Didn't all the Christmas traditions start with the birth of Jesus? Cher wonders incredulously.

"I never thought this deeply about it before. It never really occurred to me. It has just been the habit of our human traditions which we fondly repeat year after year," Grammy Rose adds.

"I never really thought that deeply about that either. I think God really knows what is in my heart," the woman answers.

"Jeremiah is reminding us of the way we should live to help us," Grammy Rose encourages.

"What you say is true," the woman says, giving a noncommittal nod and takes her turn to see the infant in the manger.

"The prophet Micah accurately foretold that a savior, a messiah would come, and that he would be from Bethlehem, where we are right now. The Creator is not limited by his creation. It seems even the stars proclaimed the birth of the savior! Cher, I believe we are witnessing the birth of Jesus, only it is not winter," Grammy Rose exclaims, turning her attention to her daughter.

"It cannot be winter," the older shepherd interjects, catching this last part of the conversation. "I cannot keep my flocks out in the fields by night, nor myself either, and the registration of all the inhabited earth could not possibly take place in the winter. The roads would be too treacherous. The mountainous roads would be covered with frost, ice and snow. That would be impassable, and dangerous."

Next it appears to be the Le Beau's turn, with Grammy Rose and the two shepherds by their side, to visit Mary, Joseph and the baby. Aunt Cher is still fuming and confused, but resolved to see the Holy Family. This topic of God has left a sore spot in her heart, since God did not give her the answer her prayers demanded. Brie and Abby are excited to see the infant, leaving what they believe about God for another day's discussion. The baby is so very tiny. Maybe they can get to hold him.

"We have some food and drink to share, if you are hungry," Grammy Rose offers.

Brie opens the tin of figs. Abby offers the water, and Aunt Cher shares the muffins. Rose presents her homemade blue baby blanket. Mary and Joseph are grateful for these simple gifts.

"May I hold the baby?" Brie asks nervously. The last baby she got to hold was Mia, her neighbor's baby, two years ago.

"Yes. How thoughtful of you. I could use a rest," Mary says graciously. Joseph lovingly takes the babe from his mother's arms and hands the precious baby boy to Brie, now sitting next to Mary in the hay. He stays asleep.

"Look how tiny his hands are!" Abby exclaims.

"Praise God for this wonderful news we have been waiting for, for so long, generation after generation! All glory and honor be to God, our Creator, who has kept his promise to send us a savior," the older shepherd says.

"Praise and glory to God forever," the younger shepherd echoes.

For days travelers to Bethlehem visit the new born babe and his family in the stable after hearing the news told by the shepherds, and share provisions they all brought for their stay for the census. Brie and Abby babysit while Mary and Joseph get rest and take care of their census registration. Aunt Cher and Grammy Rose also help with diaper changes and washing clothes when necessary down by the river.

On the eighth day after giving birth, Joseph and Mary take the baby boy to be circumcised. It is on this occasion he is given the name, Jesus, as was foretold by the angel before he was conceived in Mary's womb.

"I studied Greek and Latin. The name Jesus is Latin for the Greek name Iesous. In Hebrew his name is Yeshua or Yehohshua. It means "Jehovah is Salvation," Grammy Rose tells Brie and Abby. Aunt Cher listens, yet still not knowing what to think. Perhaps this is just a dream.

Language did not seem to be a barrier. When each person speaks, the others understand without question. Those listening to Grammy Rose appreciate knowing the meaning of the child's name. The Hebrew people had long awaited this coming of the savior, the salvation by the living God.

Joseph, Mary and Jesus again go to the Temple, forty days after the birth of Jesus, for the purification ceremony. According to the Law of Moses, they had to present Jesus to God, and to offer a sacrifice according to this law, two turtle doves.

"Sovereign Lord God, now I can die in peace. For I have seen the salvation of our God as you promised me you would. I have seen the Savior of the world which you promised in full sight of all people. He is the Light that will illuminate the veiled nations, and he will be the glory of Israel, your people," Simeon cries out in the Temple with arms raised high in prayer of thanksgiving.

"A sword shall pierce your soul, because this child shall be rejected by many people in Israel, to their undoing. But to many others, he will be the greatest joy; revealing the deepest thought of many hearts," Simeon says, speaking to Mary.

"Is this really happening? This can't be really happening. If this is true, then God is real. I don't want God to be real. If God is real, then he turned his back on me, letting me and my family suffer. God let Andre die. I prayed to God. He did not answer my prayer. I am still angry about that. How can I forgive God? I cannot. But this is taking place right in front of my eyes." Aunt Cher thinks, as a tear roll down her cheek. She is trembling. Brie notices.

Brie motions to Abby that her Mom is overcome with emotion. Seeing this, Grammy Rose gives Aunt Cher a tissue. The girls give her a big hug.

"Praise and thanksgiving to the Sovereign Lord God, for allowing me to see this day you send a savior to this world. This Jesus is the deliverance for all of Jerusalem, and the world. Before Jesus, there is no redemption. The Messiah has arrived!" Anna says to Mary and Joseph as she follows them out of the Temple.

"This is the prophetess, Anna. She is the daughter of Phanuel, of the tribe of Asher. She had a very long life with her husband, from when she was age seven to age 84. Then she became a widow. From then on she stayed here at the Temple, worshipping by praying and fasting," Grammy Rose explains to her family after Anna goes back into the Temple.

Mary snuggles baby Jesus closer to her, kissing his forehead. Joseph takes to heart all that is said about this special child, knowing full well that God, who already spoke to him in a dream to take Mary as his wife, has laid a divine charge on him to protect Jesus. Joseph takes this charge seriously in order that he be able to fulfill all that is said of Jesus. Joseph observes in quiet amazement.

From the Temple, Joseph takes his young family to live in a house in Bethlehem, where he continues his work as a carpenter for a couple of years. His workshop is connected to the house. Joseph is skilled at cabinetry and making furniture, taught to him by his father. Not only is his home filled with cabinets, tables, chairs, beds, and tools made by his own hand, but his successful career means that his woodworking also fills the homes of their friends and neighbors.

As time goes on Grammy Rose trades housing and food for herself and her family at the sheep farm for work there, transforming the wool into yarns and threads for blankets, tunics and shawls. Aunt Cher enjoys dying the wool into unique colors, learning how to use nature's organic dyes, and taking the woolen items to the open market. Brie and Abby love helping the shepherds take care of the sheep, doing everything from feeding them, and holding the lambs while they get shirred. But their favorite part is when they are able to be out in the fields with the newest little lambs. They get to know each of them by name.

Brie, Abby, Aunt Cher and Grammy Rose are visiting with Mary and playing with two-year old Jesus on the eventful day three prestigious astrologers, arrive on Bactrian camels, from the east, in the days of King Herod. Each of the impressive domesticated Bactrian camels carries a wise astrologer, bags of gifts, food and water.

"Look at the brightly colored robes and headdress each of the wise men is wearing," Aunt Cher says in astonishment since she has been working hard to get her woolen materials that spectacular.

"These camels are so big!" Brie exclaims with eyes as big as silver dollars.

"These camels have two large humps!" Abby adds.

Brie and Abby saw Bactrian camels for the first time, when Grammy Rose took them at their last visit to Southwick's Zoo in Mendon. They learned how these particular camels could tolerate widely varying degrees of temperature, from the heat of one hundred and twenty degree sun soaked summer days, to freezing minus twenty-two degrees on the most frigid winter nights.

The Bactrian camels before them right now, also have a double row of thick, long eyelashes, and a peculiar smell. Their ears are very hairy to provide protection against the desert sandstorms. Their color is also like the sand, making them almost invisible in plain sight from a distance, an advantage when they travel through dangerous lands, which the desert can be, especially at night.

"Remember we learned that the legend that camels store water in their stomachs is a misconception?" Brie asks Abby.

"Yes. I also remember that they do not store water in their humps either. It is just that they have the capacity to conserve water, but they cannot survive without water for long periods of time," Abby replies.

First the Bactrian camels bow down to let their riders off. Then the wise men bow down in homage to the child Jesus upon seeing him, knowing they are in the presence of true royalty.

"While we appreciate that you recognize us as wise men, magi, please know that we make our living as experienced astrologers. We first sought King Herod in Jerusalem, asking him where the newborn King of the Jews is now living. The new star was born two years ago. It has taken us until now to arrive here from lands far to the east. We told this to King Herod so that we can worship the babe," the astrologer dressed in blue says.

"What is your name?" Joseph asks.

"My name is Gaspar. My name means treasure. Herod and all of Jerusalem became troubled when we asked where the King of the Jews was living. King Herod secretly assembled all the religious leaders and scribes, and asked them where the Christ was to be born. It is surprising to us that King Herod did not know this himself," the astrologer dressed in blue replies.

"Welcome to our home," Joseph greets the astrologers.

Jesus peeks around his mother's light blue tunic, playing hide and seek from behind her knees.

It is the taller astrologer dressed in royal purple who bows and responds next.

"My name is Melchoir. My name means king. The religious leaders and scribes told Herod that the prophecies of the prophet Micah say the child is to be born in the little town of Bethlehem Ephrathah, evidently not such an insignificant Judean village. After all, it is from that very town that a King is to rise to rule the people Israel. However, this was news to King Herod. He did not like hearing that. As if it wasn't enough for King Herod to ask the Jewish religious leaders and scribes about this, he privately called us back in so he could figure out the exact time of the birth of the child. We only have the stars to go by, by means of astrology, but we are very good at telling futures by means of stars."

Jesus is captivated by the ornate Bactrian camels saddled with regal seats.

The third astrologer dressed in red robes smiles at the child and says, "My name is Balthasar. My name means God protect the king. We told King Herod that we first saw the new star two years ago. Herod told us to go and search diligently for the child. When we find him, we are to go back and report to him, so that he too might come and worship him. We rejoice exceedingly at the birth of this child. After such a long journey, it is wonderful to offer praise to him. The star we have followed rests directly over your house."

Mary looks at Joseph, who gives her a nod of approval.

"This is Brie to my right and Abby to my left. Cher is Abby's mother, and Rose is Cher's mother. Won't you please come inside?" Joseph introduces the family, and opens the door for his visitors.

The astrologers humbly accept the invitation and come inside. At the kitchen table, they open treasures of gold, frankincense and myrrh, offering these gifts to Jesus. Mary and Joseph humbly accept these gifts, and store them away in their home.

Jesus smiles at the astrologers as he sits on Brie's lap.

Mary serves cinnamon fig loaves, baked fish and grape juice before the wise men set up their tents and spend the night under the stars. The next morning, they share some startling news.

"Last night we were warned in a dream not to return to Herod," Melchoir says to Mary and Joseph.

"We all had the same dream," Balthasar added.

"We understand that King Herod means to do the child harm. We intend to depart to our own country by another route to avoid King Herod and his men," Gaspar concludes.

Brie holds Jesus, as he waves good-bye to the astrologers. These were the most exciting visitors he has ever had.

King Herod waits until his patience runs out. Time elapses since the visit from the astrologers, who came by seeking the birth of the newborn king. Herod's patience is replaced by an insidious jealousy that is multiplying with each passing day.

An angry King Herod now demands the chief priests and scribes be brought to him. His servants waste no time obeying the command.

"Tell me exactly what you told those astrologers when they asked to see the newborn king of the Jews!" King Herod pounds his fist on the marble stand.

"The astrologers came with the knowledge of the new star in the east that was born at that time. It is written in the Book of Micah, that the birthplace of the messiah, their new king, will be born in Bethlehem Ephrathah. But that is such a small Judean village. Can it be true? We combined this information, and told them to go there," the chief priest says, bowing before the king.

"Gather the soldiers. Tell them to ride on horseback to this same Bethlehem of Judea. My order is to kill all male boys age two and under! There is only one king. I am King! There is no other king before me, infant or otherwise!" King Herod decrees, spurred on by a dark and sinister murderous plot.

For a moment, King Herod debates his direct orders, but as the fallen star and his underlings muse over this ego-driven kingly earthling, their whispers of wiping out the Son of God overtake him, sinking King Herod into further fury and lethal action.

That night, a heavenly angel of God, appears to Joseph in a dream saying, "Get up and flee to Egypt immediately. Take the child and his mother with you, and stay there until I tell you to return. King Herod plans to kill him."

The dream was so real and moving that Joseph wastes no time with doubt or fear. His only thought is if he can save the two year old toddler in time. Without a word to friends and neighbors, Joseph takes Mary and Jesus in the middle of the night, carrying whatever provisions they could gather quickly, and leave for the journey to Egypt, taking the arduous roads less traveled. They remain there until the death of Herod, which fulfills the scripture, "Out of Egypt I have called my son."

The next morning, before daybreak, King Herod's soldiers on horseback storm into Bethlehem Ephrathah of Judah and all its districts. The soldiers meticulously fulfill the strict orders of their King. They do not confuse Bethlehem Ephrathah of Judah with Bethlehem to the north in the land of the Tribe of Asher. The soldiers waste no time, ending the lives of the boy babies who were two years old and younger. Cries of the mothers and families fill the air.

The soldiers enter every dwelling, including the shepherd's house. Brie, Abby, Aunt Cher and Grammy Rose are horrified that anyone could be so cruel. They are so scared by this terrible scene. They don't know where to turn. These are angry men wielding blood-stained swords, with no respect for the shepherd's private property, nor the sanctity of human life, not even baby boys. They are ransacking every room in an effort to find young mothers and their two year old sons. Thankfully, no two year old baby boys live on this sheep farm.

All of a sudden Brie knows where Grammy Rose would turn. Brie prays to God in her heart to save them and finds the key in her pocket. Aunt Cher clings to the girls and Grammy Rose in an effort to get out of the way. They are crouched down near the shepherd's old locked chest. Brie takes the large key out of her pocket and inserts it into the large lock in the chest, and begins turning and twisting the key in an effort to unlock a way back to the hidden library at Sturbridge Village.

"Dear God, help us!" Brie prays all the harder.

Brie never remembers ever praying this hard for anything. She may have had questions about God in the past, but right now, she is a believer. She and Abby saw Jesus as a baby in the manger and spent the last two years whenever they weren't with the sheep, babysitting and playing with Jesus. While they were here at the sheep farm, Aunt Cher learned how to dye wool and spin yarn. Mary taught Brie, Abby and Grammy Rose how to make unleavened bread. They see in real time, what they had heard in church after years of Christmases, about the killing of the innocent babies, in an effort to try to kill Jesus as a baby. Thankfully baby Jesus got away.

Just last night before they went to bed, Joseph had taken the time to teach Brie, Abby, Grammy Rose and Aunt Cher about the important customs and traditions of the Hebrew people, especially on the first night of Passover, marking what Brie knows as the first Seder Meal. Brie knows from her Jewish friends that this has been repeated every year since then. Joseph told them this Passover meal first took place on the night that the angel of death passed over all homes painted by the blood of a lamb, as God directed Moses to proclaim to Pharaoh. Houses without lamb's blood on the lintels of the houses experienced the death of the first-born child, regardless of race, age, color, creed or gender. Had Pharaoh let God's people, the Hebrew people, go from the land of Egypt, this would not have happened. But Pharaoh's heart was stubborn. He refused to let God's people go. Joseph said the Hebrew people commemorate this exact meal each year by eating symbolic foods of bitterness, and reading the history of their people.

Brie has heard this history before. The death of the first-born at the time of the first Passover actually happened. Now she and her family are here again, at a time when the answer to a human problem is to kill innocent babies, male babies this time. God protected Jesus and his family. Now to turn the key, and pray, that God will protect her family too.

Click.

CHAPTER 5

GOOD AND BAD ANGELS

"Let's check out the angel presentation over in the Parsonage. I see a fire in the fireplace," Abe says, not waiting for an answer. His frozen feet lead him right inside the door. Greg is right behind him.

"Welcome, come on in," Pastor Robbins gestures, a real pastor in modern current time, and portraying a Baptist Meetinghouse pastor in the year 1830. "Take a seat near the fire. I just threw a couple of logs on to warm you up again."

Abe, Greg and Sarah file into the Parsonage with other guests anxious to hear about the wonderful news of angels. Sarah likes to top their family Christmas tree at home with the angel holding an electrically lit candle. She loves the sweet influence of the Thomas Kincaid delicately pink, painted angel statues decorating their house she had purchased to benefit women's breast cancer research.

"Tonight in this presentation, we are going to learn about angels. Most people here in 1830 did believe in angels, both kinds," Pastor Robbins says.

Abe and Greg exchange quizzical looks.

"First, let's discuss angels in general. The Bible refers to angels as morning stars, sons of God, holy myriads and sometimes as a heavenly army. The word angel means messenger. Did you know that all of the angels, numbering over one hundred million, were each created individually?" Pastor Robbins asks, with bushy eyebrows raised.

"No, I didn't know that," Abe says.

"That's a lot of angels!" Greg exclaims.

"They are not like us, with the ability to reproduce. God made each and every one of them one at a time. Although they each have individual names and distinct personalities, they take a strong stand against receiving any worship. They defer all worship to God, the good angels, that is. The inhabitants of 1830 did not share the custom many people today have, of putting up statues of angels or paintings of angels on their walls, because they thought that amounted to angel worship, something they did not want to do," Pastor Robbins explains.

"I never thought much about that," Sarah says.

"Good angels?" Greg asks.

"Yes. Bible history tell us that not all the angels chose to worship God as their sovereign ruler. Do you remember when God creates Adam and Eve? What does he tell them not to do?"

"I know! I know!" the cute teenage girl next to Abe exclaims. "God told them not to eat from the Tree of Knowledge or else they will die."

Abe smiles at her.

"What happens next?" Pastor Robbins asks.

Not to be out done by a girl, Abe remembers Grammy Rose's answer to this question, and says, "The snake tempts Eve to eat the fruit. Adam eats it too. Then they get kicked out of the Garden of Eden."

"Anything else?" Pastor Robbins asks.

Wasn't that the end of it? The first man and woman sinned against God in that Original Sin and now all humans must die. Isn't that it in a nutshell? Sarah wonders.

No one has the answer to Pastor Robbins question.

"What was the punishment for the snake?" Pastor Robbins prompts his interested audience.

The brother of the cute teenage girl responds, while wiggling his body at the same time. "The snake has to crawl around on its belly and has to eat dust."

The audience laughs.

"Yes. Think of this. What does God first create?" Pastor Robbins.

"I know! I know!" the cute teenage girl next to Abe exclaims again. "God first creates the heavens the earth, water, sun, moon and the stars."

"God also causes the grass to grow, and seed-bearing plants and fruit trees. But one of the trees get Adam and Eve in trouble," Greg says, trying to remember what the cute teenage girl had just said.

"Was it really one of the trees that got Adam and Eve in trouble?" Pastor Robbins asks with a twinkle in his eye.

"No," Abe says. "It was the talking snake, you know, the devil named Satan in the Tree of Knowledge that was the problem. He tricked Eve into eating the fruit, even though God told Adam not to."

"What a great group of guests we have here tonight." Pastor Robbins congratulates his young audience. "God gives Adam only one rule not to break, not to eat from the middle of the garden, from the Tree of Knowledge. Later God creates Eve, a partner to go through life with, so Adam is not alone.

"One day Satan uses the serpent to talk and temp Eve. The serpent challenges that God will not in fact make them die if they eat the forbidden fruit. Rather, the devil, Satan, lies and tells Eve that instead of dying, their eyes will be opened, and both she and Adam will be like God, knowing what is good and evil. Eve was deceived and ate from the forbidden fruit. Adam, however, was not deceived since God spoke directly with him, but he ate the forbidden fruit anyway." Pastor Robbins pauses to catch his breath.

"Wait. Is this really about eating a piece of forbidden fruit, or is it something else?" Sarah asks. Her mother would often speak to her about God, but she simply did not remember the answer to this question.

"Very good question. Do you think God is talking about punishing a snake in this story?" Pastor Robbins enjoys drawing his audience to a deeper conclusion.

It is the older man with the red muffed hat who answers. "No. The snake is really the devil. He tries to tempt all mankind not to listen to God. God told Adam not to eat from the tree in the middle of the garden. But the devil lies to Eve, and says she does not need to listen to God, and that she will not die."

"Good answer. In the very first book of the Bible, in Genesis, Satan challenges God's right to rule. Satan thinks both angels and people can rule themselves, without God giving them any rules or laws, in heaven and on earth," Pastor Robbins answers.

"I have been forgetting that it was the angels who first revolted against God's authority. That's right! Some of the angels do not want to obey God. They think they can rule over themselves just as well." the older man says, as if a light switch just went off in his mind. "So, there really IS an evil force tempting us not to listen to God."

"The congregation at the Center Meetinghouse here in 1830, believe in Jesus as their Savior. They also have discovered a very important secret hidden in the book of Daniel, which you will discover for yourselves in other workshops tonight," Pastor Robbins reminds his guests. "This is why the people of Sturbridge Village were so cautious to worship God only, and not give in to the false gods and pagan religions that they believed were influenced by bad angels."

"Are they still here?" Greg asks.

"Christians say we are still under the evil influence today, with so much evil in the world. The Christians in this congregation believe in God and Jesus. They believe Jesus is God's first creation, even before all of the angels were made," Pastor Robbins explains.

"Wait. You mean Jesus was made before ANY other angels were made?" Abe begins to ferment his question.

"Yes," Pastor Robbins simply says.

"Does that mean Jesus was created BEFORE Satan?" Abe asks with huge eyes of wonder.

"Yes. That means Jesus and Satan knew each other before Satan rebelled against God, and before Satan tempted Adam and Eve to follow in his footsteps," Pastor Robbins says.

"So, we can either follow the good example of Jesus, or the bad example of Satan," the older man says.

Sarah is watching the boys, amazed at how this subject of good and bad angels has caught their attention, especially Greg.

"The 1830 Christians of Sturbridge Village believe Jesus came to earth to teach us how to live better," Pastor Robbins says, carefully choosing his words to his interfaith audience.

"Do the Quakers at the Friends Meetinghouse believe in Jesus?" Abe asks.

"The Religious Society of Friends who attend the Quaker Meetinghouse in 1830 do not all agree who God and Jesus are, nor do they agree that the Bible is the inspired word of God, despite what 2 Timothy 3:16 says. They leave the light of understanding up to the individual. Since both houses of worship are here, I am teaching you about both conceptual understandings," Pastor Robbins explains as best he can.

"Did the Quakers at the Friends Meetinghouse believe in angels?" Sarah asks.

"That's hard to say. The Friends believe they do not need rituals nor ministers or priests to lead a person to God. They do not define God to individuals, but rather allow for individuals to find this out for themselves," Pastor Robbins explains.

"A friend of mine is a Quaker. He told me they did promote the equality of women, and had women writers and preachers in the 1600's. I bet they were angels," a red-cheeked, beefy man chuckles.

The guests laugh.

"I am here to present Bible history as we are displaying for you tonight in the live manger scene outside. According to scripture, an angel named Gabriel announces to Mary that she is going to have a child, and that his name is to be Jesus. Any more questions on this subject?" Pastor Robbins asks, trying to stay on the topic for the evening.

"Are angels aliens?" Greg asks, amid giggles throughout the room.

"Another very good question," Pastor Robbins smiles. "Angels are from a higher realm. It might be more accurate to say that there are different ranks of angels that have different assignments. Gabriel is seen in the Bible as a messenger of God, but other angels serve before the throne of God, and others intervene between God and people. There is even an army of heavenly angels which are on the side of Jesus at Armageddon referred to in Revelation 19:14, 15. No matter which role they have, the good angels are always faithfully serving God. This is the common Christian thought of 1830 which is still with us today," Pastor Robbins answers.

"You keep mentioning good angels, so what are the bad angels doing at that time?" Greg asks curiously.

Pastor Robbins thinks for a moment, wanting to stay true to what Christians believed in 1830.

"Keep in mind that one of the reasons the early settlers came here from across the ocean was for religious freedom. Christians wanted the freedom to believe what they believed without religious or political punishment, ridicule or retaliation. As I mentioned with the Quaker Friends, belief in angels is not part of their creed. The Center Meetinghouse and my ministry, represents mainline Christianity, which does believe in angels, good as well as bad. We've discussed some of the roles of good angels. Now let us take a closer look at what early Christian settlers believed about bad angels.

"Remember that Christians of 1830 believe that keeping non-Christian traditions is superstitious because of their nature gods instead of the God who created nature. It is about one hundred and forty years since the Salem Witch trials. Christians in the Village believe in Jesus, not Wicca and other pagan practices and false gods, which they think are influenced by the bad angels. They oppose these practices so much, because they know they stem all the way back to Nimrod, a king in the pagan city of Babylon. He was the first king to build an expansive kingdom after the flood, which is ironic, because he was such a bad king, setting himself up as a great hunter in opposition to God, as Genesis 10:8,9 tells us. Yet his great-grandfather is Noah, a man who walked with God," Pastor Robbins explains.

"Wait a minute!" Abe says with light bulbs going off in his mind. "You mean that Nimrod was also tempted by Satan?"

"Yes," Pastor Robbins says. "Noah chose to follow God. Even though Nimrod is Noah's great-grandson, Nimrod made a conscious choice not to follow God. Nimrod gave in to the temptation of Satan. Most temptations start out as simple attractions to people, places or things. Satan plays to what our egos want to hear. He is devious."

"Sounds like families today, one generation fighting with the previous one, just to be different, and not as religious," the short man says, standing in the doorway.

"That's a good point. The bad angels we are talking about, in the minds of the early settlers and most Christians today, tempt and entice all humankind to choose selfish and greedy pursuits over worshipping God with a pure heart. Many believe that the bad angels entice the people to mix popular human customs that ultimately honor false gods, with honoring God alone. The only intention bad angels have is entice people to denounce God, challenge belief in God, and seek glorifying self, pleasure, fame and fortune at the expense of God. Any more questions?" Pastor Robbins asks.

"Sounds like what you were explaining earlier with Adam, Eve and Satan in the Garden of Eden," Sarah comments.

"What did Nimrod do that was so bad?" a boy sitting next to Greg asks.

Pastor Robbins takes a deep breath, pausing to think of the best way to be true to history, in a way his guests can hear it.

"Well, Nimrod is a good example of someone being influenced by a bad angel, or Satan. Nimrod set himself up as a god for people to worship instead of God. Nimrod created a tyranny. Does anyone know what a tyranny is?" Pastor Robbins inquires of his captive audience.

"It is cruel and unfair treatment by people, or a government, with power over others," the man in the red hat answers.

"That is correct. In a government, it is when all the power belongs to one person, the person is called a tyrant," Pastor Robbins explains.

"Now think about this, Nimrod said that the only way for people to not have fear of God was to be dependent on himself. Nimrod is the father of all other Babylonian gods. Some encyclopedias even call Nimrod the horned one. God himself speaks against this practice in the Old Testament Book of Jeremiah 32:35, telling people that Nimrod had high altars built for the fire sacrifices, something that the true God had never said to do, and had not even imagined." The pastor pauses, observing his keenly interested audience, then continues.

"This was first done, according to Bible history, noted in Jeremiah 19:5, that the place would no more be called Tophet, nor The Valley of the son of Hinnom, but the valley of slaughter. The word Tophet means "the drum." Drums were played to drown the screams of the victims in the flames." The wide-eyed audience now groans at the thought.

"Are you making this up?" the young girl next to Greg squeals.

"Unfortunately this is accurate history. Keep in mind this is also the same valley Jesus compared to the fire of Gehenna, in the New Testament Book of Mark 9:43-49, then used as a place for trash and waste matter that was burned. Fires burned there all the time in Jesus' day. It was thought to be located where it connected to the ravine of the Kidron, which separates Jerusalem from the Mount of Olives. These are real historical places.

"Those little baby angels people decorate with at Christmas are a remnant of this history. Check out "Oscilla" in the Dictionary of Greek and Roman Antiquities, third edition, volume II, when you get over to the Rome presentation. Then Nimrod threatened to have his revenge on God if he were to flood the earth again. He even challenged God that he would build a tower that the water could not reach, and there you have his unfinished temple-tower, built in the model of the Tower of Babel," Pastor Robbins says, with his hand on the Bible. "You can check this out for yourself if you would like."

"Wasn't the Tower of Babel destroyed by fire?" the cute, teenage girl next to Abe asks.

"Yes. Nimrod was furious with God for destroying that temple tower by fire, because they built it high with its top in the heavens. They were more interested in making a celebrated name for themselves rather than worshipping God the way he instructed his people to worship him. Nimrod vowed humans would never be scattered through the earth again, the way the razing of the Tower of Babel did. Even their language became confused. Nimrod used the Tower of Babel as his model to begin construction of his own mega temple tower. The city of Babel later becomes the thriving city of Babylon on the shores of the Euphrates River, in the fertile plain between this and the Tigris River, which used to be called the Hiddekel River in Nimrod's time," Pastor Robbins says as he smiles at his interested guests.

"The Christians of 1830 wanted nothing to do with Nimrod, nor the customs he started. Sometimes today, people do not want to know this. But this is historical fact. It is the origin of the current Christmas customs, and the Easter traditions. Keep in mind that Nimrod's wife is named Ishtar, pronounced 'Easter.' Both she and Nimrod came from the pagan land of Canaan. But the Easter story is for another day. It is obvious the early Christians in Jesus day, the 1830's and now, want to honor the true God, not the false god Mithra, Saturn, or Moloch," Pastor Robbins adds.

"I think I read something about this," Sarah says. "Professor Elias Austin said there was a Sumerian King with a similar name to Nimrod, if you take out the vowels."

"Yes. In those early days vowels and punctuation were not used, which is one of the reasons it is so difficult to translate the words accurately. Look at the name Nimrod without the vowels, NMR. The 'd' turns the word into a verb, so you don't count the 'd.' Professor Austin noted that there was a Sumerian king about that same time in history, who was also known as a great hunter. He said the letters "kar" at the end of a name denoted that he was a hunter. The name of the Sumerian king he found was Enmerkar. Now drop the hunter portion, the "kar," and drop the vowels. What consonants are left?"

His guests think for a moment, then Abe says, "NMR!"

"Right you are," Pastor Robbins says enthusiastically. "I think it is possible that Professor Austin is correct.

"I leave you with one last thought. Do you remember who the first Christian martyr was?" Pastor Robbins asks.

"Stephen is the first Christian martyr. I'm a devout Catholic. We celebrate the feast day of the first martyr on December 26," the man sitting next to Sarah says.

"That's right. Do you know why he was stoned to death?" the pastor asks his guests.

Silence.

"Stephen was stoned to death to stop him from preaching against what has now become our popular Christmas traditions. He accused the people of his day of following "another Christ," like 2 Corinthians 11:3-4 points out. The settlers here in 1830 cared very much about not following non-Christian, superstitious traditions, or bad angels. They believed in what Jesus taught, and stayed close to his message," Pastor Robbins takes a deep breath, followed by all his guests.

"Bible history is echoed in archeology and political history of the world. Let's turn our attention back to the good angels, the good news of the birth of Jesus, the joy of tonight's celebration, the choirs of angels singing praise to God, and join in the happy news with all our festivities. You might also like to check out one of the most fascinating living exhibits this evening is over at the Religious Society of Friends Meetinghouse. The Quakers are very instrumental in initiating the Underground Railroad. It is quite an impressive demonstration," Pastor

Robbins says, as he wraps up his talk for this session, suggesting another great program tonight.

"Let's go see the Underground Railroad." Greg jumps up, with hyperactive legs carrying the rest of him right out the door.

Abe and Sarah run to catch up to Greg, who for some unknown reason, has wandered off the main path of the circle around the Town Common, and bolted straight up the road between the Center Meetinghouse and the Town Pound.

"Greg," his mother calls in a panic. "Where are you going?"

"I think I saw a dog!" Greg answers, over his shoulder, before dashing off into the woods.

CHAPTER 6

PANIC OF 1837 AND EFFECTS
OF REV. ADIN BALLOU

Brie finds herself pulling the key out of the antique book entitled, *Heaven Helps Earth*. Abby, Aunt Cher and Grammy Rose are all huddled next to her, staring at one another. She feels bewildered and excited at the same time.

"Were we dreaming?" Aunt Cher asks, feigning denial. "Wake up! Wake up!" She exclaims and pinches herself to see if she is awake.

"If it was a dream, we all dreamed the same thing. I know I suggested for us all to put ourselves in the story, when it was time to read the book, but that was so real!" Grammy Rose exclaims, wondering how anything so strange could have possibly happened.

"Grammy Rose, didn't you say that Jeremiah says not to believe in astrology?" Brie asks.

"I'm wondering about the same thing myself. You're thinking about the astrologers coming to visit Jesus when he was two years old, right?" Grammy Rose herself is having the same question.

"Yes. If we are not supposed to go to astrologers, then why would the story about the birth of Jesus have astrologers in it?" Brie continues.

"That's a good question," Abby says reviving a bit after the ordeal.

The girls perch their heads in their hands, leaning forward for the answer.

"I'm not sure I have the answer for this, just observations. I notice that when the astrologers enter the picture, things start going bad. Joseph, Mary and Jesus have to flee in the middle of the night, running for their lives. They leave their families and everyone they know, leaving Joseph's job as a carpenter, and flee to Egypt," Grammy Rose begins.

"And those poor baby boys who the soldiers were trying to kill with their swords," Cher adds.

"History shows that the soldiers did kill all they could find. Obviously this is horrible. I've wondered about this before. This too happens right after the astrologers enter this historical account. The astrologers' appearance stirs up King Herod into a fit of anger. He uses the information from the astrologers to figure out when baby Jesus was born. I get the feeling there is more to the new star in the sky over Bethlehem," Grammy Rose drifts off in thought, trying to put all the puzzle pieces together, but they are not fitting quite right.

"What about the star?" Brie and Abby ask in unison.

"I also have a question. I have not thought out all the ramifications to this thought, and I could be wrong. Let me say that right up front. But it seems a contradiction for God to say not to use astrologers, then for him to turn around and use astrologers as part of announcing his Son Jesus to the world. The only way this makes any sense to my mind is that the Bible uses the word stars for angels. My question is, what if the star that shines over the stable at Bethlehem is not one of the good angels, but a bad angel, you know, Satan?" Grammy Rose asks.

"There. The thought is out. It has been a point of concern for many years now, how so many bad things occur after the introduction of the astrologers," Grammy Rose muses to herself.

"Oh, this is ridiculous," Aunt Cher says contentiously. "I don't even know if I believe in God, never mind the devil! I refuse to believe this."

"The Bible has many references to the angels as stars, even the fallen angels in the book of Revelation says one-third of the 'stars,' bad angels, were swept out of heaven at the battle in heaven with Archangel Michael. It is not impossible. What if it is true? And think of this, when Jesus heals demonic people later in his life, they all scream out who he is. Jesus tells them to be quiet, but first they all acknowledge him," Grammy Rose points outs.

"Grammy Rose, didn't you tell me while ago that Satan can transform himself into an angel of light?" Brie considers the possibility.

"Yes. You know my life's work was as a holistic counselor/practitioner," Grammy Rose confides. "I was taught to always 'connect to the light' before I started a healing session. I began noticing that they never say God, they only say to connect to 'light,' or 'Source.' What if the source of this light is not the God of heaven, but the god of this world who got kicked out of heaven?" She is asking this question to herself as much as to her family. This has been her life's work. How would coming to a different conclusion about this "light" or "Source" affect her beliefs now?

"Those choirs of angels singing when we were with the shepherds were shinning so brightly I could barely keep looking at them," Brie acknowledges.

"Yes. It was like looking directly into the sun," Abby adds.

"I do believe the heavenly choir of good angels sang out praises of joy and thanksgiving to God, to announce the birth of Jesus to the shepherds and the world," Grammy Rose says, considering all possibilities.

"I need a drink, or a snack to clear my head," Aunt Cher says, leaving not only to find refreshment, but to look a bit harder for another way out of the library, the pantry, and this conversation.

Brie and Abby stay in the library as the grown-ups head for the pantry.

"Abby, I need to talk to you about something that's bothering me," Brie begins to confide to her best friend.

"Sure. What is it?" Abby is all ears. She is a great listener, unlike her twin brother. Maybe it is because Abby is an adolescent female like herself. Abby and Brie are simultaneously maturing from a pre-teen and a teenager into heroic women in today's modern world. But a conflict is brewing beneath Brie's emotional, intellectual and spiritual self. Perhaps Abby will understand.

"I find it confusing. Grammy Rose says that God is real. You and your Mom sometime say there is no God. Even I say there is no God sometimes. But when I'm scared, I find myself praying," Brie confesses.

"I like the answers science and nature have," Abby answers, not really sure what to say.

"I like intelligent reasons for things too, but sometimes there aren't any good answers. For example, why is there war? Why are people starving? Why can't the world's governments get along for the good of the people? Why don't we all agree with the undeniable facts about climate change and global warming? Why doesn't everyone want to protect the environment? We only have one earth for all of us to live on." Brie confides her struggle.

"I don't have an answer for that," Abby says.

"I don't want to believe in God. Then I do. Then I don't. When I get scared, I pray. Am I a coward?" Brie finally expresses what is troubling her.

"No, Brie. You are not a coward. You are the bravest person I know," Abby says.

"You're such a good friend Abby. You won't tell anyone, will you?" Brie asks, not sure she should have shared this.

"Don't worry Brie. I don't ever say this out loud, especially to Mom. I don't want to hurt her. But ever since Dad died, I do pray to God for him. I just can't believe that this life is all that there is. Grammy Rose says that Jesus promises us all resurrection after this life. I hope to see my Dad again then," Abby admits her innermost secret to Brie.

The girls hug each other and promise to stay best friends forever.

Brie and Abby are captivated by a scene outside one of the windows at the corner of the room. Aunt Cher and Grammy Rose coming running in to look out too. An ambulance is appearing to be coming into the Village itself. Sirens blare loudly, with horns honking and lights flashing.

"What is going on?" Grammy Rose asks.

Grammy Rose feels a prick in her arm. She looks down to see a cut on her forearm near her elbow. In her haste, a pin she is wearing falls off her sweater, which she tries to catch by folding her arm up. The pin unlatched and dug into her arm.

"Ouch!" she exclaims.

Aunt Cher runs over to help her. "Let's wash this at the sink with soap. It doesn't look bad. I've got a Band-Aid in my pocket. I'm ready for anything, at any time, except maybe this adventure," she says.

"Oh, I feel so clumsy. I don't understand what is happening," Grammy Rose says.

"Don't worry Mom. You will be all better in no time," Aunt Cher soothes with a comforting touch.

Brie discovers a locked chest with leather straps on the floor under the book table in the hidden library. They had missed seeing it in the shadows cast by the flickering candles in the night. Curiosity gets the best of her, as well as the rest of the family who are flocking around her. She inserts the smallest key on the large key ring, and twists it.

Click.

Brie looks around to find herself and her family are in a retro Sturbridge Village, among the hustle and bustle of the Town Common, standing in front of the Center Meetinghouse on an exceptionally brisk spring morning. Citizens here are proud of the Center Meetinghouse, most of them helped to build it in 1832 as a Baptist Meetinghouse. She finds the women dressed in simple full, ankle length linen dresses, gathering from under the breast tied around to the back, and big puffy sleeves. They are also wearing linen day caps with ruffles hugging their faces, beneath wide brimmed bonnets with chin ties. The colors of their dresses and bonnets match. Grammy Rose finds herself in soft pink, Aunt Cher in a golden amber tone; and she and Abby are in a sky blue and navy respectively. They observe each other's attire, happy that it is not tunics this time.

Tulips and daffodils dance in the gentle, colder than normal breeze, brightening the otherwise gloomy crowd around them. The recession hit hard. It was nothing personal. It was just business.

Shell shocked, Brie and her family have just left the bank in Sturbridge Village, upon hearing that they have lost their home and land. The banker tried to explain to them that last month, on May 10, 1837 specifically, banks in New York City suspended what they said were specie payments, meaning that the banks would no longer redeem commercial paper money at full face value. In the process of this new bank policy, Brie, Abby, Aunt Cher and Grammy Rose lost their home and land on the Quinebaug River flowing through here. Not knowing where to turn next, they walked over to the Center Meetinghouse.

Pliny Freeman, with his horse and wagon, is just coming into the Town Common and takes notice of the crowd of people now all sympathizing with one another in front of the Center Meetinghouse.

"Why is everyone here?" Pliny asks, trading his morning chores at the farm for buying more milk cans from the Tin Shop. Since he is a farmer, and not wanting to get his one and only coat dirty, Pliny is wearing his waumase, a heavy wool shirt, which is warmer and easier to work in at his farm, and very popular in New England.

"We just lost our house and our land. The bank foreclosed on our property. We don't know where to go," Grammy Rose laments, speaking up for the family.

"My wife needs help to finish planting, weeding my garden, and milking the cows. Most of all, we have just shorn the sheep. Delia needs help with getting the wool ready for market; to clean and card it, and spin it on the big, walking wheel into thread and yarn. She is heavy with child now, due any day. I can trade your services at my farm for food and shelter," Pliny offers, with a smile that warms Brie's heart.

Brie breaths a sign of relief. She doesn't want her family to know just how upset she really is, especially Abby. They always look out for each other. She finds it extremely frightening when the grownups are even more scared than they are, ever since Uncle Andre passed away.

Yesterday they were neighbors. From today onward, and until they can get back on their feet, they will be the Freeman's live in farmhands in an equitable barter.

"We accept your kind offer." Grammy Rose blushes with embarrassment, but wastes no time in replying.

Pastor John Burkhart, Sturbridge Village's own Baptist minister, approaches the crowd from the parsonage, having recently returned from his horse and buggy trip to visit the Reverend Adin Ballou, the newly installed minister of the Mendon Unitarian Church. Reverend Ballou's controversial views of the afterlife have already resulted in him being disowned for being an apostate by his father's church, known as the Christian Connection, where his father was a minister at the Ballou Meetinghouse. Most recently the good reverend was fired as minister of the Milford Unitarian Church, permanently. But Ballou was invited by the Mendon Unitarian Church to be their minister, intrigued by his more humane treatment of human souls after death. Rev. Ballou, after reading the Bible at length, did not agreed with the traditional Christian that God would eternally punish his creation with hellfire and brimstone.

"Come on in to the Meetinghouse," Rev. Burkhart invites, noticing the tension mounting in his flock of souls, commiserating at the bottom of the steps.

Rev. Burkhart's heart, mind and soul is stirred to the depths of his being from his visit with Rev. Adin Ballou. He begins his opening remarks saying, "I have just returned from an inspiring visit with the Reverend Adin Ballou, the ninth minister of the Mendon Unitarian Church. There are only eight Unitarian Churches in all Massachusetts. As you know, we stopped getting federal assistance to our churches four years ago. Our Massachusetts congregations and politicians were the last holdout receiving federal money. Try though we might, we now have a separation of church and state, which is not altogether bad, since only some of the churches were receiving all of the federal assistance.

"Let me share some good news with you to help us focus on higher concepts in this dire recession. Rev. Adin Ballou has a different understanding of the afterlife, which he has paid a dear price in his ministry for promoting.

"I traveled to visit Rev. Ballou and his congregation by horseback, along Route 16, which is part of the Transportation Revolution taking place now. Many of you might find work by rebuilding the roads. There are over three thousand, seven hundred miles of turnpikes and toll roads marked for better improvements and construction in all of New England. So many of our roads are deeply rutted, and some near impossible to pass on safely. I thank God that this road is now passable, so I can share this visit with you.

"Rev. Ballou believes in a doctrine that he calls nonresistance. It is the same doctrine that Jesus introduced, replacing the Old Testament, "an eye for an eye," with the New Testament version, "love your neighbor as yourself," including loving your enemies. However, Rev. Ballou does not promote pacifism, since the good Reverend believes in the aggressive use of spiritual force through prayer, the active promotion of the good and true against every kind of sin, just as we Baptists do.

"Physical force, naturally, he is against in any form, such as from the armed violence of war to attempt or coerce a person into doing anything he is not willing to do. He is organizing and dedicating his next book, which he is titling *Christian Non-Resistance* to this moral philosophy. Consider the possibilities of the Declaration he is asking his congregation to pledge:

"... never under any pretext whatever to kill, assault, beat, torture, rob, oppress, defraud, corrupt, slander, revile, injure, envy or hate any human being – even my worst enemy;

"... never in any manner to take or administer an oath;

"... never to manufacture, buy, sell or use any intoxicating liquor or beverage;

"... never to serve in the army, navy or militia of any nation or chieftain;

"... never to bring action at law, hold office, vote, join a legal posse, petition a legislature or ask governmental interpositions in any case involving a final authorized resort to physical violence;

"... never to indulge self-will, bigotry, love of pre-eminence, covetness, deceit, profanity, idleness or an unruly tongue;

"... never to participate in lotteries, games of chance, betting or pernicious amusements;

"... never to resent reproof or justify myself in a known wrong;

"... never to aid, abet or approve others in anything sinful, but through divine assistance always to recommend and promote with my entire influence the holiness and happiness of mankind."

"This leads me to another point which I hope and pray you can hear clearly and without bias. Consider Rev. Ballou's conclusion, that it is a Christian duty to withdraw from government, because it supports war, slavery, capital punishment and other acts of violence. He says to hold an office, or even vote is, therefore, to sanction violence," says Rev. Burkhart.

An audible gasp escapes the lips of some of the congregation gathered before him. Some are taking in this knowledge as if they had never pondered these points in this view before. The congregation exchange looks to see how each other is handling this new knowledge.

"Keep in mind," Rev. Burkhart continues, "Rev. Ballou does not advocate either resistance to government or even a complete disassociation from it. He believes you can always make use of legal titles to property, patent inventions, and pay general taxes, provided that such things do not make you an accomplice in violence.

"The recession this year, 1837, has sent everyone into a panic. But I urge you to use the power of prayer to the good Lord above to spur you on to wholesome care of one another. We need to help one another who have fallen upon hard times. An encouraging book to read tonight, to help keep your mind off these troubles, in the book of Daniel in the Old Testament. We will discuss this in length next Sunday.

"I leave you with one last glimpse of hope. Upon closer inspection of the Bible, Rev. Ballou is promoting an alternative to an afterlife of hellfire and brimstone teaching you have been accustomed to hearing being preached from this pulpit. Our King James Bible, in the Book of Romans 6:7 says, "For he that is dead is freed from sin." Rev. Ballou and I discussed this point at length. That verse specifically says that the penalty for sin is death. That means, once we are dead, there is no more penalty to be paid, no need for hellfire and no need for brimstone."

Brie, Abby, Aunt Cher and Grammy Rose have smiles on their faces upon hearing this, along with everyone else in the Center Meetinghouse. As former Catholics, they were all taught about suffering the eternal punishment in hell if their sins were deemed to be mortal, and a shorter punishment but still hellfire and brimstone in purgatory for venial or lesser sins.

"Who is perfect, and has never sinned?" Brie wonders. She knows there are times when she and Abby lied once or twice so they don't get in trouble. They even blamed their brothers for eating the rest of the chocolate cake just last week.

It was as if a huge weight that had been weighing on them most of their lives, was lifted immediately off their shoulders. Aunt Cher had never believed in hell, but she had never replaced that belief with anything else either.

People begin filing out of the Center Meetinghouse. Townsfolk are talking about Rev. Burkhart's last point, obviously relieved, and in lighter spirits than when they first came in.

Pliny Freeman purchases new milking cans, and takes the cans and Brie's family in the wagon, making their way up to the farm. Brie and Abby already know how to take care of sheep since their time with the shepherds.

"I will show you how to shear sheep and feed them," Pliny tells Brie.

The Freemans are friends and neighbors of theirs. This kind offer is still humbling, but necessary. Mrs. Delia Freeman sets out hot cups of tea to warm them up on this windblown, chilly day.

"I know how to dye the wool," Aunt Cher contributes to the conversation.

"I use plant parts to make many different colors. I use everything, like leaves, stems, blossoms of the forests and flowers from the fields; roots, bark, nut hulls, tree galls, berries, fruits, pits and skins, mosses, lichens and fungi; and non-plants such as insects and shellfish," Mrs. Freeman says taking a sip from her tea.

"Brie and Abby, you can help with cleaning the wool before your grandmother and I take turns spinning the yarn on the high walking wheel. You will have to card it too. I will show you how," Mrs. Freeman adds.

"This is very gracious of you and Mr. Freeman to take us in like this," Grammy Rose says.

"In tough times like these, we all have to stick together. That's the only way we will make it. We need to keep our payments to the bank too. We understand. Think no more about it. We will work together. There's a lot of work to be done. I truly can use the help," Mrs. Freeman says, wiping her brow and holding her back to support her very large and growing baby.

"We have extra room in the back section of the barn where we keep clean hay. It will be comfortable for you there. There are extra blankets in the cabinet in the corner," Mrs. Freeman welcomes.

"When and where do you dye your yarn?" Aunt Cher asks.

"I usually do this the third week of May after the sheep are shorn, but this year I am so late since my child will be arriving soon. Thank you for offering to help us. We stoke up fires for the pots, as many fires as we have different colors of dye," Mrs. Freeman answers.

"We need to get this done quickly," Mr. Freeman adds. "We can get very good prices right now that the textile mill is operating. But we have a back log of sorting to be done." Mr. Freeman gives his wife a gentle smile.

"I'll show you girls how to card it, to give the wool the best quality for spinning. Cher, the girls might need your help with this. It gets put into a scouring solution in the hot boiling pot, for about ten to fifteen minutes, before we take it out with a stick. Next it goes into cooler water temperatures. Then you need to spin the water out by hand, by holding it tightly in your hand and waving it around," Mrs. Freeman instructs.

"Yes, but be careful not to drop it because it will be wet, and we do not want it to get dirty. Then comes the detangling process. We have a machine in the barn that has rollers with brushes that takes out the debris and separates and smooths out the fibers, taking out the dense portions, and making all the fibers go in the same direction," Mrs. Freeman adds.

"We have worked with this process in the past," Aunt Cher remembers from her recent past experiences.

"Very good," Mrs. Freeman smiles. "We have so much wool that we are able to spin both thread and yarn. Cher, since you are familiar with this process, why don't you take charge of dying the wool. Rose, you and I will spin using the walking wheel."

Fires are lit under pots of scouring solution, hot soapy water to wash out all contaminates and impurities, under the watchful eyes of Mrs. Freeman. The cleaning and dying project begins and takes most of the day.

Mrs. Freeman makes thrifty use of the outside fires for cooking a hearty cabbage, potato, carrot and beef stew after the day's task. Following the meal enjoyed on the outside picnic table, they move the wooden benches around the dwindling fire for storytelling before exhaustion overtakes them. Brie and Abby are exhausted, and head off for the clean hay in the barn. Before long Grammy Rose and Aunt Cher join them, closing the barn door behind them.

Unaccustomed to the lack of indoor plumbing and presence of outside bathrooms, Brie gets Abby to go with her to the outhouse, which is thirty-five feet behind the barn and the house, under the light of the moon. Brie takes the first turn.

A lone wolf howls in the not too distant woods. Brie and Abby quickly trade places. A second wolf howls even closer this time. Abby doesn't want to come out of the outhouse because it sounds like the wolves are very close, but her cousin is out there. They have yet to walk back to the barn.

Silently and slowly, Abby opens the creaky door and slips out next to Brie, who is now shaking dramatically. Over on the rock outcrop to their right, is a silhouette of two wolves in the light of the full moon behind them. The wolves are now looking directly at them. One of them starts to crouch down and creep towards them.

"Run!" screams Brie. Their feet are flying barely touching the ground. They can hear the growls of the wolves approaching closer behind them. As they make it back, Brie spots the lock on the door. She wastes no time inserting the smaller key into the cast iron rim lock on the barn door.

Click.

CHAPTER 7

ABE LINCOLN, CHARLES DARWIN, THE $20 BILL, AND A WOLF

"Greg! Stop!" Sarah cries out after her attention deficit son. Usually she manages to stay up with his activity, but as the night wears on, Sarah wears out.

"I see a dog," Greg yells back to his mother.

"Don't worry Aunt Sarah. I'll bring him back." Abe steps up to help his aunt, and takes off running after his youngest cousin into the woods at the start of the Woodland Walk, next to the Center Meetinghouse.

"We know this trail by heart," Abe says, trying to comfort his worried aunt. But Abe knows they usually walk it in the warm sunshine of long summer days, not running by the dark of night in the slippery winter snow.

The freshly fallen snow over the past hour is blanketing the already white trail into the woods, at least making it easier to follow Greg and the dog's tracks. The flurries tonight have been intermittent with the full moon peeking out between assorted flakes of clouds and snow, as it is now. The moon is casting long shadows into the woods, accentuating every tree.

As they trek deeper into the woods, the sounds of Old Sturbridge Village become distant, then nonexistent. What they do hear off in the distance however, makes them stand stalk still sending shivers up their spines.

A wolf howl breaks the silence in the distance, far off to the right of the path. Abe and Sarah stop for a moment to assess the situation.

"Aunt Sarah, that's a wolf howl!" Abe exclaims to his already scared aunt.

Sarah takes a deep breath. She is not the animal lover her young son is. But no wild animal is going to come between her son and herself.

"Greg thinks he is chasing a dog!" Abe exclaims, running faster to catch his energetic cousin. "Greg! Wait up!"

Greg does not answer.

Now Abe and Sarah are both running, following the footprints in the snow, exchanging the Woodland Walk for the Pasture Walk to the left, then off the trail altogether and into the thick woods behind the Freeman Farm. Pine trees and evergreens have boughs bowing with snow laden branches.

Another wolf howl, only closer this time, interrupts their thoughts. Then another wolf howl off to their right. It sounds as if the wolves are circling them.

Then Abe sees it. A lone gray wolf, looking like a large German shepherd but with longer legs and a broader head has set its strong jaws, and is standing in a stalking position about twenty feet from Greg, who is bracing himself up against a tall oak tree.

They all freeze.

CRACK! The single shot of a gun fires a few yards past Abe, at right angles to Greg. Abe and Sarah scream. The wolf drops to the ground. Greg cries, both relieved and worried about the downed wild animal.

"Please stay where you are," an unfamiliar voice demands.

"I am Willard Barnes, game warden of Hampden County," the stranger in the night says. "OK, you are all OK now. Young man, please come join your family," he beckons looking around the woods as other men with guns join them.

"Game wardens from Hampden and Worcester Counties have been tracking three wolves that have been seen in the greater Quabbin Reservoir area. I need you all to stay together with me, and I'll lead you back. These men will move this wolf back to the wild where he should be and keep an eye out for the other two wolves," Will says.

"You mean he's not dead?" Greg asks very relieved.

"No son." Will smiles. "He was shot with a tranquilizer gun, Acepromazine to be exact. It has about a six to eight hour life, which gives us enough time to move him to a better environment, away from people and farm animals."

"Thank goodness," Greg says relieved. He did not want to be attacked by a wolf, but he did not want the wolf to be dead either.

"You still have to be careful though. We think there are two wolves further out. They do not usually go after people, but you entered his domain, so he met the challenge. We have several game officials working behind the scenes in these woods, watching out for all the human and animal guests here tonight. We started following your mother when we heard her calling out for you. You should be fine if you stay to the marked areas," Will says, winking to Greg.

In no time, Abe, Aunt Sarah, and Greg, walking on rubber legs, are back at the Town Common at the reindeer attraction near the manger scene, another welcome addition courtesy of Southwick's Zoo.

"Let's get inside and rest at the Quaker Meetinghouse," Sarah says.

Spent with the night's activities, Abe sinks into the hard wooden bench as if it were an overstuffed chair. His mind is invigorated by the cold of the night, even though his body is like a limp dish rag. Greg nestles in next to his Mom, appreciating her and the warmth.

"Welcome to the Religious Society of Friends Meetinghouse. I am Gabe Coffin and this is my beautiful wife, Lily. We are relatives of Quakers Levi and Catherine Coffin who have already aided over three thousand slaves to escape since the Underground Railroad began in 1780. We like to call Levi the President of the Underground Railroad," Gabe teaches in his yesteryear persona, repeating his role in character for the night and scanning his multi-racial, bi-lingual guests.

"What was it like? How did you help?" Abe asks, looking around the room of benches filled with a kaleidoscope of people.

"Abolitionism is strong here in the north, so the 'secret' railroad is not so secret. We help as many come our way. It is quite a different story in the south. Slavery is not legal in the northern states, but if a southern slave owner comes looking for his runaway slaves, there is a penalty for us in the North if we do not turn the fugitive slaves back over to the Southern slave owners. Slavery is legal down there. There is so much unrest between the north and the south over this issue, we fear a war may break out soon, but we help the slaves anyway. We do not think people should own people," Gabe confides to his interested audience.

"Some of the safe houses are now constructing hidden passages in the larger homes, behind moving mantels, walls, or hidden rooms in their attics and cellars," Gabe continues.

"Did the Underground Railroad have real tunnels underground?" Greg asks.

"No," Lily says. "That's just a metaphor. The Underground Railroad is the name of the secret escape route they used."

"Is this the time of the book, *Uncle Tom's Cabin*?" Greg asks about one of Brie's most recently read books. She shared what she read each night at the dinner table.

"Yes. It is written by Harriet Beecher Stowe about this time. Harriet was born in 1811, goes to private school, and teaches school in Hartford, Connecticut, about 30 minutes west of here. By 1832, Harriet moves to Cincinnati where she encounters runaway slaves and the Underground Railroad. She writes *Uncle Tom's Cabin* as a reaction to the fugitive slave laws which she does not agree with. She bases her character "Eliza" on a slave she met with the same name, who was hidden in a home in Indiana. She does not think anyone ought to be mistreated like that. The book is published March 20, 1852 a little ahead of the time we portray here. It is having a major influence on the way the general public is viewing slavery. She dances in the streets when President Abe Lincoln announces the end of slavery when the Emancipation Proclamation is announces on January 1, 1863," Gabe says.

"By the way, are you aware that President Abraham Lincoln, who is championing emancipation of the slaves, and Charles Darwin, who is spearheading a brand new theory of evolution by means of natural selection, were born on the same day, February 12, 1809?" Lily asks.

"I never realized that," Abe says, with his eyebrows knitting together.

"Both famous men are changing how people think in this world. They never meet or talk with each other, but they are aware and interested in each other's life pursuits," Lily says, getting comfortable in her chair, and continuing her presentation.

"President Lincoln is not only interested in ending slavery. He is a voracious reader. His law partner, William Henry Herndon, leaves theories of Darwin and other English scientists out on the coffee table for him to read. President Lincoln was curious about Darwin's *Origin of the Species*, which Darwin wrote when he was 30 years of age.

"President Lincoln is fascinated by the notion of universal law evolution, and says, 'There are no accidents in my philosophy. Every effect must have its cause. The past is the cause of the present, and the present will be the cause of the future. All these are links in the endless chain stretching from the finite to the infinite.'"

"Did President Lincoln believe in God? Did he think the Bible was real?" Abe asks.

"Good question," Gabe says. "Yes, President Lincoln had a strong faith in God. He also read the Bible a great deal ever since he was young. William Wolf wrote, "Lincoln's knowledge of the bible was so thorough that his political opponents generally found themselves on dangerous ground when they quoted it against him. When Judge Douglas somewhat fantastically cited Adam and Eve as the first beneficiaries of his doctrine of 'popular sovereignty' Lincoln corrected him. 'God did not place good and evil before man, telling him to make his choice. On the contrary, he did tell him there was one tree, of the fruit of which he should not eat, upon pain of certain death.' Then added Lincoln pointedly, 'I should scarcely wish so strong a prohibition against slavery in Nebraska.'"

"Don't forget, President Lincoln used quotes from the Bible in his writings and speeches. They are all salt and peppered with biblical references, including many quotations from Psalms and the Gospels," Lily answers.

"The first book of the Bible, Genesis, says that God created everything. President Abe Lincoln believed that. That fact was so well-known in the President's time that he received many Bibles as gifts. He got his first family Bible, the Oxford Bible, when he was ten years old, just about your age. Have you read it?" Lily asks Abe.

"Not really," Abe says, wishing for the first time that he had. If President Abraham Lincoln started reading the Bible at his age, maybe he should too.

"I've read some of it," Sarah adds, "but not all of it."

"I've always heard that there is a conflict between religion and science," Abe says, pondering the origins of everything, failing to see the conflict.

"President Lincoln is an independent thinker and a sceptic who is influenced by Voltaire and Tom Paine. He follows Darwin's theory of evolution by natural selection, but President Lincoln believes that Darwin's theories were just that, unproven theories.

"To date, President Lincoln reasons that there is no foolproof evidence of all stages of human progression as Darwin suggests. The President sees holes in the current thought taking place in science and archeology, and turns his attention to more urgent human needs of emancipation," Lily teaches.

A rotund man at the far end of the room joins the conversation. "To this very day, we still have some missing links. From time to time, science has reversed its statements of fact on some of its findings, like the earth being flat, or that morning air causes malaria. Science only knows what it knows, until it learns something new. Then it updates its findings. Scientists still cannot create something from nothing."

"What you say is true. Darwin came up with this idea, but never worked all the kinks in it at this time in history. His theory, like life itself is a process. Time will tell," Lily responds, knowing her audience includes religious minded people and science minded people.

Gabe stands up and says, "On June 5, 1861, just two years before President Abraham Lincoln gives the Emancipation Proclamation, Charles Darwin, writes about the condition of slavery in North America. He said, "I never knew the newspapers so profoundly interesting. North America does not do England justice: I have not seen or heard of a soul who is not with the North. Some few, and I am one, even wish to God, though at the loss of millions of lives, that the North would proclaim a crusade against Slavery. In the long run, a million horrid deaths would be amply repaid in the cause of humanity. What wonderful times we live in ... Great God how I should like to see that greatest curse on Earth, Slavery, abolished."

"Even Darwin, with his theory of evolution, does not see black people and all slaves as less than all other human beings. To Darwin, there is only one race, the human race," Gabe teaches.

"Were houses around here part of the Underground Railroad?" another boy Greg's age asks, eager to learn more about emancipation stories.

"Ah, you mean "stations." Houses that assist the fugitive slaves are known as 'stations' or 'depots,' in keeping with the Underground Railroad theme. These safe houses are places where slaves, escaping for their lives, can get meals and rest. People who help the fugitive slaves are called 'conductors.' We also call anyone who helps us by contributing money, 'stockholders.' The money goes for food, clothes, and sometimes travel expenses by boat. Good clothing is important for them when traveling, so they do not give themselves away. And yes, there are several homes in this area that help move them through Worcester and Northampton," Gabe informs.

"If they went to Canada, they could not be legally retrieved by their owners, right?" Sarah asks.

"That's correct, although some are offered and accept work and lodging right here," Gabe adds.

"Does anyone remember the name of a famous conductor?" Gabe asks.

"Harriet Tubman," Greg answers, thanks to Brie sharing what she was reading recently.

"You are correct again," Gabe smiles.

"Are you aware that on April 20, 2016, the United States Treasury Department announced they intend to put the picture of Harriet Tubman on the front of the United States $20 bill, replacing former president Andrew Jackson, and putting him on the back of it? It is supposed to be coming out in the year 2020," Sarah asks, unsure if she should cross timelines like this.

"We are portraying Old Sturbridge Village in the year 1830. President Andrew Jackson is our president at this current moment. He was just elected last year, in 1829. I can tell you he remains our President until 1837, when Martin Van Buren is elected president. By the way, there is an expression everyone uses today that is attributed to President Van Buren. Does anyone know what this is?" Gabe questions.

A spindly old woman in a beautifully woven shawl raises her hand and says, "OK. The expression is 'OK.' He was from Kinderhook, New York, sometimes referred to as Old Kinderhook. 'OK' clubs were created to support his political campaigns. The expression 'OK' came to mean 'all right.'"

"Thank you. That answer is correct. Here we are, though, helping the Underground Railroad to free slaves, while our President Andrew Jackson owns slaves, even while he is serving as president. What do you think about that?" Gabe asks his audience.

"Former president Andrew Jackson owned slaves?" Abe asks in astonishment.

"Yes. Remember, it is not illegal in our southern states. President Jackson owns hundreds of slaves who worked on his Hermitage plantation, which he has had for over two decades now. We still try to free the slaves who come through here looking for freedom. Does anyone know what else President Andrew Jackson is known for, besides being a slave owner?" Gabe asks his guests.

"When he was seventeen years old, he became well-known for his role in the Battle of 1812. He won at the Battle of New Orleans, when the British army was invading there. But in 1818, President Jackson also invaded the Seminole Indian Tribe in Spanish Florida," the spindly woman says in dismay.

"Yes," Gabe agrees. "Did you know that the Seminole Indian Tribe of Florida is a federally recognized Indian tribe, the only tribe in America who never signed a peace treaty?"

"Yes," the spindly woman says. "Florida then gets transferred from Spain to the United States."

"Correct," Lily says. You know your history. Your modern day money is reflecting that. These conductors have a tough and dangerous job. First the slaves have to make a getaway from their owners by night. They know if they keep their eye on the North Star in the sky, they will reach the northern states. Harriet Tubman pretends to be a slave and goes to the plantation, then guides them on their way, since she is a former slave. She is a Union spy. She returns nineteen times and helps more than three hundred slaves to freedom. In the process, she threatens to shoot any slaves who lose heart and want to turn back, which can foil the whole escape plan."

Abe and Greg exchange horrified glances.

"Second, the operators put themselves in a very precarious position by helping the slaves. Operators are fined hundreds, and even thousands of dollars, an exorbitant amount of money at this time. In this area, not only did the Underground Railroad operate openly, former slaves, like Stephen Myers of Upstate New York, writes his own newspaper, Northern Star and Freeman's Advocate, telling about his work to help other slaves escape," Lily continues.

"That's good!" a Mexican, Spanish speaking teenager exclaims in broken English.

"Vigilance committees are formed within communities for the purpose of aiding runaways often openly advertised their meetings. These same words mean different things in different periods in history, when people take the law into their own hands for non-existent or corrupt justice. Any questions?" Lily asks.

The tall black man in the doorway asks in exasperation, "Aren't there any famous people in the southern states who were against slavery?"

"That's a very interesting question. Has anyone heard of Robert Carter III?" Lily inquires of her interested audience.

No one answers.

"This is a wealthy and prominent individual, a member of the planter class in Virginia. He is the wealthiest man in the colonies, and has owned hundreds of slaves for the past forty years, since 1791. But he is losing his popularity because now he wants to free the slaves. He says he has become convinced that to keep slaves is contrary to the true principles of religion and justice. He even feels it is his duty to manumit them," Lily explains.

"What does manumit mean?" Abe asks.

"Manumit means to release from slavery. Carter not only condemns slavery, he actually does something about it. He is freeing his slaves, but only 15 of the oldest slaves each year. He also believes there is only one race, the human race." Lily scans her guests, accessing their attention spans.

"Why release only fifteen slaves each year?" Greg asks.

"This rich businessman from Virginia, not only releases them, he cares about them. If he releases too many slaves at once into the hostile South, they might not find enough work to support themselves. He carefully releases fifteen slaves each year, so he can help them find work and survive. He just wrote a book that is still around called, *Deed of Gift*. Some of the children of the slaves are still being released in 1830. We help them through this Sturbridge Village area. Carter released approximately five hundred slaves, which is the largest emancipation by one person in American history," Lily boasts.

"Carter is so wealthy that President Jackson has borrowed money from him. President George Washington's nephew proposed to his daughter. Former President Jimmy Carter is a descendant of his. Robert Carter III's nickname was King. He was descended from William Strother, on his father's side. Everyone knew Robert Carter III was descended from English royalty, going back to Charlemagne and William the Conqueror, and many other English kings. Presidents Zachary Taylor and John Tyler were also descended from Strother. Former President Jimmy Carter also is related to former President Barak Obama. They are eighth cousins," boasts Lily, proud that the United States of America truly is the melting pot of the world. She takes a drink of water and continues.

The guests gasp at the little known revelation.

"Do you know of anyone else who has helped the slaves?" Lily asks. Again, no response.

"Let's learn about Edward Coles. He was President James Madison's secretary in the year 1809, and neighbor to Thomas Jefferson, our third president. After Madison's presidency, Coles sells his Virginia estate and moves to the Illinois Territory where slavery is not permitted. Next he releases his slaves, then sets them up as farmers. Does this sound familiar to anyone?" Lily asks.

"Seems to me," the tall black man says, "I heard Jefferson suggested all slaves be freed and removed from the United States. Illinois was only a territory then. Coles must have listened to him."

"I think you are right. Don't forget, it is not the case that all presidents who owned slaves, wanted to promote slavery. What else did they have to consider?" Lily asks.

"Their political careers," the tall black man answers, shaking his head.

"Was the Reverse Underground Railroad active here?" Sarah asks.

"Yes. Not everyone remembers this," Gabe says. "Unfortunately yes, in some northern states bordering on the Ohio River, but not so much here in this location. It is good to know who your friends are though. There are profits to be made. Black men and women, whether or not they had ever been slaves, are sometimes kidnapped and hidden away in homes, barns or other buildings until they are taken into the South and sold as slaves."

The guests sigh a disgusting groan.

"Keep heart though," Lily encourages. "Samuel L. Hill is a local abolitionist. He just purchased two properties, the Ross Farm and his house which he calls the Samuel L. Hill House. They are both in Northampton as part of his utopian community called the Northampton Association of Education and Industry. It's about nine towns to the northwest from here."

"Northampton also has the Elisha Hammond House, the Dorcey-Jones House, and the Hall Judd House, if the other safe houses are full. The Unitarian minister, Rev. Rufus Ellis also has a house on 48 Pomeroy Terrace in Northampton that serves as a station too. Exhausted slaves, running for their lives, come in from the sea, landing in Boston. But some come in by land from the south up through New York and Connecticut. Worcester is the key point northwards in the Underground Railroad system. We help out here as best we can between Worcester and Northampton. Sturbridge Village a good half way point," Gabe adds.

"It's been one hundred, forty-four years now that our philanthropy has been flourishing. We Quakers are the first organization in history to ban slaveholding. We've created several groups that promote emancipation and abolition societies, like the American Anti-Slavery Society; the Philadelphia Anti-Slavery Society and the Female Anti-Slavery Society," Lily says.

"Massachusetts Senator Daniel Webster gave a speech known as the *Second Reply to Hayne*, where he famously thundered "Liberty and Union, now and forever, one and inseparable!" In Webster's speech on January 26, 1830 before the United States Senate, he described the federal government as: "made for the people, made by the people, and answerable to the people." Does this sound familiar?" Lily asks.

"Yes," Abe answers. "President Lincoln spoke of this in the Gettysburg Address."

Lily nods. "In 1830, Abraham Lincoln has not been elected President yet. He is elected as our sixteenth president on November 6, 1860. But he is very interested in Webster's 1830 speech, so much so, that he re-phrases the conclusion of the Gettysburg Address with, '… and that government of the people, by the people, for the people, shall not perish from the earth.' It is worth mentioning that the *Springfield Republican* newspaper, from just a few towns west of here, published the Gettysburg Address in its entirety, saying it was a 'perfect gem, deep in feeling, compact in thought and expression, tasteful and elegant in every word and comma.'"

Lily adds, "Webster also noted, 'This government, Sir, is the independent offspring of the popular will. It is not the creature of State legislatures; nay, more, if the whole truth must be told, the people brought it into existence, established it, and have hitherto supported it, for the very purpose, amongst others, of imposing certain salutary restraints on State sovereignties.' Union responsibilities and State's rights were just as important to people back then as it is today."

Abe pauses for a moment, worried about Grammy Rose, and who will take care of her. Grammy Rose was just asking his Mom yesterday what will happen if her Social Security gets cut.

"Southern states, calling themselves the Confederate States, want state's rights to slavery, the impetus for the Civil War which is brewing in 1830. It is the reason for the Underground Railroad here in Old Sturbridge Village. President Lincoln is well aware that slavery is illegal in England since 1772, was abolished in New York in 1827, and also in the English colonies in other parts of the world in 1833. Sadly, the United States of America lags behind social progress and justice until January 1, 1863 when Republican President Abraham Lincoln issues the presidential Emancipation Proclamation, freeing more than three million slaves across the entire Union. Even though it is little later than the time we are portraying here, does anyone remember the date that the Civil War and the Underground Railroad finally ends?" Lily asks.

"The Civil War ended May 9, 1865," the man answers, sporting the brown woolen hat with ear muffs.

"I think that is one of Brie's high school's history teachers," Greg whispers in his mother's ear.

"You are correct," Lily says.

"Did you start any schools here?" Abe asks.

"Yes. We are interested in the education and the social progress of freedmen. We raised hundreds of thousands of dollars for freeman's relief and established many freedmen's schools," Lily explains.

"I'm glad the Quakers helped," Greg says, firmly shaking Gabe's large hand as they leave the Religious Society of Friend's Meetinghouse.

They step out into the carol-filled, brisk air of the night, looking to the right and to the left for their long lost family.

CHAPTER 8

RENEGADE NEPHILIM

Brie, Abby, Aunt Cher and Grammy Rose look right and left for their missing family members. It has been a while since they divided up for the horse drawn stagecoach ride. They must be here somewhere in one of the workshops. The lit candles in this hidden library do not seem to be diminished in their absence. The ambulance has come and gone. They are looking out of the hidden library windows. Surely they could be opened, but not in any obvious way that they can figure out, without breaking the glass.

Before anyone could stop her, Brie inserts another bigger key into the book entitled, *Noah, The Flood and The Ark*. In an effort to stop her, Abby finds Brie's hand, intent on pulling it away from the lock in the book. Simultaneously, Aunt Cher grabs hold of Abby, while Grammy Rose holds on to Aunt Cher's shoulder.

"Stop!" they all yell out loud to Brie.

Brie smiles.

Click.

"Please listen to me. It is for your own good," the man in a long tunic says.

"Who is that, and where are we?" Brie asks in shock. The area appears unsafe. Unsavory characters appearing not to have the best intentions are crowding around the big wooden structure.

"My friend, this is Noah. He is tenth in line from Adam. You must not be from this region. You have reached the city of Eridu, east of Eden. People say Noah is the laughing stock of the town. My name is Shem, the second son of Noah. He is six hundred years old this year. He walks with the true God, Jehovah, and tries to do what is right. But the people do not respect him, nor do they honor God. To them, God is a joke. They think my father is foolish for believing in him," Shem sighs.

Then turning his attention to his new guests, he asks, "What is your name?"

"My name is Gabriella, but people call me Brie. This is my cousin Abby; my Aunt Cher; and my grandmother, Rose," Brie introduces.

Brie observes Aunt Cher, apparently not believing her eyes or her ears. Aunt Cher pinches herself to make sure she is not dreaming again.

"This really is ridiculous. Who can believe any of this? I must be dreaming, too," Brie thinks.

"Noah!" Grammy Rose exclaims.

"So you have heard of the man who is trying to preach to everyone so they can repent from their evil ways, and come back to believing in the one true God so they can be safe when the flood comes," Shem says cautiously.

"Yes," Grammy Rose replies, equally on guard.

The crowd around them is distracted by Noah talking. Yet the jeers and jokes from the crowd rival a bad crowd in a bad bar. It appears no one is taking him seriously.

Brie observes a pick pocket in the crowd near them.

"Grammy Rose, hold your pocketbook close to you. I just saw a man steal something from another man's pocket," Brie whispers in her grandmother's ear.

Grammy Rose slides her shoulder bag to the front of her, under her tunic. Again, they are all in tunics and head coverings.

"My father is a good man. There aren't many of those around anymore, if any," Shem laments.

"God loves him," Grammy Rose unexpectedly says to Shem.

"Yes, he does. My father is a righteous man. He always prays to God, and does his best to please Him. It matters to my father to conduct his life according to God's will. No one does that anymore. They think God is a myth, at least, if they believe in God, they do not live their lives as if they do," Shem adds.

Brie watches Aunt Cher roll her eyes in disgust.

"Please listen to me," Noah bellows over the boisterous crowd. "God, has told me he is going to destroy all mankind, for the earth is filled with crime because of man, and the angels who have come down to mate with human women. You see the revolting creatures you have spawned. The earth is now filled with you fallen angels, and the Nephilim children, who are giants, and maligned humanity born to human women. It is too much for us to bear. You Nephilim magnify the evil, selfish spirits of your fathers. You giants are perverted bullies, carnal creatures, carrying the evil spirit of death and destruction. You are known for your unholy, violent actions, but it is God in heaven who is going to put an end to you."

The laughter is so loud from the unruly crowd that even those standing close to Noah cannot make out all his words.

"As for you men and women," Noah pleads, wiping the sweat from his brow, "God is no longer going to put up with humankind choosing to do evil, and ignoring God's just laws. They are not merely suggestions, you know. God's laws will keep you physically, mentally and spiritually healthy. You are ruining yourselves. You are ruining the earth. You do have a choice. You cater to pride which kills your reasoning ability. Do you hear me? This pride has eaten your integrity whole in one gulp." Still he continues.

"You angels materialize, possessing human forms. You freely choose to lessen your God-given glorious place and privilege in heaven, and pervert your thoughts and actions to a state of debauchery here on earth. You are rebelling against God by your misuse of free will and actions. You are sure to be confined to Tartarus and chained by the deepest mental darkness, along with Satan the devil for not obeying God's order of creation. Mankind is duped, lied to by evil beings who choose evil over good, and is rotten to the core. A flood is coming which will wipe out all living things," Noah proclaims.

The crowd roars in laughter.

"I can swim," a filthy, rotund man taunts.

"God told me to build an ark ..."

Before Noah can finish his sentence, another does "… on dry land, of all places! He is building this ridiculous ark on dry land!"

The crowd laughs all the louder. It is an odd assortment of people. Like any crowd of people, all shapes and sizes are represented. However, there is one eerie difference. Some of the tall people are exceptionally tall, measuring approximately fifteen feet in height. Their brawny bodies are topped with mean minds with violently aggressive and greedy natures. That is precisely the point. They do not seem natural at all.

Grammy Rose leans over to her oldest granddaughter and says, "Brie, I believe the tallest ones are the violent hybrid sons who are the children of the fallen angels who mated with the daughters of men, described in Genesis 6. These are the Nephilim Noah was just speaking about."

"I know I've given you a hard time about this in the past, but I think you might be right. Look at them. They are huge!" Aunt Cher admits, still confused and cozying closer to her mother.

These people are crude, arrogant and filled with nothing but selfish pursuits, void of any godly, redeeming qualities. They no longer serve God. They serve themselves as if they are gods. Why believe in God who has rules, when they can just as easily live a life without God and do whatever they please, no praise, or prayers. The crowd is clearly driven by puffed up pride and insane egos. This is the universal mark of the crowd.

"Try though I might, I can't seem to get them to listen to God's word," Noah says to his family and his new guests.

"Noah, no one can find fault with you in trying to reach them. You speak to them every day," Noah's wife, Naamah says. She turns to talk to her new guests, introducing herself and making them feel welcome.

"I am a direct descendent in the line of Cain, who killed his brother, Abel, and was banished to the land of Nod, east of Eden. Adam and Eve were also cast out by God for disobeying God by taking and eating the fruit from the Tree of Knowledge. Adam and Eve knew not to eat the fruit from this tree in the middle of the garden. God personally told Adam not to eat from that tree," Naamah explains.

"God spoke to Adam, in person?" Greg asks.

"Yes. Before Adam and Eve sinned, God spoke to Adam directly. Satan wasted no time in tempting our first parents to sin by lying to them about the life-giving commands of God. Cain was also tempted by Satan.

Cain believed Satan's lies, to his demise. God put a mark upon Cain so that no one would kill him, or be avenged sevenfold. Now our life is not only toil, but there does not seem to be any redeeming quality in people at all. Life has become perverted," Naamah says.

"The Tree of Knowledge really had a talking serpent in it?" Brie asks Naamah in surprise. "I don't really believe that a snake can talk."

"I know. In the natural order of creation, snakes cannot talk. But remember, this is no ordinary snake. What we have here is Satan, the devil in disguise. That was the first time we humans fell for one of Satan's lies. Adam, Eve and Cain used their God-given free will to believe Satan's lies instead of God's live-giving laws. That is why people now have to die. God told Adam beforehand what would happen if they ate from the tree," Naamah says.

"So Satan tricked Eve, and Adam too," Brie says her thoughts out loud.

"Yes, but they also had free will to choose to listen to God, not Satan. Their pride got the best of them. Once Satan saw how easy it was to tempt Adam and Eve, he also tempted Cain. I am descended from his lineage. Evil has grown on earth ever since that day. I'm sure you can see how things are in the world today," Naamah explains.

"We sure do," Grammy Rose says.

"But Noah has taught me about the love of God, as was taught to him by his father, Lamech, his grandfather, Methuselah, and his great-grandfather Enoch, who walked with God. Noah also walks with God. Now God has commanded Noah to build an ark and bring in male and female animals, two of each kind into the ark so life can begin again after the deluge."

"This ark is so huge!" Brie exclaims in amazement.

"We are making the ark exactly to the directions God gave to Noah." Naamah replies.

"Wow!" Abby echoes, with her eyes and mouth wide open.

"Satan was not content to simply keep on tempting us humans to do maligned, evil things as a way of turning against God. He deceived us into thinking his lawless ways were much better, enticing people to follow him instead. Then Satan and his fallen angels decided to come to earth, taking on human bodies so they can take our beautiful women and have children with them. These are the giants, as you can see with your own eyes. Humanity is ungodly, with no redeeming qualities. Noah tries to reach them, but they only laugh and make fun of him. Look at these Nephilim that have been created!" Naamah says.

"The tall ones are so vulgar and scary," Cher agrees.

"I know. No one is to be able to return to the Paradise Garden God originally made for humankind. We cannot get away from these horrible, cruel creatures! God placed a mighty angel with the flaming blade of a sword to guard the entrance to the Tree of Life, after seeing what the angel and human species did with the Tree of Knowledge." Naamah laments.

"You said Noah taught you about the love of God. What did Noah teach you?" Grammy Rose asks.

"He taught me that God promises to send us a Savior, to restore all of us to his good grace. The creation of a Paradise Garden, and humankind's place in it is God's original plan. He is sure to make it happen. I follow the ways of God closely, hoping God has mercy on all of us who believe in him and follow his ways. Noah says Jehovah God promises to save us, and that anyone who calls on the name of Jehovah will be saved," Naamah says.

Aunt Cher stands with her arms crossed across her body, and her feet crossed at the ankles. She has had about as much of this as she can take.

"You must be from far away. You seem unfamiliar with this place," Naamah says.

"We have never been here before," Brie admits.

"My father is Lamech, that is, the Lamech in Cain's line, six generations from Adam. Zillah is my mother. Tubal-cain is my brother. Unfortunately my father killed a man for striking and wounding him. He said that if Cain is avenged sevenfold, that he would be avenged seventy-sevenfold. So far this has held true. My faithful husband, Noah, has taught me so much. Noah and I are born of different seeds. I am from Cain's lineage, he is from Seth's. Yet Noah loves me, and God loves Noah," Naamah shares in an effort to reach her new guest's hearts.

She continues.

"Noah's father's name is also Lamech, after his namesake in Cain's line who is my father. But Noah's father is nine generations from Adam in the line of Seth. Both our fathers share the same name, but are very different people. It is the same thing, having two different Enochs in our families. The Enoch in my line, is Cain's first born son. The Enoch in Noah's line is five generations from Seth, and is the one who walked with God. One day God took him back to heaven with him." Naamah glances at the rowdy crowd edging closer to them.

"As you can see, not everyone in our human family wants to follow the directions God has given us. The earth is filled with a multitude of people now. We can all trace our roots back through Cain or Seth through our first parents, Adam and Eve, and of course to God who created them. But the people have turned mean and cruel, and blame God for their lot in life, rather than take responsibility for their own bad actions. It is going from bad to worse," Naamah says.

"I guess you cannot help people who do not want to be helped," Grammy Rose agrees.

"That is true. We have to put up with the fallen angels who masquerade in human bodies and suddenly appear, taking as many wives as they want. But their children are worse, truly monsters. They think nothing of killing and eating people, or having sex with animals!" Naamah laments.

"What did you say this place is called?" Abby asks, trying to get her bearings.

"This is Eridu, the city we know as 'sovereignty descended from heaven.' It is the next town over from the city of Enoch, named after Cain's first son. There are four other cities here: Larak, Sippar, and Shuruppak, all here in the Fertile Plain. But the city of Badgurgurru, the fortress of the bronze workers, is located away from here. My brother, Tubal-cain forges instruments of bronze and iron, while other men make tools of copper and iron over there," Naamah answers, sweeping her arm to the left.

"You can see the plants and animals do grow here, but we must work at it constantly. We do get fish out of the Greater and Lesser Seas, but that is also a lot of hard work. God told Noah to build this ark right here. God will save us from the flood he is telling us he is sending to wipe away all the wickedness. But no one listens. How did you travel to get here?" Naamah asks.

"We're not exactly sure how we got here," Grammy Rose answers, shaking her head.

"You can stay with us for a while. We sure could use the help. There is so much to do," Naamah invites.

"We would love that," Brie says, looking over her shoulder at the rough encroaching crowd.

"You have a beautiful name," Aunt Cher notices.

"Thank you. My name means 'the beautiful' and some say it means 'the pleasant one.' Noah has taught me that it is far more important to form a strong character, and become educated in the ways of God. He is a great man, who loves and obeys God. These people are ignorant, of God that is. They are very smart in worldly ways when it comes to working with bronze, copper and iron, and the ways of war though." Naamah says.

Turning to Grammy Rose and Aunt Cher, Naamah explains further. "Noah is from the line of Kenan, the Fourth Patriarch who lived, eight hundred, forty years, through Seth and Adam. Methuselah was Noah's grandfather. He was very loved by God and was rewarded the longest life of all people who ever lived, living nine hundred, sixty-nine years. Methuselah's father, Enoch, walked with God and lived three hundred, sixty-five years on earth before God took him to heaven with him. Enoch is Noah's great-grandfather. It matters very much to Noah to follow God's direction, not the desires of the ignorant people of this land. I am so grateful for learning this too from Noah."

Naamah relishes sharing this information with her new guests. At least these new visitors are willing to listen, rather than close their hearts and minds like the rest of the people they meet.

"This show is over. Everyone's invited to my place, over by the olive grove and Sycamore Tree. We're having a bonfire. Bring your wine and women. See you there!" A timbersome, crude, smelly vagrant extends an open invitation to everyone.

The crowd follows him, trading vulgar remarks to Noah for vulgar revelries of the night.

Shem quickly ushers Grammy Rose, Aunt Cher, and Abby closer to the ramp of the ark where Noah is speaking, but not before a thick, dark arm darts out from the crowd pulling Brie into the center of it.

"Brie!" her family screams out hysterically.

"You're coming with me. I need a wife!" the tall man in rags yells.

"She is too young!" Shem yells back.

The tall man continues to drag Brie along behind him, unleashing a string of obscenities cascading out of his mouth toward Shem.

"Tonight, we party!" the humungous man decrees, hoisting Brie over his shoulder with her back hitting the low branches of a nearby tall tree and snarling leaves in twigs in her long blonde hair.

To Brie, this gruff man appears to be a giant, at least three times the size of herself. Now they are in a clearing. Each of his galloping strides cover nearly twenty feet with each running step. In no time they reach the olive grove and Sycamore tree. There is weird music, haunting singing, profanity, obscene gestures and lots of drinking. The entire area wreaks of foreign smells.

"Trask, over here," an even taller being bellows.

Trask flops Brie down to the ground.

"Jezebam, watch her until I get back," Trask orders, loping away.

"Who is that man?" Brie dares to ask the filthy woman watching her.

"I see you have met Trask. We are proud to have him. Not every settlement has a son of an angel in their midst," Jezebam boasts.

"Son of an angel?"

"One of the mighty ones. His father is a heavenly being. These angels come to earth and take as many of us beautiful women as they want. It has been said that his father, angel as he is, took over the body of a mortal man so he could have children through mortal women. Trask is only one of his sons. You are lucky he has chosen you," Jezebam says, smiling through missing teeth.

Brie feels unreal. Grammy Rose helped her family cope with stress when Uncle Andre died. Brie begins to foster a plan for her escape, keeping a keen eye on her surroundings, and this strange woman.

What kind of world is this, where this kind of treatment is OK? What is Jezebam talking about with angels mating with women of earth? She had heard Noah say this exact thing. This is not just a myth? Isn't this whole experience a dream? Naamah talked about this too. Brie had not paid attention to much in her religious studies, other than celebrating Christmas and Easter. Now she wishes she had.

"I'm going to get a drink. Do you want one?" Jezebam asks, thinking she has made a friend with Brie.

"No, I'm fine," Brie answers, pretending to be calm.

"I'll be right back," Jezebam says and abruptly leaves.

There is a rustling in the olive grove nearby. Shem has been following at a distance, waiting for the perfect moment to spring into action to free Brie from the disgusting villain. No sooner had Jezebam left, then Shem slides into view, waving Brie to retreat into the grove of olives. In a split second, Brie was by Shem's side, shaking like a leaf.

Brie follows Shem into the safety of the ark where Noah and his youngest son, Ham, and his oldest son, Japheth, and their wives are protectively caring for Abby, Aunt Cher and Grammy Rose, showing them the progress they have made.

"Please accept my apologies for the rude greeting you and your family have received in this land. I cannot tell you how saddened I am for the failings of the rest of the human family on earth," Noah says.

"Thank you Shem for saving me. I don't know what I would have done if you hadn't done that!" Brie says, nearly hysterical. She huddles all the closer to Grammy Rose.

"Brie, we are so grateful to God that Shem has brought you back to us safely," Noah adds.

"You have already met my loving wife, Naamah. And this is Sedeqetelebab, Shem's wife," Noah beams proudly, gesturing to her.

"Over here on my left, I'd like you to meet Ham's wife Neeltama, who is from Egypt; and Japheth's wife, Adataneses," Noah says.

"We are all faithful worshippers of Jehovah God. My great-grandfather, Enoch, taught our family to lovingly and faithfully follow the laws and customs given to us by God. They are for our own protection. Enoch taught us how to pray for whatever we need. Grandfather Enoch always told us God is closer to us than our next breath, and that he draws close to us when we draw close to him. Grandfather Enoch was so faithful to the way God asked us to live that God took him up to heaven in a cloud. Then Enoch was with us no more," Noah says, adding, "Brie, we are so grateful to God that Shem has brought you back to us safely."

"Thank you Shem for saving me. That was very eerie," Brie says as she pulls a few twigs out of her snarled hair.

"I think God for helping me to save you," Shem answers with a smile.

"Yes. First we acknowledge God's saving hand in bringing you back to us. It is really bad out there. People nowadays hold fanciful traditions that do not give life; spinning their wheels on distractions, anything not to honor God, or even admit that God exists. Satan successfully distracts their minds with the glitter of material goods, teaching women to wear makeup and hair braiding for flattery, and blinds them by inflating their egos so high that they truly cannot see the forest for the trees. They choose to worship nature which God created, not God who created the nature. They are very confused," Noah explains.

"Is everyone like this?" Abby asks, shocked by so much violence.

"Yes. The fallen angels take on human bodies so that they can have relations with our beautiful women. The children born of these unholy unions, result in grotesque, mean creatures, such as you have met today. They terrify us. Try though I might, I can't get anyone to listen to God's word." Noah laments.

"Let us show our guests how the ark is coming along Father," Japheth suggests.

"Good idea, now that the crowd has left us for the day," Noah says.

With Japheth in the lead, Brie and Abby follow with Cher and Grammy Rose right behind them, while Noah explains the project of the ark to them.

"God told me he has observed how bad things have turned here on earth, and how vicious and depraved it is on earth now. He said this is not his original intention for his Creation, which was meant to be a Paradise for us. God told me he is going to destroy all mankind because of its wickedness. " Noah says sadly.

"I walk with God every day. I notice he does not tell me he is going to destroy the earth. God says he is going to destroy all living things because they have turned their backs on God and live as if they did not need him at all. They pervert all of the gifts God generously gives them, as if they are in charge of the earth, and how to live on it."

Noah shakes his head, and continues to share God's words to him to his new guests.

"God told me to make an ark. By the measurements he gave me, it looks more like an extremely large chest of resinous wood, not a ship. It has three decks, several compartment stalls and only one door on one side. Then he said to seal it with tar. It measures four hundred, thirty-seven feet long, seventy-three feet wide, and forty-four feet tall. He even said to construct a sky light all the way around the ship, eighteen inches below the roof. It has taken all eight of us nearly fifty years to build it. It has taken us so long to build this ark that the people of the area have forgotten all about God's prophecy of a flood. They only laugh at us. But God did promise to keep me safe in the ark; me, my sons, and our wives. We are faithful to Jehovah God," Noah says.

"This ark is so huge!" Brie gasps at its enormous size.

She guesses it to be nearly four football fields laid end to end long, and only five feet narrower than a football field in width. The three decks made the wooden structure forty-five feet from the ground to the top roof, about as tall as a five story building. It is a tarred, wooden rectangle.

"Sedeqetelebab, Neeltama and Adataneses are a great help to me. We take great care to fill the grain bins and food supplies that are to last for many days. Not only is there food and water for us eight people, we have water, straw, grasses and grains for the wildlife as well. Plants, seeds, nuts of all kinds and vegetation are stocked in an organized way for when the great waters subside, allowing for our new beginning," Naamah says to acknowledge all their hard work.

"Japheth, Shem, Ham and I made these necessary provisions for cooking stations, milking stations, and prep stations to make cheese and other food items," Noah beams, giving a nod of appreciation to his sons.

"Look! On the mountain over there," Brie exclaims, pointing her right index finger in all directions.

They are coming by air. They are coming by land. They are coming in pairs of like-minded birds, beasts, and every creature and critter imaginable. They are quacking, honking, tweeting, croaking, mooing, whinnying, barking, and purring. But most of all, they are patient, friendly and orderly.

A huge lumbering line of animals, birds and reptiles is heading for the ark without aggression, stalking or incident. The procession is marked by peaceful gentleness and overall cooperation, and quite a sight and sound to behold. The earth is trembling with the rocking of the soil to the pulse of the pairs of paws, claws and countless hooves pounding them all closer with each step they take, all without any assistance by Noah, or anyone else.

Brie has seen enough of the Nephilim, and the violence and shame of this generation of humanity. Grammy Rose always says that God fulfills his prophecies one hundred percent of the time. Just in case, Brie begins praying for God to save herself and her family from the prophecy of the flood to come. She prays an earnest prayer, holding onto Abby's hand. It was not one of those, "If there is a God" prayers, but a real, heartfelt prayer to God, for the safety of her family and herself. She reaches for the key in her pocket and spots a huge bronze lock lying on the ground, next to a tree where her family is now huddled, watching the parade of wild and tame animals, birds and reptiles majestically climb, crawl, slither and fly into the ark as if they all had number tickets to take their turn.

Brie inserts the key in the lock and firmly gives it a twist.

Click.

CHAPTER 9

SHOCKING MEDE-PERSIAN EMPIRE ANCESTRY

The cheerful sound of sleigh bells fills the air. Abe, Greg and Sarah see the stagecoach waiting for them at Fenno Barn. Arthur Benson, is just arriving for his stagecoach driving job. Another carriage driver, Ralph Osgood, has been filling in for him until he got there, since Clyde switched back to driving the toboggan-like sleigh around the outer roads of Old Sturbridge Village.

"May we have a trip over to Bullard's Tavern?" Greg asks.

"Perfect timing my young man. I have room for three passengers. Sorry I'm late. The snow is falling harder in Worcester. I was stuck behind a three car accident on Route 290. It took me until now to get here," Arthur says, shaking his head, thinking about the insane, mindless, crazy driving on that road from hell.

"No worries. Gitche and Manitou didn't mind at all. These two Morgan horses love everyone, even me," Ralph chuckles.

Once at Bullard's Tavern, they trade the nine-passenger Hartford and Worcester Stagecoach on wheels, for the horse drawn sleigh waiting for them on freshly fallen snow.

"This entire event is so picturesque. Abe, would you take a picture of the living Christmas manger in the Town Common with your cell phone camera so we can use it for our Christmas cards?" Aunt Sarah asks.

"Yes. I have already been taking pictures. I took one of that camel as it was looking right at me," Abe says.

Belgian draft horses, Jerry and Jim, perk up as Clyde, their favorite driver, comes to the front of them to give the duo some fresh water before climbing back into the high driving seat of the toboggan-like sleigh. Clyde barely has to touch the reigns and makes a clicking sound with his mouth.

Jerry and Jim come to life, all four thousand pounds of them.

"These horses are huge!" Abe exclaims.

"Yes they are. Each of these two Belgian draft horses is eight hundred pounds heavier than each of the Morgan horses pulling the stage coach tonight. While the Morgan horses are also known for being wonderful work horses and for pulling weight, they are better suited to pull the stagecoach in the packed snow. It is harder to pull the sleigh in snow because it is dead weight. We assign our strong Belgian draft horse team to this task. We try to make the ratio of pulling weight according to their weight, and have them only pull one-tenth of their body weight. That's why we are limiting the sleigh rides to three or four people including me, depending on their sizes," Clyde explains, as the horse drawn sleigh rocks and squeaks at the second left hand turn at the Knight's Store corner.

Tonight a multitude of stars seem to dance in a brilliant show in the indigo sky above them, alternating with moments of cloud bursts of flurries. It is a peaceful, quiet ride with the gentle rhythm of bells keeping the beat of the horse's hooves, taking them past the Town Pound to their right and the local shoe shop to their left.

Horse tails swish like a clock's pendulum from time to time, brushing off some new-fallen flurries. Their manes, once cropped in the summer giving them a sophisticated style, have grown out for the winter to keep them warmer. Red velvet bows grace their manes, keeping the tempo of their strides. Their heads seem to be pulling them along with each step, as much as their hooves driving them onward and upward. Snow caressed trees hug the one lane path.

The oil lamp held by Clyde casts long shadows into the woodland scenery.

"Hey, look at that fox!" Greg shouts in a high pitched shrill.

The fox runs. The horses gallop. The sleigh of two Benoits and one Le Beau scream. The two Belgians to shift gears quicker than a Subaru Impreza WRX. Each muscle of these highly defined animals springs into action like a lean and eager racehorse. It is a wonder that the entire sleigh did not take flight.

"WOAH!" Clyde coaxes. "W-O-A-H!!"

It takes a minute, bells ringing loudly, for the muscular beasts of burden to slow down and stop, their flowing manes following their shaking heads. The families' braided bodies bounce back into their seats. Clyde applies his brake and gets out of the impressive high seat.

"Is everyone alright?" Clyde asks, turning to his guests.

"Yes. We're fine," Sarah assesses, after a quick investigation.

"OK. Please stay in your places and be nice and quiet. I am going to calm them down."

Clyde stands near the horses, patting them, and speaking so softly to them that the trio could not hear his words. The horses seem to have a trusting affection for Clyde.

"You may disembark if you would like to go in to the Mede-Persian Empire presentation. I will wait for you," Clyde suggests, noticing they have stopped in front of the school house.

"Thanks," Greg says, beating Abe and his Mom into the school house.

"Welcome, welcome!" Mrs. Edith Torrington invites. She is the would-be 1830's all grades school teacher. "We have a nice warm fire going in here to keep us warm."

Abe and Greg huddle together nearest the crackling fire in the small fireplace, along with Greg's Mom.

"Tonight you will notice that Old Sturbridge Village is celebrating its seventieth anniversary in grand style, with extra workshops and presentations taking place, more than in past years. In keeping with the Old World Empire theme from the Bible book of Daniel we have going on tonight, and its effect on the community here in Old Sturbridge Village in 1830, we are quickly going to take a snapshot view of highlights. Let's start with the Medes. Do you know where they began?" a slightly frozen Mrs. Torrington asks. She has just arrived from the walk in the cold from the center of town.

Blank looks stare back at her.

"Have you heard in tonight's workshops about Noah and his sons?" the teacher asks.

"Yes," Abe replies. "Noah had three sons, Japheth, Shem, and Ham, before the flood. Ham's son Canaan is born after the flood." Abe remembers their first presentation tonight at the Salem Towne House.

"You are a good student," Mrs. Torrington replies. "The Medes are from the line of Japheth, coming from Japheth's son, Madai. You will find him mentioned in Genesis 10:2. They live in Media, near the Caspian Sea, in the Zagros Mountains of Assyria. That is a mountainous plateau three thousand to five thousand feet above sea level. They were great breeders of horses, which their invaders often sought. We know their history from the Greeks, and from Assyrian texts, since they left no written material for our history books.

"The Medes have constant incursions by the Assyrians, and finally allied forces with the Babylonians. Now this is the interesting part. This is the time of King Nabopolassar of Babylon, Nebuchadnezzar's father. The Medes capture the city of Asshur in 634 B.C.E. Do you know who the city of Asshur is named after?"

Abe and Greg look to Sarah for the answer, but she only shrugs.

"The city of Asshur is named after Asshur, the son of Shem, Noah's son!" Mrs. Torrington exclaims with a twinkle in her eye, sharing this little known knowledge.

"Really?" Abe asks in a surprised voice.

"Yes. I find it interesting that going back through history, we find family fighting family, a sad theme that keeps repeating itself. For example, to this very day, we have the remnants of two sons of Abraham fighting, Isaac and Ishmael, otherwise known as Israel fighting the Arab and other nations, and vice versa. But that is later in the time than what we are discussing tonight. I only mention this to point out the family connection, and battles between them are a theme to be continued throughout history, even to today's time," Mrs. Torrington says.

"I never thought of it that way," Sarah ponders.

"Tonight, we have the lineage of Japheth, known as the Medes, fighting the lineage of Shem." Mrs. Torrington teaches, rubbing her hands together near the hot fire.

"Shem is also the start of many other Semitic peoples, not only the Assyrians. Shem's lineage is also the start of the Elamites, the early Chaldeans, the Hebrews, the Aramaeans, who are also known as Syrians by the Greeks later on, a variety of Arabian tribes and most likely the Lydians of Asia Minor," the teacher adds, reaching for another woolen blanket to put around her shoulders.

"So Shem's descendants are responsible for populating southwestern Asia, clear across to the Fertile Crescent," Sarah observes.

"Yes. Shem's descendants are also living in a major portion of the Arabian Peninsula," Mrs. Torrington says, walking over to the large, round, hand-drawn poster pinned to the wall, pointing to the oldest known map of Europe, Asia and Africa. "Isidore of Seville mapped out the world as it was known on January 1, 900 AD based on the territories Noah's sons inhabited. You can also check this out on your computers at home.

"The neat thing about Shem is that Abraham descends from his line, through Shem's son, Arphachshad. Some think it is Shem who has the title of Melchizedek, the same king-priest Abraham pays tithes to in Genesis 14:18-20," Mrs. Torrington teaches.

"Doesn't history have its own facts written down and documented in books other than the Bible?" Sarah asks.

"The history books of antiquity, often look to the Bible for historical facts, matching up history recorded from other sources to confirm what we can, and deduce plausible explanations. Remember, before there were books of history, there was the Bible," Mrs. Torrington says.

"Cuneiform texts tell that Mede King Ishtumegu, whom Greek historians say is Astyages, gave his daughter Mandane in marriage to the Persian ruler Cambyses. It is a common practice for marriages to take place, hoping for peace keeping futures. In this case, their child was Cyrus, who grows up and ultimately seizes the Median capital. What do you think is the connection between all of this, and the people of 1830's Old Sturbridge Village?" Mrs. Torrington asks.

"That's a good question," Greg says, remembering the globe of the world in his room, and able to pick out some of these countries. "But aren't they across the Atlantic Ocean, and a long, long time ago?"

"Yes," Mrs. Torrington agrees. "But there are two churches here filled with people who care about their faith. These empires not only affect the people way back in those days, but we see this today with the descendants of Isaac and Ishmael. Even though history happened a very long time ago, the ramifications of actions at that time, and continued actions in every generation, affect relationships between countries and people to this very modern day. Just because an event happened in history a long time in the distant past, does not make it irrelevant. The actions and reactions of people back then have a direct effect on the people of Old Sturbridge Village, back in 1830, and still today," Mrs. Torrington explains, with a careful eye on her young audience.

"I thought matters of faith were up to the individuals who choose to believe whatever they want to believe, or not," Sarah comments, a bit defensively, thinking how her sister would take this information.

"That is true. People have the freedom to believe whatever they want to believe. But it is my job as a teacher of history, to teach history as accurately as I can. History does not stand alone in time. History also shapes our future, not only in our beliefs, but also helps us not to repeat past political, military, social, economic and many other mistakes, even in education and religion. History also encourages us to become better people, at least, I think it does," Mrs. Torrington says.

"The Medes and the Persians from this point in history become known as what?" asks Mrs. Torrington, getting back to her topic for the night.

"The Medo-Persian Empire?" the teenage next to Abe guesses questioningly. He just came in, walking up from the Town Common.

"Correct. It is interesting that many of the Bible reading church-goers of Sturbridge Village say this very empire is written about in the Book of Daniel 2:32, 39 and Daniel 7:5. It tells of the Medes and the Persians conquering Babylon in 539 BCE, which is approximately the same time our secular history books document it. The Bible is historically accurate when it predicts hundreds of years before hand that Cyrus will be the one to decree the return of Jews to Jerusalem.

"In conclusion, I have one more consideration before you go. Does anyone remember who the first king of Babylon was?" Mrs. Torrington asks.

"I know! I know!" Greg squirms, wiggling his arm wildly in the air. "I know this one!"

"Alright Greg. What is the answer?" the teacher asks.

"Nimrod! The answer is King Nimrod. We just learned this tonight over at the Salem Towne House," Greg beams, giving his first correct answer in the school house class.

"Correct. Secular history books will tell you of the battles between the empires, how the Babylonians, Canaanites, Assyrians, Medes and Persians fought. These empires are also mentioned in the Bible. But a deeper understanding of the origin of these empires reveals that they all stem from Noah's sons, grandsons and great grandsons. Tonight we learned about the families of Noah's sons Shem, Japheth, and Ham. And now we finish tying them all together remembering Nimrod is the son of Cush, the son of Ham, the son of Noah. Nimrod is the famous Babylonian king. This is truly a family affair," Mrs. Torrington concludes.

They climb back into the sleigh next to the school where Abe, Greg and their cousins had attempted to walk on stilts and played jump rope outside last summer, pretending to be children in 1830, now with a fresh blanket of snow.

"Thank goodness the boys are enjoying this," Sarah thinks, eyeing her attention deficit, hyperactive son. "A good meal full of protein and stimulating conversations really do slow him down, and engage his mind," she chuckles to herself.

"Are we going to be able to stop to see the Pottery Shop?" Sarah asks.

"Sure thing," Clyde says. "This is a special night. Something on your Christmas wish list?" Clyde muses.

"Nothing in particular. I just appreciate homemade pottery," Sarah answers.

Back in his seat, Clyde turns his attention to his Belgians, urging his horse drawn sleigh through the winter woodland wonderland again. Clyde's oil lamp is bright, but the full moon appearing from behind a cloud is brighter.

The bells ring louder as the reins guide the Belgians, the family, and Clyde up the hill. Abe and Greg know this place. Grammy Rose takes them here every year, but usually when it is warmer, and they are walking on the dirt roads.

"Greg, grab that big blanket near your feet and cover us up," Abe notices.

Even Sarah climbs under the blanket. Off they go into the darkness, trading the familiar sights, sounds and aromas of the Village taverns, houses, churches and school, for the intense smell of pine trees, horses, leather and hay.

"We'll be coming up to the Pottery Shop pretty soon on your left. The kiln, however, is on your right. You will see the fire glow from the kiln. It will certainly keep you warm." Clyde shivers, with exaggerated flair.

"We will make a quick stop in case you would like to see the kiln in action, or if you would like to see the pottery, or buy some. If you are chilly, you can stand on the outside of the kiln, but do not get too close because it is really hot," Clyde cautions.

"It takes one to four cords of wood for each firing by the potter. The inside temperature can get to 1,900 degrees, so please be very careful. We have set up a rope around the kiln for the protection of our guests. You may not get any closer to the kiln than the roped off area. Please stay outside the rope," Amos Green says, the kiln attendant for the evening.

Sarah walks into the potter's shop and watches the potter at the wheel. He takes a lump of clay, and with wet hands, begins working the clay into a mug, while his feet pump the wheel to go around. But the mug is not coming out to the liking of the potter. He picks up the clay, forms it back into a ball, slaps it down on the wheel, and wets it the clay with his sponge. The process starts all over again.

"This is just like the verse in Jeremiah 18:6," the potter chuckles, "As clay is in the hands of the potter, so are you in my hand."

"It is really a nice thought, that God can reshape us when we ask for his help. On our own, we do not shape ourselves, our lives, or even governments in the best way without him." Sarah ponders the potter's comment.

"I love the mugs, and the crocks," Sarah says to the boys. In no time at all, Sarah is the new owner of old fashioned, homemade pottery to add to her platter collection at home. For this evening only, a special businessman, an associate of Scrooge himself, is set up in a corner of the potter's workshop, assisting in the sales of his goods.

"Greg! Don't lean over the rope!" Abe exclaims, shooting a quick glance at the horses to make sure he didn't make them start again.

"I was just trying to feel that heat on my face. I know what I'm doing. It is way too hot to touch, anyway," Greg justifies.

"Alright you two," Sarah says, catching up with them. "Let's get back in the sleigh, and remember to be quiet now."

Nestling under the blanket, the three of them snuggle as frosty wreaths of exhales form from their mouths and noses. Snow covered fields come into view on their right, now reflecting a sheen of full moon light. In the distance, they can see the silhouette of the farm house and barn etched against the night sky.

CHAPTER 10

How Christmas Came To Be

Brie, Abby, Aunt Cher and Grammy Rose find themselves comfortably seated in over-stuffed chairs in the library, pondering the spectacular and curious events of the evening. Candlelight gently flickers soft reflections in the windows and across each of their faces. Warmth from the cozy fireplace welcomes them back to the hidden library. At first, they remain silent, drinking in the evening's amazing events. The snap back to their present time is a stunning, loud silence. The sturdy table in the center of the room still holds the large antique leather locked books, with one of the huge keys sticking out of one of them.

Brie and Abby get up and begin pushing and tapping all the walls and casings to the doors and windows with the hope of finding the gingerbread contest room, dining room, or any other room in this historical place. But no walls, windows or doors revert into anything familiar.

Back at the books, Grammy Rose examines the old volumes closely, deciding Joshua surely must have done his research here. He covered history, both Bible history and world history, much deeper than she remembers studying. She reads the titles again slowly, *Heaven Helps Earth*; *Noah, The Flood And The Ark*; *The Revenge of Nimrod - Sumerian King Enmerkar*; *Slave Away*; *The Creation Of Creation*; *Jeremiah In Egypt*; *World Powers Foretold by Daniel*; *Living In Jesus' Time*; *Revelation of the Greek Myths* and *Constantine and The Roman Empire*.

Aunt Cher carries a tray of drinks to refresh them. They are recouping from what feels like a long journey.

Brie and Abby give Grammy Rose a big hug, thanking her for this special holiday treat, as Grammy Rose curiously removes the large key out of the *Noah, The Flood and The Ark*; and inserts an older looking key in *The Revenge of Nimrod* book, twisting the key.

Brie, Abby and Aunt Cher gasp.

Click.

In their next breath, they find themselves is a huge, cold, damp, stone room. There is a roaring fire in the oversized fireplace with seemingly little if any effect at all. Brie and Abby are hiding behind an enormous marble pillar, next to a similar pillar hiding Grammy Rose and Aunt Cher. They listen carefully, not sure if they should be eavesdropping on the royal couple speaking at the head table.

"Nimrod, you are truly a giant of a man, the first of all kings. Let me show you how to party like a Canaanite, in real world style," Ishtar jests to her husband, king of the most expansive and beautiful city within all of Mesopotamia, Babylon, nestled in the fertile plain between the Euphrates and Hiddekel Rivers. Ishtar bats her eyelashes, heavily laden with black mascara and shimmering eye colors from Tarshish adorning her eyelids. The bangles from her gold bracelets sound like a soft tambourine to each dramatic move she makes. Between the two of them, they own the world.

Nimrod claps his hands. Immediately his chief servant is by his side.

"Gather the hunters, and saddle the camels to carry the game home. We go into the forest to begin our Saturnalia celebrations, honoring Saturn, the god of sowing," Nimrod bellows his orders.

"Your Kingship, your horse is ready. The hunters are awaiting your orders." King Nimrod's personal assistant bows.

"I will lead the ride to the woods. You will laden the camels with the game I shoot. Canaan, you will chop down the tallest and fullest evergreen tree you can find for the Saturnalia feast in the Palace Banquet Hall, and haul it back on the sled. Your son Sidon will assist you. Heth, you are in charge of collecting the evergreen branches for the yule logs and the wreaths. Take three men to assist you and gather mistletoe as well. Tonight we kick off the grandest Saturnalia and the wildest winter solstice ever we have ever had!" King Nimrod commands, pointing to the three men to his left. He couldn't care less about family connection to Canaan, his illegitimate uncle.

Nimrod's reputation as a tyrant precedes him. Nimrod knows the righteousness and integrity of Noah, his great-grandfather, baptized and blessed by Jehovah God through the great Flood. Nimrod sees God's mark in the sky, a colorful rainbow, a sign of the promise to Noah that God will never again flood the earth. However, that is not enough for Nimrod, who decides to set himself up in opposition to God.

Nimrod and Noah could not be more different. Nimrod does not have a problem with Noah. Nimrod does have a problem with true, living God of Noah. God had destroyed the tower of Babel, and confused the language of all humans. Most recently Jehovah God had caused the great Flood, wiping out all living things.

Nimrod, tempted by Satan himself, choses to denounce God, and replaces himself as the god of the land. Why should he have to obey God when he could be a god himself?

All the other hunters along with Nimrod on this hunt, obey Nimrod, not the God of Noah. They are all part of the same Canaanite family, thanks to the unholy deed done by Ham, Nimrod's grandfather, on that fateful night so many years ago.

Nimrod recalls the story of Canaan on his way to the great hunt. The first grapes from the vines from the ark were finally ready after the Flood. For the first time, Noah had been drunk from the over-abundance of wine on the day that Ham violated the trust of his mother and father mother. Ham had the audacity to brag about this abuse to Shem and Japheth, who then took a robe and walked backward to cover Noah and his wife. Unfortunately, Canaan was born, and was cursed by Noah.

Nimrod remembers this curse laid upon his uncle. Who could forget it? Noah had said, "Cursed be Canaan; a slave of slaves shall he be to his brothers."

Nimrod's Great-Grandfather Noah told this curse to Nimrod's Grandfather Ham, how Canaan is to be cursed for the rest of his life. Canaan is to be a slave to Ham's two other brothers, Shem and Japheth. The retelling of this family history occurs on every summer solstice feast, affecting Nimrod in many sinister ways. If it is a revolution God wants, Nimrod is glad to give it to him.

Nimrod also remembers this blessing his Great-Grandfather Noah gave to Shem and Japheth, "Blessed by the Lord my God be Shem, and let Canaan be his slave. God enlarge Japheth, and let him dwell in the tents of Shem; and let Canaan be his slave."

Canaan carries the curse with proud arrogance. The haughty nation of Canaan is now the spoil of Nimrod's capture by his Babylonian expansion. The land of Canaan continues to be filled with evil, carnal creatures, prone to killing, gross immorality, idolatry, Spiritism, violence and war. Flagrant pride and insane ego is the fruit of their caving to temptations by the first of all rebels, Satan. The entire land of Canaan, now part of Babylon, is cursed with depravity void of any redeeming quality.

Unlike Noah, Nimrod, has chosen to turn his heart cold, with a violent disposition, hunting not only animals but also mankind, anyone or anything that stands between himself and his deceptive tyrannical rule. His professed purpose is setting himself up in opposition to God. Nimrod refuses to take the correction that the flood wiped out the evil choices of mankind. He is here and the world is going to have to deal with him.

Nimrod decides to take things into his own hand, refuses to obey God, and substitutes himself in place of God. In his tyrannical rule over the people, first he uses deception, instituting false gods and goddesses, promoting paganism and false philosophy. If that plan fails, he resorts to fear and terror tactics. He finds holding the life and death of people in his grips very effective.

Horses' hooves thunder against the early morning quiet, snapping his attention back to the present moment. After leaving the fertile low lands, they make their way to the prolific hunting grounds in Nimrods' newly acquired territory beyond the Hiddekel. Leaving his newest shining cities of Ninevah and Calah behind him, Nimrod enters the oak and verdant forest.

Nimrod releases the arrow directly into the hearts of gazelles, a lion, sheep and goats. The fowl of the air also become food for the feast.

"Load the beasts upon the camels," Nimrod demands, shortly after the hunting begins. They head back to the Palace. Ravaging the land does not take long.

Once in his Palace bedroom chamber, Nimrod calls for his personal servant, who assists him out of his hunting skins, and dresses him in the exquisite royal robes made just for the Saturnalia feast tonight.

"See to it that the final plans for the Saturnalia celebration are complete with music and dancers for the feast tonight. Light the candles. Decorate the tree with the gold and silver ornaments from Tarshish, only the best for our sun god Saturn, and fasten it with hammer and nails so it will not fall over. This year we cut down the tallest and thickest fir tree in the forest. Have the women make the yule logs for the tables, wreaths for the walls, and hanging mistletoe for all the entrances.

"Have the children decorate the tree with the painted clay cherubs they made last month, in memory of the children who have already walked through the fire in years gone by, for our own enlightenment. We shall gorge ourselves with food and drink. Organize the food and wine taste testers. Report back to me on your progress."

The chief servant in charge of the festivities bows before King Nimrod and departs quickly to follow his orders.

King Nimrod and Queen Ishtar make their way through the marble Palace hallway leading to the Palace Banquet Hall to make sure this evening's Saturnalia celebration is perfect.

"You must be so proud, King of the grandest empire in the history of the entire world," Ishtar beams, as they stand near a crackling fire roaring in the large stoned fireplace.

"Yes. Look what we have done. Educational pursuits thrive here. Through our own effort, we have New Age religious, cultural and political thought in this international capital. No longer is the world at the mercy of archaic tradition like the pre-flood days of my Great-Grandfather, Noah," Nimrod agrees, sweeping his hand across the room.

"Who says Noah is God's only voice when the world now has you!" Ishtar exclaims.

"You are right. Much blood, sweat, wars and tears is the purchase price I paid for all of Babylonia. Victory does have its price. But it is worth it. Look at the empire I am amassing," Nimrod exclaims, opening his arms wide.

The fragrance of freshly cut evergreens fills the Palace Banquet Hall. There is still time before the chief servant returns from his assignments, so Nimrod continues reminiscing.

"The world begins with God's own people. Yet look how God treats them." Nimrod scoffs, challenging the God of Noah, and continues.

"God in his brilliance wipes them all out with a flood. Why? Because they used their free will not to believe in him, live the way they wanted to, with no rules. I decree that will never again happen, if I have anything to do with it, and I do. I am ruler in the largest empire since the Deluge, my empire, my rules. Of course these people fear that kind of God. Who wouldn't? I will show my people not to fear this God. I will show them how to live," Nimrod says to his wife.

"We are both royalty. We both claim Ham, son of Noah," Ishtar boasts, playing with her hair. "To you he is your grandfather; to me, my father. You, my dear husband, are the great and mighty hunter, son of Ham's oldest son, Cush, while I am the daughter of Ham, "Semiramis, Night Goddess of the Moon." While you were first my son, now you make a fine husband for me."

"Let us never forget our royal lineage. I am proud to have the land of Canaan by conquest. It stays in the family. I already invaded and captured Shem's territory to the north to build my new cities. Now we go from sea to sea." A haughty laugh escapes Nimrod's lips.

"Canaan made up his own rules. He was banished, yet has become the father to his tribe in the region near the Great Sea, spanning from the mountains to the lowlands. This land of the giant Anakim, once Canaan's land, is now mine as well," Nimrod boasts.

"You and I both grew up in this land of Canaan. It's a merchant's paradise, rich in trade on the coast of the gorgeous Great Sea. We began our own Saturnalia customs and holiday celebrations of our many gods, like Mithra. No more celebrations of Noah's God, and having to repent in ashes. The people worship you now as a god, and say you will never die. We can believe what we want, with no interference from Noah's God. Who needs that kind of God?" Ishtar agrees.

"What enrages me is that Great-Grandfather Noah curses Canaan, making him a slave of his brothers, while in his next breath Great-Grandfather Noah asks God to bless Uncle Shem and Uncle Japheth in sharing their prosperity. Grandfather Ham is left out in the cold to witness all this misery. Great-Grandfather Noah thought that was an acceptable punishment for Ham's abuse. No wonder Canaan left to start his own nation. And what a nation Canaan has become. Now it is mine," Nimrod says, proudly patting his chest.

"After the feast this evening and before the dancing would be a good time to decree the new religion of Babylon," Ishtar prompts.

"Enough of the God of Noah. Reformation is at hand. Yes, tonight we have a double celebration, the victory of gathering all these cities under my rule, not God's rule; and the finest winter solstice celebration in honor of our own gods, Saturn and Mithra. What kind of god drowns people and animals of the entire earth? Tonight I state my revenge on God if he ever floods my people again." Nimrod has no problem threatening God.

"Yes, tonight we also celebrate the progress of my highest temple-tower and greatest sacrificial alter built into it. Surely that alter will be higher than any flood water can reach! Noah's God scatters people who challenge his leadership and lifestyle. Not only that, he confuses the original language given to Adam. My temple-tower will reach higher than any other!" Nimrod defies, with fists raised to the sky.

Brie, Abby, Aunt Cher and Grammy Rose remain like statues in their hiding places behind the huge white marble pillars near the side of the room, intently listening to the enlightening conversation. Brie has never heard anything like this before. They take the tan tunics and grey head coverings in stride, more concerned about what is going to happen next.

"Servants! This is not the kitchen! I should have your heads for sneaking into the King's Palace Banquet Hall, but we are short staffed. You will just have to follow me. Next time it is death to you." The chief servant berates them.

Brie jumps out of her skin.

"You, help out with the bread making in the kitchen. We want all three hundred kinds of bread this time. No skimping in this celebration!" the chief servant says to Brie. She is glad she remembers how Mary made bread in Bethlehem.

"You, fill the clay jugs with wine. You must be new here. No standing around. After you fill the jugs with wine, start filling the smaller jugs with water from the well outside the kitchen," he says pointing to Abby.

"You two," instructs the chief servant to Aunt Cher and Grammy Rose, "to the vegetables for preparation with you. This time clean them better. The last feast still had dirt on the carrots. No more lingering around."

The chief servant darts down a dark stone corridor and into the kitchen already filled with more servants consumed with meal preparation. It is hot. The work is hard. Vast mounds of vegetables that lay before them. They labor for hours.

Brie worked from Sumerian and Akkadian bread recipes, taught to her by Ada, first kitchen bread maid. They worked with barley and other cereals which first had to be ground into flour. Then they mixed their batches with oil, milk and beer. Not all were leavened. Some were sweetened with honey, some with date sugar, while others they flavored with spices and fruits. The bread kitchen was smelling delicious.

"Shape the bread in different sizes and shapes. Use your own imagination, a heart, a head, a lion, anything you want. Or you can use any of these fifty traditional molds under the counter. The King wants variety this time," Ada teaches.

"Ada, your recipes are very sophisticated, rich and refined," Grammy Rose notices, glancing over the shelf of garlic, onions and leeks. Above that shelf was another holding mustard, cumin, coriander, mint and cypress berries.

"It is nice to have an experienced group of servants this time. Use the semolina, flours and malted barley to thicken and smooth out the gravies and sauces. When it is not such a special occasion, we have used blood also, but not today," Ada instructs.

Finally the food is prepared and set in glazed pottery bowls, just like the ones at Old Sturbridge Village. They are hot and heavy to carry with no potholders to help. The King's table is heavily laden with wooden platters of roasted beef, pork, various poultry, sea and freshwater fish, turtles, crustaceans, shellfish and lots of trays of fried locusts. This feast also boasts of many cooked vegetables and fresh fruits, tender bulbs and roots, truffles, and mushrooms all seasoned with herbs from the palace garden outside.

"I am very impressed with your use of milk, butter and other fats, both animals and vegetable oils, and especially how you work honey and salt to enhance the flavors," Grammy Rose says.

"These are my mother's recipes. The King likes them too," Ada says proudly.

"Let the music begin," King Nimrod orders to the minstrels.

Instantly the lyre and harp come to life. The reed flute and trumpet players slowly circle the palace banquet hall, while the drums to keep the tempo of the dinner music.

After serving King Nimrod and Queen Ishtar at the head table, and several rows of enormous palace banquet hall tables for the attending governors and their guests, the kitchen help stands at attention on the side of the wall. The taste testers come out to sample each of the dishes to make sure no one poisons the King. The wine from the jug poured for the King is also taste tested. No taste testers die. King Nimrod begins to eat, followed by the governors and guests from each village, hamlet, town and city in the ever expanding Babylonia.

Satisfied after what seemed like hours to Grammy Rose and her family, King Nimrod rises with goblet of wine in hand.

"The world now belongs to me. The tower is almost completed, thanks to my vision. It is no small task for the millions who slaved away to create the tallest temple-tower ever to be built in the history of mankind. Because this temple-tower is to reach to the highest heaven, no more will we have to scatter or have our language affected. Tomorrow this platform temple will receive a baptism by fire at my decree. I am the representative of the fire god Baal, but the next twenty-four hours celebrate Saturn, the god of sowing, as well as my victories.

"Now for a toast to the gods of Saturn and Mithra. Raise your goblets and drink with me as we celebrate the beginning of the One World Government on this Saturnalia. It is my New World Order. Since the flood wiped all people off the face of the earth, I decree that it is good for men to have more than one wife," King Nimrod institutes, as an audible sigh of approval cascades throughout the room.

"My father Cush and I are promoting the worship of many gods. In one week's time, we will also celebrate the Sun God of Righteousness, Mithra. From now on, Saturnalia will not only be a grand one-day of celebration on December 17, we will suspend work from now to December 25, Mithra's feast day. Enjoy yourselves. Eat, drink and be merry. There are no rules here. Anything goes!" King Nimrod announces, standing tall before the feast table.

"You are our god now," one governor yells out, pounding his fork on the thick wooden table, joined by the entire room of guests, sounding like thunder.

"You will never die," another governor adds, not to be outdone by the first. Elections for governorships will be coming up in a few months, and now is the time to gain some political ground.

With his goblet still raised, Nimrod states, "The symbol of the gods will be the snake, sun and fire. Our human sacrifices begin tomorrow night, even though the temple-tower is not yet finished, the sacrificial altar is completed. Have no more fear of the God who sends floods to kill you. You can reach enlightenment by sacrificing your first-born infants to the fire tomorrow night. This is an order." King Nimrod sits down was a wave of shock goes around the room.

Grammy Rose feels the same pit in her stomach as she had when she heard Joshua describe it. The family trade horrified glances not noticed by King Nimrod.

All guests appear to trade fear of God to fear of Nimrod, but at least now, they get to live loose lifestyles, indulge in magic, spell-binding, astrology, Spiritism, incest, sodomy, bestiality and speak vulgar and crass words; and eat meat and drink blood without fear of breaking this or that outdated rule in the ever-expanding Babylonia. The minds of men are now in charge.

Hunting animals is not Nimrod's only game prize. No price is too great, not even conquering Shem's son Asshur, in his namesake city in Assyria, is off limits. Nimrod is bloodthirsty, violent and notorious, claiming Shem's territory as his own, just as he did to Ham.

The enormous map chiseled in the furthest wall depicts all of the cities, hamlets and villages which have been conquered. The Babylonian Empire now extends from the mountains north of Nineveh, one of the Assyrian cities, in addition to Rehoboth-Ir, the city of Calah, and Resen, which is nestled between Nineveh and Calah. These are the first cities he built to start his kingdom, including the battle-scarred remnants of cities left behind.

The Babylonian Kingdom now extends to the southern and prosperous city of Ur, across the Arabian Desert all the way to Tema and the Red Sea; and from as far west encompassing all of Mesopotamia to the Euphrates River, clear to the Upper Sea, and all the cities in between.

To the west, Nimrod's conquered lands reach as far as the highest mountains west of the Tigris River, and further west of the Elam region. Included in his coveted cities are his beloved Babel and Erech in the land of Shinar Chaldea. Some people in the region are affectionately calling this entire region Babylon, warming Nimrod's proud heart.

The region at the mouth of the Tigris and Euphrates Rivers empty into the Lower Sea, and is a fertile area where crops, trade and people flourish. Nimrod boasts he owns and rules the cradle of civilization itself, rebuilt after God's wretched flood destroyed it.

Brie and her family take a break behind the incredibly tall and thick marble pillar, just outside the kitchen to the left, and watch history unfold before their eyes.

"Finally the cities have ripened enough to be plucked. That flood ruined every living thing, and killed everyone, all but Noah, Japheth, Shem, Ham and their wives. Some God they believed in. I believe in myself. Only now have my conquests succeeded. There is no other king in Babylon greater than me. Look at my cities: Ur, Erech, Babel, Accad Calneh in Shinar; as far to the east as Susa, and as far south as Tema. But my prized city is my precious Babylon.

"Servants!" King Nimrod bellows, clapping his hands. "Away with the food, let the dancing begin."

Brie, Abby, Aunt Cher, and Grammy Rose snap into action, clearing plates and bowls of food, some barely touched. They will get to eat in the kitchen when the banquet hall is cleaned up. From inside the kitchen, they peek out into the banquet hall at the loud ruckus echoing over the sound of the minstrels.

"The double crossing of Nimrod worked!" the leader of a band of seventy-two co-conspirators brags. He is protected by armor under their clothes.

The leader has a curious look on his face. King Nimrod's guards, full of feast foods, seem unaware of the sinister plan. Before anyone has a chance to react, the leader draws his sword and slashes Nimrod through the chest.

Nimrod shoots the tall man a pained look and falls to the floor.

"Let the world know, that today your pretend eternal god has died," the leader yells, over the deafening screams of the unsuspecting and horrified guests.

"Our god Nimrod will never die," a governor screams, raising a fist.

"See for yourself!" the leader declares. No one is going to take the place of his Sovereign God, Jehovah.

The Palace Dining Hall is in upheaval. The seventy-two co-conspirators rush to Nimrod with swords drawn, quartering him and chopping him into little pieces for the governors to take back to their hamlets, cities and towns, proving beyond any doubt that King Nimrod is no more.

"There is only one God, the God of Noah and Adam. Nimrod is not a god. Take these pieces of Nimrod back to prove that this fake god is in fact dead," the leader yells, as he and his entourage flee the frantic scene.

Seconds later, Semiramis, Night Goddess of the Moon, quickly plots to continue her Queen status. No governor or anyone else is going to strip her of her title and fame. Time is of the essence. Her fear of a coup is significantly greater than the shock and horror at the gory death of her husband.

"Governors and guests, your Queen is speaking. Guards, set out immediately to chase after Nimrod's killer. Bring him to me when he is bound," Ishtar orders, with her right hand raised.

Queen Ishtar stands with shoulders back and head held high. "This very night, we keep all of the Saturnalia traditions, despite the murder of Nimrod, and even because of him, another living sacrifice. All first born babes this year will walk through the fire, appeasing the fire god Moloch, if you wish to receive enlightenment from the gods. Be at the temple-tower at sundown. The soldier guards have already been sent out to go through all houses in Babylonia to make sure this order is followed," Queen Ishtar demands.

The dark Queen expects that, with the love of the community and the popular traditions behind her, they will be done with the likes of the conspirators and their God before too long.

Queen Ishtar enjoys her self-given name, "Semiramis, Night Goddess of the Moon." In the circles of her self-inflicted New Age religion, a compilation of antiquated pagan religions both she and Nimrod started, she picks out the most appealing holiday traditions, while retaining the child sacrifice practice. There must be an element of fear of her, for her worshippers to remain. It is by Queen Ishtar's name that she continues to politically rule her beloved Babylon.

"We love you Queen Ishtar!" the closest governor bellows. "You are truly the Night Goddess of the Moon! We love the human traditions you and King Nimrod have given us."

"Agreed!" the next governor joins in. "Look at how popular your god and goddess holidays are now. They are too ingrained into our society now to forgo."

Ishtar beams with pride far greater than the sorrow over the death of her husband, and far greater than the fear of losing her position.

"I wish to speak for all the governors," the third governor says, perceptively noticing that the Queen is commanding the room. "We express our sympathy to you and our heartfelt condolences at this time. We are here to assist you in any way you see fit."

They love the presents, the revelry and debauchery of the immoral orgies, the breaking of every civil-legal-moral law, the food and feasts, the fairy tale myths, mistletoe and the evergreen decorations, especially the decorated tree with silver and gold ornaments. They even love the depravity of the dark side, the guilt of purgatory, the hell-fire-brimstone which keeps the clans in line. It is the extreme partying that brings the brightest joy through it all. This winter solstice celebration adds such joy to the darkest time of the year.

Clinging to her feast table for added stability, Queen Ishtar stands with her finger pointing to the governors and says, "From now on, I decree under penalty of death that we will worship Tammuz of Babylon, the sun god, just as we celebrate the birthday of Nimrod at this winter solstice celebration. You all come from different lands in all of Babylonia. Since the fall of the Tower of Babel, when our one language became many, I understand that each population has their own interpretation naming the sun god. Most of you here know the sun god as Mithra; while some of you call him Baal, Marduk, Ahura, Mazda, Gott, Anton or

Dagon. What we are really celebrating is the re-incarnation of Nimrod as *the* sun god."

A loud applause breaks out in the chaotic palace dining hall. Obviously Queen Ishtar is still in charge. Equally loved by her people are the celebrations at the spring equinox complete with all the fertility symbols of bunnies and eggs. These Queen Ishtar dubbed "Ishtar bunnies" and "Ishtar" eggs. Ishtar pronounces her name as "Easter." The pagan May Pole is also their creation, a treasured dance of spring.

Queen Ishtar regains control of the room. "No longer must you follow the archaic rules from an archaic God who chooses to drown those who do not obey him. Now I say, you do as you like. Take your pleasures where you will. Nimrod and I have instituted many pagan celebrations for all the holidays and feasts, being handed down from generation to generation."

Again the governors give rousing applause.

Semiramis, Night Goddess of the Moon continues.

"Rather than outdated laws, look to the joys we have given you. You now have sprites, fairies and gnomes in the summer. In the autumn you have the hallowed reincarnation, Spiritism, astrology and interfaith beliefs. We are proud of all metaphysical approaches to life, anything to take attention and worship away from Noah's God. The true God of Adam and Noah is still our enemy and the enemy of the vast throngs of pagan worshippers. Man's thoughts are the measure by which to judge and live by, not the outdated Ten Commandments of God. We have evolved. We have the right to rule ourselves. From now on, we will teach that we are all gods and goddesses."

With that the Queen collapses in her seat. Her attendants come to her side and refresh her with wine and fruit. When the color returns to her pale cheeks, she orders the room to be cleared of guests so that there is enough time to prepare for what comes next.

Governors and guests leave the Palace Banquet Hall, their minds spinning in the wake of the evil aftermath, catching a few late rays of afternoon sun and a fresh breath of air before the twisted twilight agenda. The dark Queen expects that, with the love of the community and the popular traditions behind her, they will be done with the likes of the conspirators and their God before too long.

The riders ride the thunderous sad sound of pounding horses' hooves throughout the Babylonian Empire, carrying out orders, bringing back with them all the precious cargo of soon to be infant sacrificial victims by sundown.

Wailing of mothers whose hearts are torn by sorrow, fills the air, while dancers with streamers leap for joy in circles around them, all to the heavy beat of the deathly drummer's dirge. The yearly Saturnalia and Feast of Mithra celebrations demand these innocent deaths for the first time under King Nimrod; to appease these manmade gods. No one dares to challenge this death decree, which the king had promised to bring enlightenment to each and every one who participates. Participation is mandatory, under penalty of their own immediate deaths.

The altar fires are lit. Huge crowds of agnostic and atheist worshippers attend the mandatory temple-tower ceremony, soon to be christened with innocent blood. Mothers continue crying for their children, but are drowned out by the thunderous beating of the temple drums, and the loud singing of dirges.

Wafts of smoke pour down the side of the temple-tower, into the open windows of the Palace kitchen where Brie, Abby, Aunt Cher and Grammy Rose are finishing cleaning the banquet hall and kitchen, following Ada's orders. They are all crying, partly because the smoke is burning their eyes, mostly because of what they realize is about to happen. Soon the sacrifice of babies for selfish religious, political and financial gain takes place.

"Put the glazed pottery bowls in the large wooden chest with leather straps in the corner of the room over there. Make sure to lock it when you are done." Ada points to the heavy chest which is currently opened, awaiting its fill. She hands Brie the key.

As soon as Ada says this, Brie, Abby, Aunt Cher and Grammy Rose quickly fill the chest with the ornate pottery bowls. Brie knows what she has to do, and locks it shut as they all pray silently to the God of Adam and Noah, to save them from this horrible period in time. It feels natural to pray. This is only a few generations from their last visit when they saw the cruel and selfish Nephilim first hand. Now they are in the land of Canaan where the rebellion to God got a resurgence, thanks to Nimrod. Brie and Abby hold hands while Brie whispers a prayer to God, that they return safely, and to never again allow the murder of children be the solution for any human situation. Even Aunt Cher silently prays again for the safety of her children, her mother and herself. Grammy Rose prays for God to help them all, for history not to repeat itself, and she makes sure to pray in Jesus name. Amen.

Click.

CHAPTER 11

DICKENSIAN TIME

"It won't be long. We are making our way to the Freeman Farmhouse," Clyde says, with a hearty laugh. "First we'll stop at the barn. Then you can go into the farmhouse where we have hot chocolate waiting for you inside."

"Meet Franklin Johnson," Clyde introduces, as his charges disembark from the sleigh. "He is getting the cows, heifers and oxen bed down inside the barn tonight."

"Hey, look at the red cows!" Abe remarks in surprise.

"Yes, this breed of cow is called Red Devon. They came from England to this country a long time ago. They look very much like the breed that are around here in 1830. They do not mind the cold." Franklin winks.

"What is this one's name?" Greg asks, as he reaches for some hay to feed her.

"Why this is Betsy. She is our milking cow. The whipped cream for your hot chocolate which is waiting for you inside the farmhouse tonight comes from her," Franklin beams, the eldest and wisest farm hand on the property.

"These two heifers next to her are Button and Bonnie," Franklin teaches.

"What's a heifer?" Abe asks curiously.

"They are called heifers because they have not had a calf yet. In the next pen we have Lance and Henry. Do you know what kind of animals they are?" Franklin quizzes.

"I believe they are oxen," Sarah says, appreciating the enormous size of the animals.

"That's right. And over here we have two calves, Rainy and Summer. Summer was named that because they was born on the summer solstice." Franklin pauses to pat the gentle animals.

"Over here are the Horned Wiltshire sheep. As you can see by their coats, they are of what we call the unimproved variety of sheep, like the kind that are around here in the early 1800s, with the looser quality of wool. I am happy to say we have six lambs here, three sets of twins, born in the spring. But, the improved variety of sheep over at the town barn are a different breed that look mostly like the nineteenth century Merinos that you might be familiar with. There was a lot of modified breeding taking place to result in finer wool, which is important to the textile industry. Make sure to visit the textile workshop this evening next to the cider mill. The town barn is on the other side of the cider mill, so you might like to visit those sheep also. Over there you will find thirteen sheep in that flock including five lambs, five ewes, and three weathers, which are neutered males," Franklin teaches.

"What are in those buildings?" Greg asks, pointing to the out buildings past the cow barn.

"That is where we house the chickens, and that one over there is home to our pigs. We protect all our animals at night because of predators. We have special lights on inside to keep their homes warm in the winter months," Franklin says.

"We saw wolves tonight. One had me up against a tree. But the game wardens saved me," Greg recalls.

"That's good! We are always ready for all kinds of predators," Franklin assures him.

"It must be hard keeping this barn clean in the winter. It seems like a lot of upkeep," Abe ponders out loud.

"Most of our work caring for the barn takes place in the warmer months. Sometimes the men who are farmers nearby help one another with the men's work of repairing barn roofs, building adequate storage space in our barns for blankets, tarps, feed, animal medicines, and barn tools. There are rusty and broken hinges to be fixed, gates and fences around the barn to be painted, and broken windows to be replaced. Just before winter, we clean out all the old hay and scrub the place clean to avoid allergens and mold. Do any of you suffer from allergies?" Franklin asks.

"I do," Greg admits.

"Allergies also affect the animals. Then we insulate the barn with hay bales and corn stalks. You'll notice we also pack the outside of the barn with snow. But we do have to make sure not all the windows are sealed too tight, or else fresh air for the animals to breathe won't get in. We also check for safety inside the barn by making sure there are no ropes or wires hanging around, and make sure no toxic cleaning supplies or medications can be accessed by the animals. We do not keep any toxic materials near any of the animals," Franklin explains.

Fire in the farmhouse fireplace crackles, as Belle, Scrooge's former fiancée, greets them, pointing to the table and chairs waiting for them.

"Would any of you like some hot chocolate to warm you up? We have some nice whipped cream I whipped up for you from milking Betsy this morning. Sit at the table by the fire to warm you up," Belle says warmly.

They all accept.

"Why did you not want to marry Scrooge?" Abe asks curiously, dropping into the beloved popular story.

"I see you have read the latest novella by Charles Dickens. "*A Christmas Carol*" was just published by Chapman and Hall December 17, 1843 in London. I have a new copy of the book here on the table. It is an instant success, even the critics like it," Belle brags.

"To answer your question, when I first met Scrooge, he had a fear of being poor. He told me the hardest thing in the world is poverty. He said that poverty severely condemns the pursuit of wealth. I fear he succumbed to his greatest fear. He focused so much on material poverty that he planted seeds for relationship poverty. He dwelled on making money so much that it consumed him, making his heart hard on every other human need, even his own. I do wish him well. But now I have a wonderful life on this farm with my husband and with our children," Belle beams.

"I love all of Dicken's books," Sarah says.

"Me too. I like his *Pickwick Papers*, but I liked "Oliver Twist" better, published in 1838. We already got to read it," Belle boasts.

"Brie had to read *Great Expectations* in school," Greg says.

"I also liked *David Copperfield*, and *A Tale of Two Cities*," although they were a bit dark," Sarah says.

Belle winks at the family and says, "The books you mention will be written in about another ten or so years," she says, keeping in her 1830's-1840's persona.

"We can relate to the struggles of Dickens' youth, and his humanitarian vision. We call it the Carol Philosophy, because his books are based on his humiliating experiences as a child, the plight of the poor. The children born in the 1830's -1840's, which we exhibit here at Old Sturbridge Village, can relate to these messages," Belle says.

"Didn't he also base some of his writing on Washington Irving's writings?" Sarah asks.

"Why yes he did. We have a copy of Irving's *Sketch Book* on the table by the bed in the other room. It was published in 1820. You are correct." Belle smiles.

"What time were you up milking the cows this morning?" Abe askes, changing the subject.

"I'm up at quarter to four, and milking Betsy by 4 a.m. It takes a long time to milk by hand. Have you been here early in the summer when we have the guest hands-on milking contest?" Belle asks her guests.

"Not yet. Is it fun?" Greg asks.

"Fun, no; work, yes," Belle comments, as she pours three mugs of hot chocolate.

She takes the whipped cream, and scoops generous amounts on top of each cup of hot chocolate.

"You notice all our lighting is by candles and the fireplace. All our farm and house equipment is human powered, horse powered, or water powered," Belle explains.

"Thank you for your hospitality," Sarah says, standing up and heading for more adventures the night holds.

"And thanks for the hot chocolate," Abe says.

"And the homemade whipped cream," Greg adds, donning a whipped cream mustache.

"I enjoyed your mugs from the Potter's Shop. I bought some to take home with us," Sarah adds.

"I hope you enjoy them as much as we do. Come back anytime." Belle waves as they load into their waiting sleigh.

CHAPTER 12

SLAVE AWAY

Brie, Abby, Aunt Cher and Grammy Rose gaze into each other's tear-streamed faces. The other family members are nowhere to be seen. Now they are sitting around the table filled with pies, finding themselves still behind the moving wall, and in the pantry. It's a good time to take a break. Grammy Rose smells the fragrant aroma of coffee permeate the air. Someone has made coffee. The silver coffee urns on the large counters to the side of the room by the windows are hot. Glazed white pottery mugs are stacked near the coffee ready to go. Grammy Rose pours two mugs of hot coffee for herself and Aunt Cher, and two half-filled mugs of coffee so Brie and Abby can add milk to their cups for coffee milk. Just a tad more sugar and all cups are set.

Aunt Cher gets pie for all of them. As she gathers the forks from the drawer, some fall to the floor with a loud chiming sound. Some of the fork tines hit Grammy Rose's arm in the process, giving Grammy Rose a cold shiver up her arm.

"Talk about interactive learning. I do not understand this experience at all. Let's stay together. I love you so much and I do not want to lose you," Aunt Cher says to Grammy Rose.

Finally they recline on the comfortable chairs in the library, discussing the events of the evening, before a crackling fire they had not noticed before. Warmth fills the room.

"What do you make of all these adventures tonight?" Brie asks Grammy Rose.

"I notice I did not hear the Bible stories like this in the Catholic Church before I left, that is for sure. There are so many inconsistencies between the Bible, the Catholic Church, and these experiences tonight," Grammy Rose observes.

"I think it is all hogwash. Religion is for fools. Sorry Mom. I don't mean that personally. It is just that if God listens to prayer, he does not listen to mine. I am no different than you. You say God listens to your prayers. I prayed, to no avail. Why would God not listen to my prayers? I don't think God exists. If he did, Andre would still be alive," Aunt Cher laments callously.

"There is so much cruelty in the world. If there is a God, and is supposedly a God of love, then why is the world in the condition that it is in? Children are starving. Countries are at war. We now have global warming, extreme floods and droughts, earthquakes and tornadoes. I'm beginning to think God is a joke too," Brie says, trying to comfort her aunt.

Brie feels torn in her heart. Seeing Aunt Cher so sad since Uncle Andre died has affected the whole family. Brie believes in God one minute, then does not believe in God the next. Oddly, she feels a struggle in her heart. It seems to her that it matters, in the bigger scheme of life, one way or the other. She has gone to enough church services to hear Jesus saying that evildoers get cast out, and those who do what Jesus says get to be with Jesus in the Kingdom of Heaven forever. Maybe it is all a fairytale, or is it?

"I do not pray, and good things happen to me. I do not need God to be happy," Abby adds, siding with her cousin-friend, and her mother.

"This is a personal decision," Grammy Rose admits. "But, I cannot deny my experiences, with God and with prayer. I find prayer and meditation calms my mind. I feel peace when I invite God into my heart. When I don't know what to do, I ask God's Holy Spirit to help and guard me. I really do feel God's Holy Spirit."

"I feel peace when I meditate, sometimes, but I don't bring God into it. I used to believe in God. Sometimes I still want to believe in God, because I would like to think Andre is in a better place. I just feel cold and empty about God," Aunt Cher says.

"Jesus said we could go to him with our troubles, and he would give us rest. He says to learn from him. He is gentle, and that we will find rest for our souls. He says his yoke is easy and his burden light," Grammy Rose says, trying to uplift her daughter's heart.

"I could use some gentle rest," Aunt Cher agrees.

Brie sees Aunt Cher struggling with the same faith struggle she is experiencing. Abby is also going through this. Why should it matter? But it does. Brie figures she could have a condescending attitude, like some of her friends, but she finally decides to allow room in her heart for more education, not less on this matter. Still, her questions persist.

"Is it really all taking place in the same night? What is all this talk about Noah? All the grandmothers of my family and friends I know are religious. But Grammy Rose is educated, has degrees, and is intelligent. Isn't believing in God for less educated people? Isn't religion the opium of the masses? Aren't we supposed to be the change we want to see in society? Doesn't that mean we have to denounce believing in God, so we can leave our own mark on the world? We are not supposed to be followers, are we? Does science deny God? Does religion deny science? Can science and religion be understood together?" Brie is flooded by a barrage of thought provoking questions.

Brie saunters over to the books to look at the titles again. She is wearing a mischievous grin. "What about …"

"No!" Abby, Aunt Cher, and what is left of Grammy Rose rush toward her.

Too late. The key is turned and the *Slave Away* antique volume opens.

Click.

They are in a crowd of people who are laughing and making fun of the young man who is speaking to them. The more he talks, the more they laugh. They look on the young man's face is earnest, even pleading. He pauses to take a breath.

"Oh Jeremiah," an older man scoffs, "how can you say that if we do not reform our ways, change our actions and obey the voice of Jehovah our God that you are telling to us, that he will bring us to ruin? Will God really kill his people simply for having a little fun?"

"That's right," says another with his fist pumped into the air. "How can you say that the city of Jerusalem will fall, and the Temple be destroyed? This is ridiculous! What do you know? You are just a young man. King Solomon built this Temple four hundred years ago. It is made of the finest cedar from King Hiram of Tyre, and the choicest stone blocks quarried for its foundation. The Temple was built with such fine materials that King Solomon had to pay off an additional twenty towns in Galilee to King Hiram. There is no way this Temple will be destroyed. This is ridiculous!"

"God is going to punish you, all of you, if you do not stop worshipping false idols that honor your pagan gods. He has told me to tell you this, so that you will return to the one, true and living God. A punishment is coming upon you. It is death to you. Jerusalem will fall and the Temple will be destroyed!" Jeremiah exclaims, unfazed by his harsh critics.

"Go home. Don't you hear your mother calling you?" a rotund man jests.

Another man whispers behind his hand to his friend. Men and women alike are laughing.

"You are trading believing in God for believing in evergreen trees as if they are magic. Yes, they are living while they stand in the forest, but even a living tree eventually dies. The God in heaven will never die," Jeremiah stresses as he preaches in the courtyard of the house of Jehovah.

"Only some of us worship trees. We enjoy the custom of cutting down evergreen trees and tying them up in our houses, and decorating them with silver and gold ornaments. It makes the house smell fragrant and festive. Who are we hurting?" a woman clad in purple asks. "Nature is alive in all people, plants and animals. Even the seasons are in rhythm. We can see this life."

"God only you must worship, not his creation. The Creator is greater than his creation," Jeremiah insists.

"We worship the many gods of nature, and the gods we fashion with our own hands, from the gold melted down from our own jewels. We believe these manmade gods reveal the greatness of the gods beyond our understanding. We hurt no one when we celebrate these traditions handed down to us for generations. We place equal value on our traditions, the same as we believe in our own faith. God gave us free will, or don't you believe in that?" the woman asks in disgust.

"Don't bother with him. He is just a child. My son is older than he is. What does he know of life? What can he possibly know of this God of his?" The man on the opposite side of Jeremiah insults him.

"There is only one, true God; only one Creator. His name is Jehovah. His name is full of power, no other name, only the name of Jehovah; not a title or label such as "Lord," only the name of Jehovah has power to save you," pleads Jeremiah. The burden to share such an important message from God bursts forth from him.

"O save me! Save me!" a man dances in circles before Jeremiah, mocking him.

"And what are we to do with our precious and costly idols, statues and heirloom keepsakes?" an elderly, confused woman asks, who has been celebrating the feasts of the gods Saturn and Mithra since she was a child.

"Look at your idols. There is no life in them. You wise men know better than to worship these things. Why, you make these idols yourselves out of sheets of silver from Tarshish and gold from Uphaz. You skillful goldsmiths make idols, clothe them in kingly purple robes made by our local tailors, and worship these manmade idols as if they were gods," Jeremiah says, scanning his increasingly hostile audience.

"He does have a point," a young man says cautiously. "Our idols are not real."

"We are not worshipping a hunk of metal, you stupid boy," an older man says, just joining the crowd growing hotter and less reasonable with each passing second.

"We know what our idols stand for. They represent more than their workmanship, you fool," another voice yells. "Use your head."

"You even idolize non-living things. You are having trouble because you idolize your customs and traditions, things that God has not told you to do, horrible things like making your precious children walk through the fire. You are replacing what God has told you to do, and how to celebrate. But you replace the words of Jehovah God with your own. You think you know better. You misuse the free will God gave you for your own selfish pleasure and ideas, as if the way of God needs to be updated. It does not. Your made-up gods and your traditions are frauds with no power or life in them. They are all worthless and silly. It is shameful what you have done. All these idols will be crushed, and their makers will perish," Jeremiah continues undeterred.

"Jeremiah," a woman taunts in a yellow tunic and blue head covering, "we have been celebrating our many gods with all our human traditions which we love, for over 1,000 years now. We mark the year as it goes by according to our feasts and celebrations. It is only for fun. We have been celebrating these customs since our forefathers came into the land of Canaan. You don't think we are simply going to stop this fun, just because you tell us to stop, do you?"

"He thinks the walls of the Temple are going to fall into ruins," a loud man snaps, slapping his leg for hysterical emphasis.

"I do not give you my own words. I am telling you the words Jehovah God is telling me to tell you. Stop following other gods, serving them and bowing down to them. This offends Jehovah. There is going to be a punishment for deserting the One, True God, and following after false manmade gods. This entire land will become a desolate wasteland. All the world will be shocked at the disaster that befalls you. Israel and her neighboring lands shall serve the king of Babylon for seventy years." Jeremiah announces the words God has given him to say.

Not enough people are taking Jeremiah seriously. So many years have gone by since the beginning of Creation of the world that the Israelites have fallen into a pagan god coma. They vacillate from worshipping the living God of Adam and Noah; to worshipping both this living God *and* celebrating pagan god holidays and traditions.

There are even some who denounce the one, true and living God and worship only the manmade pagan gods, forgetting the God who created them and their free will. Manmade idols of clay, metals and especially gold fill their homes on miniature alters, and in their yards as shrines adorned by flowers and trinkets. Their places of nature worship are filled with such abominations.

"Jeremiah must be stopped. He is not in charge of our customs of Judah and Egypt," the princes of Israel say to one another, under the heavy influence of false prophets proclaiming peace. A remnant in the horrific line of Nimrod over one thousand years earlier is brought back as an undercurrent of manmade gods, rituals and beliefs; all part of the Babylonian system many fondly revere.

"When Jeremiah comes into Jerusalem next week, let us capture him and do away with him," the other leader replies, speaking in the shadows.

Word gets around that Jeremiah and his foolish message will be done away with. Grammy Rose knows how this story ends. Brie, Abby and Aunt Cher do not. They find themselves slaves to a farmer named Eanasat. He is also known in the region as a very busy merchant at this time of year, demanding that they keep their ears open when they go into the city to sell his fruits and vegetables. There is much profit to be made during the holidays, with such merriment and family feasts large and small.

Each day they return to the farm on the outskirts of the city of Jerusalem. Brie is the one designated to handle the money, not the women. Eanasat is not aware that Brie has disguised herself as a boy, calling herself Gabriel. Now that the crops have come in, they are sent into the city each day to sell the farmer's goods. They also sell Saturnalia favorites including evergreen trees, wreaths, holly and mistletoe sprigs, and yule logs, which they have painstakingly cut and created, for the benefit of Eanasat's coffers.

"When you return to me, tell me what Jeremiah tells the people. But more important, tell me what you hear the princes of Israel intend to do about it," Eanasat orders.

"That was a hard day," Brie says to her family after returning from handing the day's earnings to Eanasat.

It has been a long day. Slaving away for Eanasat is not easy. They are up before dawn, first gathering the crops, then preparing the baskets laden with tree and vine fruits like quince, grapes, dates and figs, almonds and other nuts, root vegetables, olives and olive oil. Once the baskets are full, they place them in the saddle sacks on two donkeys and walk to the city. Eanasat has secured the selling spot for them, right beside the city walls where everyone must walk by. The second donkey carries the added burden of festive yuletide evergreens, holly, mistletoe and trimmings. The holiday trees are delivered weekly, sailing down the mighty Jordan River from the forests of the Lebanon Mountains before the weather gets too bad. Eanasat's business is quite an expansive enterprise. They are allowed one piece of fruit in the morning, a hand full of nuts at mid-day, and a slice of bread before bed. They guard their precious skins of water with great care.

"Hey! Come back here with those figs," Brie demands, chasing after a small boy with quick hands.

Brie knows hunger. She also know the grip of Eanasat's fat fist, gripping her arm. Eanasat knows exactly how much produce and product goes out each day. Brie is also in charge of the weight scale, and dares not mess with their meager meal and sleeping arrangements.

"Arwia! We must pay for those!" Arwia's mother scolds.

Brie gratefully accepts his payment.

At twilight they return to the farm, and carefully unpack the donkey saddle packs. At this point, the family splits up. Brie and Abby take care of the donkeys, feeding them and giving them water, brushing them down and giving them a fresh bedding of hay for the night. They take especially good care of this detail because this is where they also sleep, and guard the animals by night.

Meanwhile, Aunt Cher and Grammy Rose bring the baskets into the root cellar at the beginning of the cave, and soak any root vegetables that are left, so they can plump back up before morning. Then they dry them and place them in a cool spot. The baskets must be cleaned and aired out.

"My hands are extra dirty today. Look at my nails!" Brie exclaims.

I know Sweetheart," Aunt Cher says, putting her arms around her niece, who appears to be getting thinner by the day.

"My hands are getting split in places. Some of the buyers noticed it today. I was able to get some olive oil on them, which helped a lot," Grammy Rose says.

As the family gathers together, each on their own spot of hay covered by their shawls, a blanket of exhaustion covers each of them. They are asleep in no time. Days blur into weeks, and weeks into months. This time the family has no concept of time, nor how long they have been there. They are considered to be Hebrew slaves.

The rooster crows the day awake. The donkey wants to be fed. The day is off.

"People do not own people. There is only one race, the human race," Grammy Rose has said repeatedly to her family, when no other ears were listening. She and her family have had enough.

The weather seems to be past spring now, perhaps even to the end of June, if the first grapes of the season are any indication.

"You are not listening to the word of God! He has told me to tell you these things. Stop worshipping manmade idols, and false gods which are only the fancies of human divining, and false religions. God says he will destroy Jerusalem!" Jeremiah says demonstratively, standing before the Temple. "I know some of you want to kill me. As if that will keep the God who created you quiet! If you kill me, you will be killing an innocent man!"

The princes of Israel decide to let Jeremiah live. Time will tell if he is correct. The Israelites for their part do not change. No young whippersnapper is going to correct them.

King Nebuchadnezzar is unaware that the God of Jeremiah is going to use himself to fulfill the prophecy Jeremiah has been proclaiming.

Back at the farm, Eanasat orders, "Gabriel, take these gold necklaces, rings and gold idols, handed down through my family for generations. Your women are to stay here at the farm, since you will be traveling by cover of night. Bring the gold items to the servants of the King inside the city gates at daybreak. King Nebuchadnezzar is ordering all in his land to bring all gold items to him. The King's accountant will give you a record of all the items I am giving to the King. Make sure all items I am giving you are included, or it is lashings for you. Take Ettu, my archer, with you. He will defend you. Saddle the camels for more protection against marauders. Be quick about it. Come back as soon as you have completed my order."

Eanasat is not only a farmer, but also one of the chief servants of the King. He must obey.

"You must stay here until I return," Brie says to her cousin, aunt, and grandmother, appearing wiser than her years.

"But Brie, you are too young to go by yourself," Aunt Cher protests.

"Aunt Cher, I have no choice. We must obey our master. I have heard about what he does to slaves who do not obey him. He even withholds food. We barely have enough," Brie says, omitting the lashings threat, with a mature voice that even she does not recognize.

"Hurry back!" Abby cries, not liking to ever be separated from her these days.

"Let me give you a great big hug," is all Grammy Rose can offer.

"OK, but come right back," Aunt Cher agrees.

The inky black sky is perfect for the midnight treasure ride. Two wild Bactrian camels have recently been domesticated, not always taking kindly to riders. Brie's camel is smaller, with a full-sized dose of nippy attitude. Ettu's camel is much larger, taking longer strides, a challenge to keep up with from the start.

Brie is carrying the priceless treasures under her cloak. They have been carefully packed in a box that barely fits in her left hand. Nothing is showing that would tell on her, or give any cause for other passers-by in the night to suspect these two are on anything other than a hunting expedition, with Ettu's bow and arrows strapped to him.

Brie's camel seems more intent on nipping her off his back than following his larger counterpart. Brie takes a loud crying offense to his camel's latest bite. Brie hits the camel away from her leg, causing the camel to trip on a rock lying in wait, rather than watching where it is walking. Camels are known for being sure footed, but not this one.

Maybe it is the whack of the box in Brie's left hand hitting the camel's neck, or maybe it is the awkward, unexpected, sideways jolt of the camel tripping on the rock, but whatever it is, the result is the same. Brie flies off the back of the camel, desperately gripping the box of treasures before she hits the ground.

If only she could suspend herself in midair.

Brie crashes to the ground, strewing the golden jewelry and idols all over the sand beside her. Horrified, Brie tries to sweep her hand over the top of the sand to save what she can.

"Wait! Stop!" Ettu demands. "If you do that, the gold will sink into the sand!"

Brie freezes. Ettu climbs down off his kneeling camel and lights his oil lamp. The gold items glisten in the light of the lamp.

"Thank God!" Brie says, as she gingerly picks up each piece of gold she finds. The box gets filled back up to the brim as it was before the fall. Brie takes extra care to remove the sand from each piece.

"You must work quickly," Ettu says, always on the lookout for thieves known to rob people who travel these roads by night.

It is too late. A band of thieves in black cloaks approach out of nowhere. Ettu helps Brie back up between the two humps of her camel, but does not have time to get in the saddle of his own camel.

"Get inside the city gate as fast as you can. Do not stop for anything. I will catch up to you," Ettu bellows.

Camels can move fast when they want to, evidently, and Brie's camel is now running a gangly run that nearly bounces her out of the saddle once again. Brie looks back.

Arrows are flying through the air. Thieves are yelling out in pain. The pounding of hooves is fast approaching Brie.

"That should slow them down considerably," Ettu says, meeting up with his charge for the night.

"Are we safe?" Brie says.

"Safe as you can be out here. One more turn in the road and we are there," Ettu says, huffing and puffing.

Rounding the bend, sunrise welcomes them to the city gates. They are the first to be let in to the gold gathering tables. The mini treasure chest is opened and all gold items accounted for. Brie guards this tabulation with her life, presenting it to the farmer on her return.

King Nebuchadnezzar takes all the gold collected and makes an idol in the image of a golden calf to be worshipped. It is nearly ninety feet high by nine feet wide, set it up in the plain of Dura, in the province of Babylon.

"You princes, governors, captains, judges, treasurers, counselors, sheriffs and rulers of all the provinces of the Babylonian Empire, as you stand here today, when you hear the music of the horn, zither, harp, bagpipes, stringed instruments and other musical instruments; you are to fall flat on the ground to worship King Nebuchadnezzar's golden statue. Anyone who refuses to obey will immediately be thrown into a flaming furnace!" the herald announces loudly.

God wastes no time. The people have been warned by Jeremiah, and have had ample time to soften their hard hearts. But the people want what they want; the false celebrations to false gods, and human customs win out over matters of faith which the prophets of God taught as reminders to his wayward people Israel.

Meanwhile, Brie, Abby, Aunt Cher and Grammy Rose remain as slaves to Eanasat. They have brought the grapes they picked in the morning, marking the end of June, as they know the calendar. Times here have definitely changed. The family no longer feels safe.

There is much unrest in the city of Jerusalem. Eanasat tries to make sure his goods are safe. They are not. King Nebuchadnezzar has changed his mind. Day after day the destruction of the walls is taking place at his command. It is not safe at Eanasat's farm either. Perhaps it was a greater mistake to think they would be safer inside the city walls, now that King Nebuchadnezzar is tearing them down. Jerusalem is not the beautiful city it once was. Babylonia is spreading rapidly, like a contagious disease that is creeping across the desert, snuffing out the breath of life to the lungs.

All of a sudden fire is breaking out all over the city, everywhere they turn. They must flee with the rest of the Israelites. Worse yet, they are all being taken prisoners to Babylon. Jerusalem is being captured. The city is burning before their eyes. They hear the news of King Zedekiah's sons being slaughtered. Even King Zedekiah was blinded and bound, and was taken prisoner to Babylon.

Nebuzaradan, King Nebuchadnezzar's chief of the bodyguards, is now capturing everyone in Jerusalem. Fear seizes them all. First they are slaves, and now prisoners!

Grammy Rose knows this is the fulfillment of God's prophecy that was delivered by Jeremiah. The year is 607 BCE. She knows it does not end well for the Israelites at this time in history. She is also worried for her family. The Temple built by King Solomon does in fact get destroyed as Jerusalem gets sacked. They must stay close to one another. With her arms encircling her family, Grammy Rose says a heart-felt prayer to God.

"Help me God. I don't know what to do. I need your help. I pray in Jesus name. Amen." That was all she could think to pray.

Brie spots a lock on a main gate next to her. People are screaming as they run by her, trying to escape. Her family sticks to her like glue. Before anyone notices what she is doing, Brie inserts the key and turns it.

Click.

CHAPTER 13

GREEK PANTHEON INITIATION

"This night is so amazing! I never put Charles Dickens and his *A Christmas Carol* in the same time period as Old Sturbridge Village," Abe says as he climbs in the sleigh and nestles in between his cousin and his aunt.

Sarah is relieved that there is enough activity going on in the many workshops to keep Greg's mind occupied.

"The next stop is over at the Blacksmith's Shop around the corner. They are portraying the Greek Empire, if you are up for it," Clyde announces.

"Sure we are," Greg answers, before his mother has a chance to reply.

Sarah gives Clyde a quick smile of approval. That's all it takes for Jim and Jerry, with hooves muffled under the freshly fallen snow, to carry their human cargo to their next workshop.

"Welcome to the Greek Empire presentation. Does anyone know what the Greek Empire is known for?" Matthew Templeton asks. He is the ancient historian visiting from Archeological Society of Ancient and Medieval History, through a grant by the Worcester Museum of Cultural and Natural History.

"I know about the Trojan horse, how they filled the large wooden horse with soldiers. When they took this apparent gift inside the city gates, Odysseus and his men came out and conquered the city of Troy," the little old lady wearing wire-rimmed spectacles says.

"Yes. The Trojan War takes place around the year 1180 BC," Matthew says.

"The first ancient Olympic games started in Greece," Sarah says, flashing back to her college ancient history class. "They built the Olympics on mythology, and attribute Zeus as the father of all their gods."

"Yes. The first Olympiad ever held took place in the year 776 BCE. Did you know that Alexander I participated in the ancient Olympic games?" Matthew asks his guests.

"No," the teenage blonde boy says, sitting next to Greg.

"Alexander I, who is a predecessor of Alexander the Great, could only participate after he proved his Greek heritage. These Olympic games were always held where?" Matthew quizzes his audience.

"Olympia! The Olympics then were always held in Olympia, Greece," Greg answers before anyone else got the chance. Brie told him and his mother all about the Olympics, and Plutarch and lots of things about Greece one day at dinner.

"That's right. Now, place yourself in this setting. King Phillip II and Queen Olympia, have a son, Alexander III. At that time, it was the Greek tradition to attribute to the people and situations, various gods and goddesses. Who did the Greeks say Alexander's father was?" Matthew asks, getting excited about his topic for the night.

The old lady wearing wide-rimmed spectacles raises her hand and answers, "Zeus! The Greeks figured if the Babylonians could make up their own gods and goddess, they could also. They begin the Greek Pantheon. They believed their human leaders to be gods. The mythology they created spread like wildfire."

"Very good answer. Does anyone know the name of the famous tutor Alexander has until he is sixteen years old?" Matthew pauses, not expecting anyone to know this answer to this question.

"That's only three years older than Brie is!" Greg exclaims.

A hand shoots up from the old man with a cane, sitting next to the woman who had spoken earlier. "That would be Aristotle. He taught Alexander to be one of the greatest tacticians the world has ever known. Aristotle taught him creative thinking and martial theory. That is why he won so many battles. That's why they called him Alexander the Great."

"You are correct! Alexander the Great was undefeated in battle," Matthew exclaims, enthused over having such knowledgeable guests attend his workshop. "You know your history. Alexander was only eighteen years old when as a prince, he takes charge of the cavalry. As a matter of fact, Alexander the Great was so great, that he conquers not only Persia, but Egypt, becoming king of the empire, as well as pharaoh to Egypt. One of his shining moments is in building the city of Alexandria, which is named after him."

"Plutarch said he thought it was a sign for Alexander to return home after Alexander sacked Persepolis in 331 BCE," Sarah says, with Brie's review fresh in her mind.

"Does anyone know in what country Persepolis was located?" Matthew asks.

It is the old man with a cane who answers. "Persepolis was located in what is known today as Iran, and was quite a spectacle to behold. First of all, it was built on the top of a manmade terrace, with a very wide staircase, which also went through the Gate of All Nations. This impressive gate depicted extremely large bulls with wings and human heads."

"Correct. What was your life's work sir?" Matthew asks, curious about his guest's accurate knowledge.

"My wife and I are a retired college professors of ancient and medieval history. We could not possibly miss the program tonight. It is shining a light on some of the world's most forgotten history. It is wonderful Old Sturbridge Village is offering mosaic snapshot glimpses of times that trickle down to the 1830s, in an interesting way through the Center Meetinghouse Church discovery. It is an enlightening backdrop to what and why we do the things we do even in this modern day." the old man smiles.

"Thank you for that acknowledgment sir," Matthew says, as he continues on. "They used symbolism in the construction of their buildings, like the Hall of 100 Columns, thought to have had bull-headed capitols, and still has ornate stone reliefs on their doorways."

Then turning his attention to Sarah, Matthew asks, "You said Alexander the Great sacked the city of Persepolis in 331 BCE. Some history books say the year is 330 BCE, while other historical sources say the year is 331 BCE. It is still the same conquering of the same city. Do not worry. Back in ancient and medieval history, they were not focusing on writing down accurate history for modern day history books. The further back we dig, the fewer accurate dates we find. Do you know why Alexander the Great sacked the city of Persepolis?"

"Yes," the woman professor replies. "It was retaliation for the Persian army, led by King Darius, attacking Athens, Greece."

"Correct again," Matthew compliments her.

"Brie said Alexander the Great heard that some of his men were threatening mutiny," Abe says, remembering his sister telling him all about this exciting part.

"But that backfired, didn't it?" Matthew's twinkling eyes smile at his guests. "In the year 324 BCE, Alexander the Great executes all the leaders of the mutiny on the banks of the Tigris River, at Opis."

The guests sigh a collective groan.

"What have you learned tonight about the world empires so far?" Matthew asks.

"We learned at the Salem House from Horace about the Babylonian Empire," the teenage boy answers.

"Don't forget, our archaeologists point to the Akkadian Empire. Today there are seven thousand texts attributed to the Akkadian Empire, which practiced a Sumerian religion. Some Babylonian texts also acknowledge this empire. What happens to the Akkadian Empire?" Matthew challenges his guests.

"Archaeology shows that the Akkadian Empire came to a quick end due to a dramatic climate change," the male professor says.

"The flood!" Abe exclaims.

"Yes. The Flood is dated to 2370 BCE. Think of this, geologists refer to a scientific explanation of the dramatic weather change that occurred at that time is known as the 4.2 kilo year BP aridification event," Matthew explains.

"What does BP stand for?" the blonde boy next to Greg asks. "I know that arid means dry, and there is desert over there, which makes sense."

Matthew scans his intelligent audience and says, "Some say BP stand for "Before Present," while other researchers say it more accurately stand for "Before Physics," that is, before nuclear weapons testing artificially interfered with proportion of carbon isotopes in the atmosphere, making carbon dating after that likely to be unreliable."

"However, science has other means of dating historical periods," the blond boy's father says.

"Let's list some of the ways we now know about dating some of these finds," Matthew says. "Spot dating is usually run in tandem with excavations. Today we have what is known as absolute methods for dating periods of history, such as studying amino acids, archaeomagnetics; and argon-argon or potassium-argon for dating Homo Sapien and extinct species of manlike creatures like Neanderthal, Cro-Magnon, and Denisovan remains. There are many creations in Creation. Even the Bible says all life forms were created according to their kinds," Matthew says with the light of knowledge in his eyes.

"Yes, but, don't forget that science is mutable and changes what it calls facts each time it discovers something new," the man in the handlebar moustache notes.

Matthew nods his head. He enjoys sharing his love for history as unearthed through archeology, so he continues.

"That is not all. There is also dendrochronology for dating not only trees and objects made from wood, but also used in calibrating radiocarbon dates. Still other dating methods use lead corrosion, obsidian hydration which is a geochemical method, optically stimulated luminescence; and radiocarbon dating, which of course is only valid for the past fifty thousand to sixty thousand years, due to the nuclear weapons testing incident messing with the isotopes in the atmosphere I mentioned earlier."

"The earth and Creation was around for billions of years prior to the Creation of people. It must be impossible to date back billions of years. I think it is interesting to date back as far as we can. Do you think it is possible to date back to the Akkadian Empire and the dramatic climate change that ended it?" the man with the handlebar moustache asks.

"Do you mean to say the flood is the same as the ice age?" an apparently hyperactive, high-school aged red-headed boy asks, all excited about this possibility, which he had never entertained before.

"I'll save that for one of your next workshops," Matthew winks, continuing his list of ways modern science dates archaeological finds.

"Other dating methods include rehydroxylation and thermoluminescence for dating ceramic and other inorganic materials. There are other markers for archaeological dating, such as using ephigraphy which is the study inscriptions, numismastics which uses dates imprinted on old coins, and of course paleography which is the study of ancient writing in manuscripts."

The woman professor in the wire rimmed glasses adds to the growing list of ways of dating people, places and things. "Don't forget that the earth tells on itself by stratigraphic markers, like paleomagnetism, which takes into account that the polarity of the earth changes at a knowable rate. This polarity is stored within rocks, which can be dated. I like the method called oxygen isotope chronostratigraphy. It is sometimes also called marine isotope, or marine-oxygen isotope chronostratigraphy. It is based on the climate change using deep sea core samples to determine the cold and warm stages experienced over what is called "deep time," say over the last interglacial one hundred, twenty-five thousand years. And there is one more dating tool I think ought to be mentioned, tephrochronology, which is the study of volcanic ash. Did you know that each volcanic eruption has its own signature?"

"Yes. Is there anything else," Matthew asks.

"We can also date the time period through archaeological digs, not only by the items or bones found, but also by what is going on in the stratigraphic layers of the earth. Take the sedimentary layers of volcanic ash for example, or the other things found, like buried stone walls, or obvious construction sites of buried floors, walls and other such things. There are other dating methods such as fluorine absorption, the Harris Matrix and the vole clock, which some scientists say is the most accurate dating method, using vole teeth. But I think we've made the point that there are other methods to date people, places and things, other than carbon dating, which as we stated earlier, is not always reliable. I think it is fun to think about," The woman professor removes her glasses and smiles.

"I can't remember all that!" Greg exclaims.

"I never knew all that either," Abe says.

"I know. That was a lot of information. We think it is helpful to place the dates of the empires on an historical timeline. That is why we do that.

Sometimes we have to make adjustments when we find we have made some errors in calculation on historical dating. The changes science makes in these areas is always based on new information," Matthew says, acknowledging what some of his guests said earlier in his workshop.

"Science only knows what it knows at the time. When something new comes to light, they update their findings," the woman professor says.

"What other empires have you learned about tonight?" Matthew asks, trying to bring the discussion back on track.

"At the school house with Mrs. Torrington, we learned that the Medes and who else?" Greg half answers, looking to his mother for the missing part.

"The Medes and the Persians conquer Babylon," his mother finishes.

"Correct. That takes place in the year 539 BCE. Do you remember what takes place two years later, in 537 BCE?" Matthew quizzes, to see if tonight's historic timeline is making any sense to his audience.

"Cyrus orders the Jewish people to return to Jerusalem," the male professor answers. "The funny thing about that though, is that Cyrus is not Jewish, and did not know he was fulfilling a Bible prophesy by doing so."

"That's right," Matthew confirms. "Cyrus allows the Israelites to begin re-building their temple in Jerusalem, which takes twenty-three years to complete, during the sixth year of Darius the Great, in 515 BCE. Who do you think the Greeks use to conquer Persia in 331 BCE?" Matthew asks, to see if his audience is still following him.

"Alexander the Great!" Abe deduces, knowing he was mentioned at the beginning of this workshop.

"Yes. Do you know what I find very interesting? Alexander is said to have fought with the light of Mithra! Do you remember him from another workshop tonight?" Matthew inquires with eyebrows raised.

"Yes!" Greg exclaims. "He is the first manmade god from Babylon."

"Yes, sir. You will see those manmade gods and goddesses keep coming back. What about their language?" Matthew asks his eager audience. This has been the best group of the night.

"Many books were translated into Greek. It became an international language for the educated," the woman professor says.

"Yes. Greek becomes the worldwide language, because Alexander the Great has conquered much of the known world at that time. Don't forget, up until that time, the First Persian Empire, also known as what empire?" Matthew asks, just for fun to see if the professors are as sharp as they seem.

The male professor rises to the challenge and says, "The First Persian Empire is also known as the Achaemenid Empire. It became the largest empire, and was founded by Cyrus the Great, whom you are talking about. It spanned from the Balkans and Eastern Europe proper on the west, to the Indus Valley on the east. It was a huge empire that Alexander the Great, two hundred years after Cyrus the Great, conquered for Greece. The popular custom of that day was for all countries to use Greek as the universal language."

"It is a pleasure to have you in this workshop professors," Matthew bows graciously to his esteemed guests. "The interesting forgotten history discovered by the people here in Old Sturbridge Village, is that they have pieced together history, from ancient history books, including the Bible, to find out some very unique ancestry. Can anyone guess what this might be?" Matthew draws the captive audience in. All eyes are on him, but this time, no one has the answer.

"Assyrian cunciform texts, as well as Persian and Egyptian writings call the Greeks, Ionians. This name comes from Javan, the son of Japheth, grandson of Noah," Matthew answers his own question.

The audience gasps at the revelation.

"You guessed it. Here we have another of Noah's family, exploring the world, settling and becoming the early people of Greece and the surrounding islands including Cyprus, and parts of southern Italy, Sicily and Spain. In the Old Testament, also known as the Hebrew Scriptures, the Book of Isaiah 66:19, tells how God will use the people of Javan and the faraway islands to ultimately tell of his glory. Does anyone have any questions?" Matthew checks his audience.

"Yes, more than once tonight we have heard of Tarshish, where blue makeup for women's eyes came from, like Ishtar wore. But tonight, you said Tarshish is a son of Javan, a grandson of Noah?" the woman in the bright blue scarf asks.

"You are very observant, and correct," Matthew says. "As you have seen many times tonight, the people who conquered the land named cities after them, like the city of Asshur, son of Shem, and Canaan, son of Ham; and even Alexandria after Alexander the Great. Tarshish, the city, was in the region of Spain, conquered by Noah's grandson, Tarshish."

"Why are we discussing Noah's sons again? What is their connection with Alexander the Great?" the gruff man who just walked in asks, with his curiosity stirred.

"Let's take a closer look," Matthew says. "The Greek period is also known as the Hellenistic period. Does anyone know why the name came to be known as Hellenistic?"

Abe had not learned this so far in school. No one comes to Matthew's rescue to answer the question, until the gruff man raises his hand.

"Is it because of Helen of Troy?"

"No, that is a common misconception," Matthew explains. "The name Hellenistic comes from the man named Hellen, son of Deucation and Pyrrha. This is the Greek version, using god and goddess names, of the famed flood of Noah's ark. The Greek people chose to associate themselves with the Greek Pantheon, but history shows that while the cultures used different names to refer to the flood, it in fact is the same historical global event."

"Not many people know this, but in the New Testament of the Bible, also known as the Greek Scriptures, there is a reference to the people of Greece also being called the Hellenes. It can be found in Acts 20:2. History shows that the Hellas have a connection with Elishah, one of Javan's sons mentioned in Genesis 10:4," Matthew continues.

"Do you mean that the people of Greece also have a Bible connection?" Greg asks, connecting the dots of new information in tonight's program.

"Yes. It is mentioned in the very first book of the Bible. This ancient history fact is important to the people of Old Sturbridge Village belonging to the Baptist congregation here. They practice their faith at the Center Meetinghouse. It is quite an interesting observation," Matthew says.

"Are the Baptists really in this area in 1830?" Sarah asks.

"Yes," Matthew explains. "Don't forget, the Baptist Church has been around since 1638, when Roger Williams established the first Baptist congregation in the North American colonies. Right now, in 1830, there is a growing movement in the Great Awakening all across New England and in the South."

The young girl sitting across from Abe raises her hand. "I have heard of Elishah, but who did you say Javan is?"

"That is another good question," Matthew says, with smiling blue eyes. "Genesis 10:2 says that the sons of Japheth, who is one of the sons of Noah who was with him in the ark, were Gomer, Magog, Madai, Javan, Tubal, Meshech and Tiras, all born after the flood. Just for clarification, all of the sons of Japheth, Shem and Ham are born after the flood, so Japheth's sons I just mentioned, were not with him on the ark."

"Why do all the presentations tonight keep mentioning the Bible? Didn't history happen first, and all that Bible writing come after it?" the slightly annoyed gruff man now standing in the doorway asks.

"Yes, but pre-history did get written down before people forgot it. Moses wrote the first five books of the Old Testament in the Bible. He wrote the books of Genesis in 1513 BCE; Exodus and Leviticus in 1512 BCE; and Numbers and Deuteronomy in 1473 BCE. Current historians and archeologists in our time use the Bible to validate many of their finds," Matthew explains.

"I didn't know that," the gruff man said, now with his interested peaking.

"The ancient scrolls of the Bible, first written in the Aramaic language, pre-date history. There is a lot of pre-history recorded in the Bible. The study of ancient history is a rich, in-depth investigation from as many sources as possible. Only a small portion of history was written down in comparison to actual history. We go back as far as we can in what was written down. After that, we confirm our data, find ancient historical sites, and tract down genealogies through Biblical records whenever possible. It is amazing how accurate they are. We have found many ancient buried cities and locations in this way," Matthew answers.

The gruff man nods.

"Genesis 10:4 says that the sons of Javan are Elishah, Tarshish, Kittim, and Dodanim. The next verse goes on to say that their descendants became the maritime nations in various lands, each with a separate language. Greece included part of the southern part of the mountainous Balkan Peninsula, and the islands near it, in the Ionian Sea on the west, and in the Aegean Sea to the east, and the Mediterranean Sea to the south. So you can see how accurately the Bible places Greece exactly where it is," Matthew teaches.

"Now, the northern boundary of Greece at first was unclear because in the earlier periods, the Javanites were not together as a group, like the Canaanites. Their vision for setting up kingdoms was not important to them," Matthew adds. "Seems like it was a family trait."

"Remember the people of 1830's Old Sturbridge Village, have been trying to discern the meaning of King Nebuchadnezzar's dream, written about in the Book of Daniel. It is connected to what we are talking about," Matthew says.

"Why?" Greg asks.

"Many theories have been tossed about. As a Baptist congregation at the Center Meetinghouse, they are also interested in understanding how the prophecies have come true. It is a major reason they put faith in the Bible, because all the prophecies have come true, except for the last prophecy yet to take place," Matthew adds, taking a sip of water before he continues.

"Alexander the Great is the person they think God uses to fulfill the prophecy in Daniel, at Daniel 2:39, comparing the Greek kingdom to copper in the king's dream. The reason we are taking a closer look at this dream is because this is what the people here in 1830 think they have figured out. It is very exciting to them," Matthew concludes.

"Wait. If the Greek Empire refers to copper in the dream, what do the Babylonian and Medes and Persian Empires refer to?" Abe asks, reviving with connections to the empires suddenly taking shape in his mind.

"So happy you asked," Matthew beams again. "You'll have to read Daniel, chapter two. There you find King Nebuchadnezzar has a dream that no one could interpret. Finally he calls for Daniel, who is well-known for interpreting dreams. The king has a dream of a huge statue, with a head made of gold, chest and arms made of silver, a body and thighs made out of copper, legs of iron, and feet made of a combination of two materials, partly iron and partly clay, which is the weakest of all. Daniel tells King Nebuchadnezzar that the head refers to King Nebuchadnezzar, king of which empire?" Matthew asks.

"Babylon," the quiet man from the back declares.

"Correct. And who conquers Babylon?" Matthew asks.

"The Medes and the Persians," the group answers in unison.

"Now you are on a roll," Matthew smiles. "And who conquers Persia?"

"Greece!" the guests answer emphatically.

"Guess who the iron legs will be," Matthew challenges.

"Rome," the group answers again, knowing the schedule of workshops listed on the program for this special night.

"Who are the feet, made of clay and iron?" Abe asks.

"Remember we are dealing with people of 1830. They do not understand this last part of King Nebuchadnezzar's dream, because certain historical events have not yet unfolded which will help to shed some light on this prophecy in years to come. They suspect that it will be more than one nation, formed together, but not as sturdy as one may think. Daniel explains to the king that the mixing of the two materials is the clay mixed with people, but they do not stick together, just as clay and iron do not mix. I will leave you with that. This is what is capturing the minds and hearts of the Center Meetinghouse congregation at this time," Matthew says.

"Thank you all for attending this presentation on the Grecian Empire. The workshop on the Roman Empire wraps up all the empires we will be discussing this evening. They are all part of King Nebuchadnezzar's dream, one of the most fascinating historical times that have all come true as Bible prophecy," Matthew says.

"Isn't this all a matter of personal choice whether or not to believe any of this?" the gruff man asks, again shaking his head.

"Everyone has a right on what to believe what they want as to matters of faith. However, tonight in the workshops we are looking back on real history. People can decide on what they want to believe about faith. But the historical facts of everything we have presented tonight are true and accurate," Matthew explains.

The crowded workshop guests all thank Matthew for making history come alive, and file out into the night.

CHAPTER 14

FIRE THREATENS THE SHIP

Brie, Abby, Aunt Cher and Grammy Rose are mesmerized by the flicker of flames dancing in the cozy fireplace of the hidden library. Were they just dreaming? Had they dozed off?

"Hey!" Brie exclaims. "Look! I still have Eanasat's money bag filled with coins in my pocket. I never had the chance to give it to him in all the ruckus."

"Let me see!" Abby exclaims.

The family crowds around Brie for a closer look at the old world coins.

Abby flashes a mischievous grin to Brie as she inserts the second to longest key into the thickest antique volume with gold lettering imprinted in its thick leather hide, *Revelation of the Grecian Myths*.

"Is everyone ready?" Abby asks as her mother, grandmother and Brie attempt to stop her.

Click.

It is too late. They find themselves huddled around a roaring campfire which Brie has started in an effort to dry out their soaked, seafaring clothing. *Heir of the Ark*, their sailing ship, is anchored down in the harbor. Captain Dodanim is making his way up the sandy pathway leading to a tall wall of rock, perfect for the heat of the fire to bounce back to warm his crew. Dodanim joins them on the largest log. After the fish fry, they all lean back on the rock wall for another of the Captain's fantastic tales.

"Well now, let me tell you what I have just heard directly from the mouth of my distant cousin, Nimrod," Dodanim begins.

"You are related to Nimrod?" Grammy Rose shrieks unexpectedly. "How are you related?"

"My father is Javan, son of Japheth, oldest son of Noah. Nimrod's father is Cush, third son of Ham, son of Noah. Cush and Javan are cousins. We come from an impressive genealogy. Noah is Nimrod's and my great-grandfather," Dodanim boasts.

He takes a swig from his wine skin and continues.

"Noah's sons took their land by casting lots. Shem, Noah's second son takes the land near Mount Ararat, where the ark finally landed. Shem's son Asshur built a city in his name, in that region. Ham and his son Mizraim decide to take the Nile River south and claim the land of Egypt, while Cush explores further south along the Nile River and takes the land of Nubia. Egypt and Nubia were two of the earliest civilizations to the north and east of Africa, along the Nile River. Ham's son, Canaan, is born after the flood. He settles the land of Canaan near the Greater Sea, which is really Shem's land. Canaan knows this is his uncle's land, but he takes Shem's land anyway. I will tell you about them in a minute.

"Now I will tell you the history exactly, word for word, how my grandfather, Noah, told it to me.

"The animals large and small, winged creatures and slithering ones, in all shapes and sizes, came aboard the ark by their own merit when it was finished, each going to its own stall or space constructed for them. They were peaceful and regal, with a calm spirit among them all.

"As soon as the ark was filled, the ground beneath it cracked open and trembled. The whole earth quaked and shuddered. The sound was deafening. The family was all on board when God himself shut the massive door. Water came up from the ground and down from the firmament of heaven. They heard the sound of the people pounding on the door to let them in, screaming, crying and begging to be let in. But the door would not open.

"Many days were spent inside the ark. During the day they would take care of the plants and the animals, making sure the animals and people were all fed and watered. At night, Noah spent the time recounting his family history. This is what he said."

Four pairs of eyes were riveted on the Captain.

"In the beginning, before the world and before the stars, before the planets and before the galaxies, before all creation, before the constructs of matter and voids, before hot and cold, before silence and sound, before anything else existed; there was and is God. God always was and always will be. God is eternal, the Alpha and Omega. All energy that is seen and unseen first originated in God. Undefiled, boundless energy is his mark. His spirit is holy, pure, light, innocence, love, wisdom, peace, perfect, free, expansive, magnanimous, loyal, generous, incorruptible, kind, thoughtful and complete. Among all God's attributes, his greatest quality is Love that knows no bounds.

"God is spirit and Father of all Creation seen and unseen. God resonates with the perfection, power and active force, yet it is gentle and nurturing, radiating with the wholesome, compassion and empathy, and fearsome awe. Since God is love and wisdom, his Creation is life-generating, blessed by his breath of life, and encouraged by his spirit of holiness. God's first of all Creation in heaven, is a Son in the image and likeness of himself. Together, God the Father and the Son manifest every other Creation. In the process they introduce the concepts of time and space. Through it all there is Love.

"The realms of the heavens burst forth in veils of sight, sound and brilliance. A countless multitude of angels appear, each created uniquely. Creation of matter and void is generated over billions of years, ever expanding, seeded with innumerable possibilities and variations. Through it all there is Love.

"The Father and the Son, through the wisdom and power of the Father's holy spirit, act on the external creative force, generating life in spiral fashion, in a perfect formula of symmetry, color and dimension. Solar systems and galaxies appear in the void where once nothing was. The introduction of substances, gases, vapors, mists, clouds, motion, centripetal and centrifugal forces, high energy and lack of energy forces, wind, action and reaction play upon the earth. The great waters are gathered and the land appears. Seeds of all kinds of life are generated in every possible habitat. Through it all there is Love."

Captain Dodanim pauses to catch his breath. It is important to retell the story exactly how his great-grandfather, Noah, told him in order to keep the Oral Tradition and history accurate. Eight eyes are still glued on him, so he continues.

"There is no void in God, no lack or depravity of any kind. There is balance, fairness and free will. With the addition of this last quality, other energies emerge. The Father and the Son create millions of angels individually in the heavens above, and the Creation of Man and later the Re-creation of Woman on earth. All the angels witness the Father of Creation telling his creatures the best way to live, what to eat and to not eat, since their flesh is a living, pulsating form of matter, made from the dust of the earth. They are more aware than the beasts of the field and the birds of the air. This Man and this Woman are created a little less than the angels. God names the Man, Adam, meaning "Man from the red earth." God names the Woman, Eve, meaning "Life." In time God reveals his name, Jehovah, meaning "He who causes to become." Through it all there is Love.

"Misuse of free will continues to give birth to ego, sparking unbridled pride in some of the angels. The rebellion in heaven has started to take shape with Satan at the helm. The rivalry is born, fueled by jealously, envy, misguided pride, anger and all negative emotion, but only in some of the angels. Most of the angels remain faithful to Jehovah God. For the impressionable angels duped by Satan, rather than dismiss the misguided thoughts, these angels foster them, giving birth to sin. The improper desire of wanting to be worshipped instead of worshipping Jehovah who created them, feeds their lust to be sovereign rulers themselves. Lesser angels follow Satan's lead rather than worship Jehovah. The first born Son before all other Creation and the angels choosing to follow Jehovah, are saddened at the depravity of their angelic family members with which they once shared so much love and creativity. Through it all there is Love.

"What is intended for beauty, magnanimity, integrity and generosity becomes twisted by these demonic angels for selfish pursuits. All of the angels watch as the birth of mal, which means evil, takes root in their intentions. Now they must make a choice of their own. Do they follow the sovereign rule of their Creator, or follow rival Satan, a creation of the Creator? Through it all there is Love."

Dodanim pauses, looking deeply into the eyes of his crew. He has captured their attention, so he continues.

"Most of the angels choose to think, say and do good things, out of their abundant love. However, about one-third of the angels choose mal and malevolent, malicious desires, challenging the sovereignty of the Father God to rule over his Creation. They reason, with all of their individual and collective powers and free will, they have the right to rule also, since their abilities are so great," Dodanim recounts.

"Through it all there is Love," echoes Brie and Abby.

Captain Dodanim smiles, happy that his crew is enjoying his storytelling.

"God creates the Paradise Garden on earth for Adam and Eve which he intends to be eternal and flourish with nutritious foods from shade trees. God tells Adam and Eve they may eat from all fruit trees in the garden to satisfaction, except from the tree of the knowledge of good and evil. From this tree in the middle of the garden, God tells them they must not eat. After seeing the misuse of free will with some of the angels in heaven, God tells Adam not to eat from the Tree of Knowledge of good and evil, or he will surely die. God treasures free will. This is a test of Adam and Eve's understanding of God's sovereignty. The angels, for the moment, have the ability to go between heaven and earth. Some of the angels revolt against God's sovereignty. What will humankind on earth do?" The captain looks at his crew and smiles.

"Through is all there is Love," Brie, Abby, Aunt Cher and Grammy Rose repeat.

"Now Satan challenges Jehovah's right to rule on earth. Satan lies to Eve, saying that she will not die, rather she will become like God. Satan desires to be worshipped as a god in his own right. The Father of Lies begins his lying crusade on earth. Deceiving humans on earth is not as difficult as deceiving the angels of heaven, since they are with Jehovah every day. Adam falls for the lie too, even though he has walked with God on earth. The lust for self-rule and rebellion is born. Adam and Eve also foster the rebellious ideas instead of dismissing them. The continued fueling of these impure desires, giving birth to sin against God who made them. They knew beforehand the price they will pay, and their children after them." Dodanim stops and looks at his crew.

"Through it all there is Love?" they say with uncertainty.

Captain Dodanim nods.

"Adam and Eve are cast out of the Paradise Garden their Father and the Son created for them. In the middle of the Paradise Garden, Jehovah commissions his faithful Cherubim to guard the Tree of Life, whose fruit is eternal life, by a flaming sword. Now Adam and Eve and all of their future children cannot return, eat from this tree and live forever in their sinful, renegade state. Adam is doomed to toil over the land for food. Eve is to bear children in great pain and anguish. Both of them, and their children after them will also die. The perfect union between God and Man is broken. Innocence is lost."

One last time the captain looks at his crew and responds with them. "Through it all there is Love."

Dodanim takes empties his wine skin with his last swig. Brie, Abby, Aunt Cher and Grammy Rose watch him with wide eyes, waiting for more. At this point, Dodanim brings them to his current time in this genealogical history of the beginning of time.

"Now let me tell you about my family," Captain Dodanim interjects. The wine is kicking in.

"Adam and Eve have a three sons, Cain, Abel and Seth. I'm sure you know that Cain kills Abel, then gets sent away. My great-grandfather, Noah, is in the line of Seth. So is Noah's great-grandfather, Enoch, who walked with God on earth. He is a very holy man and shares many of the ways of God with the family. He teaches Noah how to worship and honor Jehovah God in heaven. Enoch is so pleasing to God that one day God takes Enoch to heaven with him, forever. You must know the story of Noah, and how we are saved saved from the flood," the Captain says.

"Yes. This is a reoccurring theme," Abby says.

"Theme? This is my family lineage. You see, Noah and my great-grandmother Naamah have three sons, Japheth, Shem and Ham at the time of the flood. Japheth is my grandfather, who was on the ark," Dodanim says, proud of this fact.

Brie and Abby get up to stretch their legs and add more wood to the dwindling fire. Grammy Rose and Aunt Cher get up to warm themselves now that the fire is well stoked. The captain continues.

"Great-grandfather Noah told me this family sea story himself. It is handed down from generation to generation. Are you ready for another yarn?" Dodanim asks.

"I have not heard that reference for story in a very long time!" Grammy Rose exclaims.

"I remember you saying that, when I was just a child," Aunt Cher says with a deja vu memory flashing in her mind.

"Yes, more, more," Brie and Abby say, jumping up and down. This adventure sure is an exciting historical trip both girls love.

"Aye, Aye." Captain Dodanim stands with his back to the rock wall, now reflecting heat from the fire.

He takes a couple of drags from his pipe and continues.

"After the flood, Noah grows magnificent vineyards after the flood, since the land was now so fertile. One night when the family is enjoying the wine, Noah becomes intoxicated and falls asleep. During this time, his son Ham violates Noah by an unholy deed in the tent. When Ham brags about this to his brothers, Shem and Grandfather Japheth are shocked, and immediately cover their father with a cloak without laying eyes on him. Noah told Ham he curses Canaan, the result of this unfaithful act done by Ham. Part of their punishment is to be sent away from the rest of the family.

"At the same time, Noah blesses Shem and my father, Japheth. Canaan takes the land bordering the eastern Mediterranean Sea, even though it is cast by lot to Shem. I'm sorry to say Canaan is now known in our family as the first squatter of history, by overtaking this portion of Shem's land. Canaan is cursed by Noah so we do not have much to do with that part of the family.

"My cousin, Nimrod, does not care about his family at all. What matters to him is expanding his empire. He captures the land of Shem and Shem's son Asshur to the north, and overtakes Canaan's land along the shores of the Greater Sea. Grandfather Japheth told us many times how he would rather have his adventures out on the open sea than to deal with the likes of Nimrod. Now we are mariners. We claim this land of Greece clear over to Samothrace and many islands around here. Sailing is our life."

Dodanim draws closer to the fire to throw another log on the red hot embers. He continues.

"Since Japheth is my grandfather and Javan is my father, I am blessed too because of Noah's blessing. We are maritime sailors and claim this beautiful coastland of Greece on the Aegean Sea as our own. We want to get far away from cursed Canaan and his cursed land. All kinds of malevolent living takes place in the land of Canaan," Captain Dodanim says.

"Abby, remember our experiences with Nimrod and the Babylonians?" Brie quietly asks her cousin, mother and grandmother.

"Yes! No wonder Captain Dodanim wants to get away from there," Abby whispers back.

"Satan and his maladjusted angels are still leaving their mark. They do not obey God at all. They misuse the freedom they have between heaven and earth, between the spiritual and the physical. A darker agenda fills the thoughts of these angels. They are in spirit form, not physical. Each of them are created individually. They do not reproduce. They do not mate. They covet this gift to humans that they do not experience. Their ability to go from heaven to earth and donning physical bodies is the cover they need in order to experience mating with beautiful women.

"Mating between angels and women is taking place in the land of Canaan. You should see the ungodly giant beings, Nephilim walking upon the earth. They are a vicious and vulgar lot, with no respect for the God who made them. That's where my cousin Nimrod lives. It suits him well. My family wants nothing to do with Canaan and his land," the Captain interjects into the story of Noah.

Brie and Abby's eyes are as open as their mouths. Aunt Cher and Grammy Rose are speechless. Brie remembers all too well being kidnapped by one of the Nephilim.

"Nimrod claims the fertile land between the Tigris and Euphrates Rivers and beyond. He calls it Babylon. Of course he would build upon the site of the former Tower of Babel. Grandfather Japheth wanted space away from his brothers, and especially Canaan, so he decided to sail the ocean and settled here."

Dodanim eyes his audience. The young and old alike are hanging on every word. They know the geography of the world, but had no idea how the ancient civilizations actually got started. The Captain observes the twinkling stars above, mesmerized by their glow. He is tempted by the success of Nimrod, not by the man himself, but by love his people have for him. They do love Nimrod's new holiday traditions he has started. There always seems to be a party going on, for one reason or another.

Captain Dodanim warms his hands over the fire, thinking how he can integrate Nimrod's idea of creating a pantheon of new gods and goddesses, just for fun. Evidently the Babylonian Empire has the backing of his people, even the common folk. The popularity of these new holidays and feasts, with a touch of fear of retribution, keeps them in line. It is working famously.

Brie and Abby wonder about the captain's story as they stare into the fire. Aunt Cher and Grammy Rose are also soaking in the warmth of the fire, glad that they are now off the ship and done with dinner.

The captain shares new information now with his crew.

"I have just received scuttle-butt from the captain of the boatswain grain vessel that just left the port at Joppa. Nimrod is revolting against the God of Noah because he sent a flood to wipe out all sin by men and angels on the earth. Because of this, Nimrod and his wife Ishtar, are replacing God and the Ten Commandments, with their own gods and goddesses. They are even acting like gods and goddesses themselves. It is catching on like wildfire over there in Babylonia. They are making up their own religion and the people are loving it, having wild parties, feasts; doing anything they want. Nimrod is getting so much more work out of them. They do not realize what he is doing. I think it is a genius plan!"

Captain Dodanim takes off his sailor's kerchief and scratches his head, not realizing he is giving in to temptations from bad angels. He fails to ask God for guidance. Rather than monitor his thoughts as either Enoch or Noah would have done, he ferments these disloyal thoughts. The process of each new manipulation of his thoughts is addictive. The more he continues in this line of thinking, the faster the thoughts come.

"I think this will work. If my long lost cousin can do this, so can I." His *thoughts wander off into the direction of the fire.*

"Did your Great-grandfather Noah ever tell you any stories of the time before the flood?" Brie asks the Captain.

"Aye! Indeed, he did. These stories are real. As fantastic as they sound, they really did happen. Would you like to hear some?" the good natured Captain winks to the girls.

Brie and Abby are up for another good story. Today is a much needed break from their seafaring jobs.

"Back in the day, Great-grandfather Noah said that his Great-grandfather Enoch, pleased God so much in his life that Enoch walked with God on this earth. Can you imagine walking and talking with God?"

"That had to be amazing," Brie says.

"Enoch would sit down with the family, as many as could gather together each night, to learn from him the things God told him. Noah took to heart all that Great-grandfather Enoch told him. Because of this, God wanted to save Noah and his family. Noah's immediate family and his life were so pure. I remember Noah telling us how the animals walked right on to the ark." Dodanim stuffs his pipe with more tobacco and continues.

"Did you know Enoch's son Methuselah is known to be the longest living human to ever have lived?"

"How long did he live?" Abby asks.

"Methuselah lived for nine hundred, sixty-nine years! But not all people were good. Don't forget, since Adam and Eve first sinned in the Garden, we are all prone to sin. Cain even killed Abel. And then there are those angels who came down from heaven. That was a bad plan from the beginning. The mating of two different kinds of creation, is something God never said to do. The women had no choice. They gave birth to giants, like Goliath."

The family shudders upon hearing this, remembering their first hand experiences with Noah. The darkening skies now cast eerie shadows on Dodanim's very expressive face.

"Evil is upon the earth. This is where temptation to do bad things comes from. Every day we need to choose good things over bad, and choose God over Satan. These evil spirits are very real, you know. Have you ever thought about where evil inclinations come from?" Dodanim asks.

"No," Aunt Cher says.

Dodanim takes a deep breath. Unbeknownst to him, he is being influenced by an insidious impulse emanating from a hoard of dark, maligned angels hovering above him. They are quietly working in secret to cover the dastardly seeds of thought they are supplanting. Dodanim is excited to have his creative senses stimulated in this new way. He fuels these foul, tainted thoughts with the energy of focus and mounting unbridled ego. Pride masks his self-willed amnesia, inducing him to forget everything Great-Grandfather Noah shared with his family. He mimics the gods and goddesses of his cousin Nimrod, in his manmade pantheon. His thoughts escape his lips.

"One thing the bad angels like to do is hide the truth of their horrendous schemes from us humans. They like to confuse the issue of good and evil, because if they do, people won't know what to believe. It makes it more credulous not to believe in them at all, making it easier for these evil angels to influence us. At the same time, we are duped into thinking it is our own free will that is affecting our decisions. Oh, don't get me wrong. People make their own decisions all the time. But they are so also tempted and are unaware of that." Dodanim ponders out loud, equally duped.

"Nimrod is a good example of this. I think he is totally influenced by evil. Just look at what is happening in his area of the world. He is inspiring everyone in Babylonia with his outlandish scheme. They do not realize they he is bribing them with fantastic holidays, then over-working them to the bone. The people there do not have a choice. He will kill anyone who does not follow along." Dodanim rubs his chin as he ponders his next move, vacillating between thoughts of good and evil.

"We needn't kill anyone. We will elevate the mind. We will take the story of Noah and the Flood, and create a deluge story of our own! I've been thinking of this for a while now. I think this can really work." He adds more wood to the fire, as he justifies his thinking.

Grammy Rose and Cher share a knowing glance. They already know the long standing tales of Greek Mythology.

"We can say man first sprang up from the earth, just like the tender plants and flowers did. They came from nature, and nature provided homes on earth for them, like caves in the rocks, and under the boughs of the dense forest to protect them from bad weather. We're ocean people, so why not have some of the gods and goddess come from the ocean?" Dodanim slaps his knee, getting excited with every new idea.

A swarm of evil energies darken the thoughts of Dodanim. Brie, Abby, Grammy Rose and Aunt Cher are wary of condoning the promotion of false gods and goddesses, after their first-hand experience at the hands of Nimrod and Ishtar. An eerie sense of doom forebodes them. They remain quiet.

"Imagine this, primitive man becomes tamed by the gods and heroes who taught them to work with metals. In reality, that is just what the fallen angels did. They taught the men war and how to make war tools. The fallen angels taught the women how to accessorize themselves with makeup. We can say our new gods taught men how to build houses and how to become civilized.

"We'll say that over time, primitive human beings became so depraved that the gods resolved to destroy all mankind by means of a flood. Let's give them proper names. We'll say Deucalion, who is the son of, let's make up interesting names here, Prometheus, and his wife, Pyrrha, since they are so strong in the faith, that they are the only mortals saved. Sound familiar?" Captain Dodanim chuckles.

"You can do this?" Abby asks quite surprised to be at the beginning of the fabricated myth.

"Why not? People are really loving this stuff over in Babylon. I will get rich by starting my new religion. People will pay for this stuff I make up," Dodanim muses, adding, "Of course they know the real history of how we all got here. But this fanciful version adds an element of mystery and intrigue. It gives people innovative concepts to celebrate to keep the calendar feasts happy amid the drudgery of work. We will mandate the people to celebrate the new holidays, as a short break from their labor intensive work."

Dodanim keeps going.

"Let's say Deucalion is commanded by his father to build a ship for himself and his wife to take refuge during the deluge. Let's not have it last as long though. We can say the deluge lasts for nine days, after which we'll have the ship land on our Mount Parnassus. And how about this, we'll have Deucalion and his wife consult the oracle of Themis to see how best to restore the human race." Dodanim seems happy with his progress.

Captain Dodanim spends more time in the waning light of the fire figuring out an entire mythical pantheon of gods and goddess, what their special powers are to be, making them attractive enough to be heralded for thousands of years to come.

"This is only the beginning. Nimrod thinks his beloved Babylonia is the spot of Paradise," Dodanim says in a spirit of competition that is now consuming him. "But we can call attention here by saying that the site of Omphalos in Delphi is Grandmother Earth in the form of Goddess Gaia. We'll teach that we need to venerate this spot, and make it be the exact naval of the earth, since we have that magnificent spring that gushes forth from the earth there. But we need more than this idea. I know, we'll make an oracle and call it the Oracle of Delphi. It will have rules, order and a system of devotion and respect.

"Delphi is located in the upper central region of Greece. It will bring people to this most beautiful land. We can use Mount Parnassus as the breathtaking backdrop for the new shrine at Delphi, about one hundred miles north and west of our beloved Athens. This is a good location because we have multiple plateaus and terraces naturally occurring along the slope of Mount Parnassus. Why, we will include a Sanctuary of Apollo along the way. We can make up the story that he killed his mother's enemy, a serpent called Python, when it was taking shelter at the Shrine at Delphi. Sound familiar?" Again Dodanim chuckles, seemingly at his own invention.

"Apollo's story can be that he came here from the sea, of course, as a dolphin, carrying Cretan priests on his back. We'll have him be the son of Zeus and Leto. Let's have Zeus be the son of Rhea and Kronos. They will all have their reflection in the real stories of history. But, why not turn our stories into not only a religion, but also a tourist attraction here. One thing I know is, if you want to catch people's attention, you make up stories. But if you want to capture their minds and hearts, you make up a religion. That will pour people to Greece and be great for our economy." Dodanim is more satisfied with his plan with each passing minute.

"Here's another great concept. Let's have a priestess named Pythia, who Apollo will speak through. She must be an older woman of a blameless life, chosen from among the peasants of the area. That will include more people as "Pythia" needs to be replaced. Older peasant women will be vying for this title. People will be able to come to ask her questions, and Apollo will answer. We'll do this once a year, on Apollo's birthday. Oh, that's a good one!" Dodanim haughtily laughs.

The growing, sinister swarm of rebellious legions of angels are proud to foster the promotion of illicit birthdays. These dark beings offer nothing good in their diversions away from truth.

"The people will have to go through the priests of the temple to ask questions of her. Pythia will bath in this holy fountain, and drink from the holy spring. She will inhale the ethylene fumes that rise from the chasm in the rock where we will build the temple. Those fumes put everyone in a violent trace who breathes them. People will believe that. But, she really will be mentally affected by those fumes, so we will have to have the priests interpret her words for the crowds. If the priests are confused, I'll suggest they use double entendre, to get them out of a bind. She will be speaking loudly enough for the priests in another chamber to hear her." Dodanim pauses for his stream of ideas to catch up with himself.

"We'll dress her in white and have her carry a branch of laurel. Why not have her sit upon a tripod in a sanctum that is closed off from the temple priests. Again, does this sound familiar?" Dodanim is enjoying his own double entendre myths he is fabricating.

"We need sport. Not everyone is into myths and religions. We need physical exercise of some sort to bring competition to Greece. Why don't we begin the Pythian Games, where we will present a laurel crown to the winners of the contests? We can even include young boys able to cut laurel branches from the trees in the temple, to re-enact the slaying of the Python!"

"Wow! I am on a roll tonight," Dodanim thinks, filled with fierce competition against Nimrod.

"There will be temples raised for the various gods and goddesses, and of course, priests and priestesses to serve in them. There will be ribbon cutting ceremonies, fourteen mile long processions on foot or by carriage to the temples, oracles, sacrifices, ritual worship, our own doctrines, and various ages or ranks. Let's not forget the caste systems. That keeps people in order. This is the stuff people love. We will decree generations that are above war, leaving that for the lesser mortals." Dodanim adds smaller pieces of wood to keep the fire going.

Dodanim knows that the city of Delphi sits about a little over nine miles away from the harbor city of Kirrha on the Corinthian Gulf. He makes plans to raise the Sanctuary of the Gods that will be as a beacon to all people who will seek enlightenment.

"It would be good to include that after death, souls go to Hades. That notion also keeps people in line. We'll say that once their human bodies die, their spirits will keep ministering to the living, in a kind of perpetual life. Nimrod is not the only one who can make this stuff up. In that way, no one will be left behind. It sounds comforting, exhausting if you ask me, but comforting to those left behind. Yet the people of earth keep doing evil, so, let's see, we'll have a god called Zeus to let loose the water-courses from above, unleashing his anger to drown out every evil person on the face of the earth, except for Deucalion and Pyrrha, of course. Yes, let it take place like that."

The captain is getting excited as his myths begin to take shape. So many ideas are flooding his mind. Some are conflicting. Soon enough he will settle upon the stories he wants to promote.

"Prometheus will be a Titan, son of … Iapetus, to form man out of clay. Let's promote that Prometheus is chained and tortured by Zeus for stealing fire from heaven and giving it to humankind. Great-grandfather Noah told me angels are made of fire, so there is another analogy for the educated minds." Dodanim ponders for a moment to make sure his stories fit together.

"Then we will need a creature I will call Athena to breathe life into his soul, like God did in real life. We can make this goddess be the daughter of Zeus. Not only that, let's plan to have Prometheus be so full of love for mankind which he has made that he intends to elevate the mind of man, and improve his condition in every way. He will teach them astronomy, mathematics, the alphabet, medicine, and one of the more popular ideas, the art of divination."

Dodanim knows everyone is aware that these things aren't real. It is the building of a new culture he is interested in. Greece is growing rapidly.

"Before we are done, we will have hundreds of gods and goddesses, all with different gifts and jobs. We'll have the strength of Hercules and the troubles of Pandora. While we're at it, let's have Medusa, a gorgon, you know, an ugly repulsive woman with hair of snakes. One look at her will turn the onlookers to stone. Why not, God turned Lot's wife to a pillar of salt when she looked back upon the demise of Sodom and Gomorrah."

Dodanim grows tired. Brie, Abby, Aunt Cher and Grammy Rose grow worried.

He forgets taking what is pure and mixing it with what is not, is not God's way. He is sidetracked by his own pride and ingenuity, tempted by Satan and his minions. The idea of creating a new fantasy pantheon comes quickly and easily. The more he acts on these thoughts, the faster they come to him.

Down below, shrieks and screams snap Captain Dodanim back to reality. Flames from an oncoming ship arriving in port seem to be headed straight for his ship. Some of his crew beat the captain to the anchors, while others raise the sails as fast as humanly possible. Brie and the family barely board the ship in time. Dodanim mans the helm, turning the wheel sharply to the left.

The captain commands Brie and her family to assist with the sails. As soon as Brie's sails fly, she spies a lock in the captain's lucky bag, the chest which stows the captain's clothes, but it is in Captain Dodanim's cabin. Time is of the essence. Brie races to the chest with key in hand. Her family is still hoisting their sails. She hopes it works.

"Hey!" yells one of the mates passing by the room at exactly the wrong time.

Brie turns the key.

Click.

Brie finds herself alone in the hidden library. Her cousin, aunt and grandmother are nowhere to be found. There is only one thing to do, turn the key and hope she gets back to the right place at the right time.

Click.

"Hey! What are you doing in the Captain's quarters?" an angry second mate demands.

"I was just ..." her words are buried beneath the boisterous orders of the Captain.

"All hands on deck, NOW! Man the oars!"

The second mate does not wait to obey the captain's orders.

"Out of the room with you!" he snaps.

Brie runs out of the room. Panicked and trembling with legs like rubber, she searches for his family amid the chaos of the ship. Aunt Cher and Grammy Rose have completed raising the sails and are heading for the portside of the ship along with Abby, away from the oncoming blazing ship when they spot her.

"Quick! Over here!" Brie waves her arms wildly in the air.

Abby, Aunt Cher, and Grammy Rose waste no time following Brie into the captain's quarters.

"Stay close!" Brie screams over the loud ruckus of the ship. With trembling hands, she again inserts the key into the lock and turns it.

Click.

Finally they are all in the hidden library, safe and sound at Old Sturbridge Village.

Brie peers into Abby's frightened eyes. The complexions of Aunt Cher and Grammy Rose appear flushed.

"This just proves there is a God," Grammy Rose says emphatically.

"If there is a God, he is mighty cruel!" Aunt Cher says angrily. "I haven't ever told you all how worried I am about the adventures we are having. And who knows where Abe, Greg and Sarah are. No one even knows we are in here. And these adventures!"

"It's OK Aunt Cher. We are all OK. I'm sure Mom is taking very good care of Abe and Greg," Brie says in a comforting voice to soothe her aunt.

Brie has heard her aunt's tirade before. No wonder Abby was so influenced by her mother's atheist belief. It makes no sense to Brie not to believe in God at all.

If creation did begin with a big bang, where did the first two elements, forces or whatever they were, come from? Everyone knows that no one can create something out of nothing. And where did the motion come from? Was it magnetics, or electromagnetics and gravity, or centripetal and centrifugal forces that chaotically banged together? Where did they come from? What kind of coincidence could make any kind of random chaos results in complete order of the universe, the earth or the intricacies of the human body? Brie is flooded by a barrage of burdensome questions.

"Enough of this room. Are you ready? It's my turn." Surprising herself, and gasping family members, Aunt Cher inserts the key hanging from Brie's wrist into *"Constantine and the Roman Empire."*

Click.

CHAPTER 15

SANTA CLAUS, CHESTNUTS AND ABRAHAM LINCOLN

"Ho, Ho, Ho," Santa Claus beckons to a very excited Greg, who is dashing in to Bullard's Tavern faster than the legs of his cousin and mother can take them.

"Wo, Wo, Wo, young fella. You have snow on your shoes. The floor in here is wet and slippery. We don't want you to fall and get hurt," Santa says, as Greg comes up to Santa with a sliding halt.

Greg runs his hands over Santa's soft, white fur on his outfit. Abe and Sarah join him as others fill in the room. The scent of chestnuts roasting over the fireplace welcomes everyone to what is sure to be one of the most enjoyable programs of the night, at least in Greg's eyes. Everyone is seated along benches spread throughout the room.

"There are many stories about me out there in the world today. Some have me confused with other people. I will tell them to you to see what you think." Santa Claus winks has he takes some roasted chestnut out of the fire, and places them on the table in the center of the room to cool.

"When these are cool enough, help yourself to them. Parents, please make sure you test them first, as they stay hot for a while after taking them off the fire."

The parents nod.

"I will start with the oldest stories first. Then, I will tell you the famous stories of St. Nicholas, who was a real bishop in the third century.

He attended the Council of Nicaea in the year 325 AD. I will share with you how some of the people living in Sturbridge Village celebrated, for those celebrating Christmas here in 1830. But not all of them did. Even Abraham Lincoln gets in on the act. Are you ready?" Santa asks the awaiting crowd.

Cheers and applause erupt from his crowd of all ages.

"OK then." Santa takes a deep breath and begins.

"Once upon a time, in the land to the north called Vilhalla, there was a Norse mythological god named Odin with a long, white beard." Santa begins the tale while stroking his own long, white beard.

"Some know him as Wodin. He would fly through the night sky during the winter solstice, right around now. Be on the lookout for his eight-legged white horse named Sleipnir. During his flight, Odin would reward the good children and punish the naughty ones. Has anyone here been naughty?" Santa asks the children with one bushy eyebrow raised.

"No!" the room full of children squeals, with the most innocent eyes any parent has ever seen.

"What a relief," Santa says demonstratively wiping his brow.

"Next we have the story of the Norse god, Thor. Are you ready for another story?" Santa asks assessing his young audience.

Again thunderous applause breaks out.

"The Norse people made up their own gods and goddesses just like all the other cultures. Now, Thor was a god of the peasants and the common people. Norse mythology represents him as a very jovial and friendly, elderly man with a rolly-polly belly. Remind you of anyone?" Santa expressively raises both eyebrows and turns to give the room his round belly profile.

Contagious giggles spread throughout the room. Even Santa laughs.

"Thor's element was fire, and his color was red. Because of this, fireplaces in every home were sacred to him. Don't forget, these myths began in Iceland, where it is very, very cold. Of course Thor liked fireplaces."

Lots of little heads are nodding.

"Now this is the part you might like to know. It was said that Thor would come down the chimney through his element, which is what?" Santa asks.

"Fire!" Greg and his counterparts yell out.

"Correct," Santa says. "Thor was known to drive a chariot drawn by what?" Santa asks.

"Reindeer!" the excited little blonde girl answers.

"No," Santa corrects.

"In this story, Thor rides in a chariot pulled by two white goats named Cracker and Gnasher. Thor successfully fights ice and snow giants, so he becomes known as the yule-god. And of course he lives in his palace in the Northland among the icebergs. BBRR" Santa says crossing his arms and shivering for effect.

"BBRR," the children mimic him.

"Are you ready for another Santa story?" Santa asks his very excitable guests.

"More! More!" they shout.

"And now, for our next legend, we will discuss my many names over the centuries like St. Nicholas, Sinterklaas, Santeclaus, and Christkind. Also, did you know that in many countries, like Germany, I had a companion who helped me?" Santa asks.

"Elves?" Abe asks.

Santa shakes his head. "Not exactly, more like a weird, mysterious sidekick that people know by many such names as Knecht Ruprecht and Black Peter. In the Middle Ages, Knecht Ruprecht appeared along with St. Nicholas. But while St Nicholas was known to give presents like bags of candy, chocolate, gingerbread, peanuts and mandarin oranges, to the children whose behavior was good on St. Nicholas Day, which was on December 6; Knecht Ruprecht would give switches and coal to children whose behavior was bad. Knecht Ruprecht wore either a brown or black robe, or fur. He also had a long beard, and carried a bag of ashes. Like St. Nicholas, he also rode a white horse.

Knecht Ruprecht is also connected in German folklore with Black Peter, because of the soot that covered him from his sliding down chimneys. Black Peter was a lot like the mythical house spirits and elves who were known to punish the misdeeds of children." Santa eyes his young listeners.

"Why?" one young voice asks so quickly that no one knows who spoke.

"This story circulated so parents could maintain order in their homes and in society. These little dark, impish characters were also known as Pelznickle, Ru-Klas, Swarthy, Dark One, Dark Helper, Hans Trapp, Krampus, Grampus, Zwarte Piets, Furry Nicholas, Rough Nicholas, and Julebuk." Santa pops a roasted chestnut into his mouth and chews.

"He is also known as demon, evil one, the devil and Satan. That's what has the people of Sturbridge Village upset in 1830. Why would they want to celebrate anything with the devil?"

"Are you serious?" a surprised parent asks.

"Yes, I am. This is history, not opinion. Let's take a closer look at St. Nicholas. He only enters the Christmas scene in the third century. He is not around at the time most Christmas stories begin. The story most often told about St. Nicholas begins when he is a small boy, about your size," Santa says, pointing his white gloved finger at the boy in the front row.

He smiles.

"Unfortunately, his wealthy parents die. He goes to live with his uncle who is a priest. Later Nicholas becomes a bishop and is known for helping out a poor family with three daughters. They were so poor that they did not have dowries to get married. The night before the first daughter was to be sold as a slave, she had washed her stockings and left them in front of the fireplace to dry. In the morning she found a bag with gold in it. The same thing happened with the second daughter on the next night, and the third daughter on the night after that. They discovered it was Nicholas who saved them from being sold into slavery. He did not believe that people should own people. From then on, he was called St. Nicholas, helper of the poor, and of children.

"Here is another quick story of how St. Nicholas helped a child. The oldest story of St. Nicholas did not become known until well after his death. In the town of Myra, which today is Anatalya in a Province of Turkey, the townspeople were celebrating the Feast of St. Nicholas, December 6. All of a sudden, a band of Arab pirates from Crete, the largest of the Greek islands, came into the district, stealing treasures from the Church of St. Nicholas, to take as booty. As they were leaving, they kidnapped a young boy named Basilios, and brought him to their king to make him a slave.

"The Arab king chose Basilios to be his personal cupbearer, because he did not know the language, and would not know what the ruler was saying to those around him. Basilios did this job for a whole year, while his mother grieved for him and missed him very much, especially since he was her only child. As the next Feast of St. Nicholas Day came, the mother did not celebrate it since it was a day of mourning for her. Instead, she offered prayers for the safety and return of her son.

The children are eager for the story, so Santa continues.

"Meanwhile, as Basilios was doing what he had been doing every day that year, serving the king, he was suddenly whisked away. St. Nicholas appeared to him, blessed him, and brought him back to his home in Myra. He appeared before his parents, still holding the king's gold cup. Sailors took this story across the seas to other lands. This is how St. Nicholas also came to be known as the patron saint of sailors." Santa sits down and eats another chestnut.

"I have just enough time to tell you how all this affected Sturbridge Village in 1830. The story of Christmas began to change in 1821 when a poem mentioning Santeclaus was sent anonymously to New York City printer, William Gilley. In it, the poem based on the stories of St. Nicholas, mentions Santeclaus riding in a sleigh pulled by a single reindeer.

"Then on December 23, 1823, "*A Visit from St. Nicholas,*" or as it is known today as "*The Night Before Christmas,*" was written by Clement Clarke Moore. He was a professor who owned an estate on the west side of Manhattan. His holiday poem was published anonymously in a newspaper in Troy, New York. Moore made radical changes to the storyline. He described the details that were completely new. He moved the gift giving to Christmas Eve, not December 6. He changed the story to having eight reindeer and giving them all names. He even came up with the idea of called St. Nicholas, St. Nick."

Santa Claus is beaming as much as the children and parents are.

"We can all thank American Cartoonist Thomas Nast for my more modern look," Santa says with his arms outstretched.

"Nast was a magazine illustrator, the same one who created campaign posters in 1860 for which presidential candidate?" Santa eyes the older children.

"Abraham Lincoln!" Abe shouts out.

"You are correct," Santa says. "Nast did such a great job with my depiction for the magazine, that Harper's Weekly hired him in 1862. I know it is a little past the time we are portraying, but this information is so amazing. Get this, it was said that Abraham Lincoln himself requested *the* resulting cover, from the Harper's Weekly dated January 3, 1863. It depicts me in my sleigh, which had just arrived at a U.U. Army camp festooned with a "Welcome Santa Claus" sign, and a picture of Santa Claus visiting Union troops!"

Hoots and hollers ring out from the veterans in the room.

"Look at it. I am donning a suit of stars and stripes of the American flag while I am handing out Christmas packages to the soldiers. One soldier is proudly holding up a new pair of socks, a sorely needed item in the Army of the Potomac," Santa says, tapping his chest.

"Nast kept drawing illustrations of Santa Claus every year after that. It is also Nast who gave me my new home at the North Pole, my new workshop, and the many elves who now help me every year!" Santa concludes, a bit tired from the night. The next thing he knows, elves are coming in with trays of cookies for Santa Claus and his guests.

CHAPTER 16

JESUS SPEAKS AGAINST SATURNALIA

In a flash, Brie, Abby, Grammy Rose and Aunt Cher find themselves in a totally unfamiliar place, amid a crowd of people sitting outside on a mountain top. There is a speaker addressing the group. They look at one another in utter amazement. They have brown veils on the heads, and tunics with long shawls. What just happened?

"Isaiah aptly prophesied about you hypocrites, as it is written, "This people honor me with their lips, but their hearts are far removed from me. It is in vain that they keep worshipping me, for they teach commands of men as doctrines." You let go of the commandment of God and cling to the tradition of men. You skillfully disregard the commandment of God in order to keep your tradition."

"Who is this speaking?" Grammy Rose whispers to the woman sitting to her right.

"This is Jesus. I have never heard anyone speak as clearly as he does. I try to follow him wherever he goes, when I can. I never thought of this before. He speaks to my heart," the woman says. "My name is Hannah. What is your name?"

"My name is Rose. These are my grandchildren, Brie and Abby, and this is my daughter, Cher."

Hannah nodded.

"You've got to be kidding me," thinks Cher, shaking her head, "Jesus? Really?"

"He began by talking to the Pharisees, about the extra requirements they added to the law. He also explained how all of us have added to God's commandments by our human traditions, which we keep because we love them so much. Before you got here, he was explaining that Saturnalia often coincided with December 25, which is the birth date of the mystery god Mithra, who we know as the Sun of Righteousness," Hannah says. "We celebrate the god of the cattle, the harvest and the water and the sun which makes it all grow."

"He is telling us that Saturnalia is a godless practice that honors false gods, not something the living God wants us to practice. He is telling us that Mithra is a false god. We celebrate many of the god's celebrations, and also believe in the living God he speaks of. But you know how hard it will be not to practice Saturnalia!" Hannah says in exasperation.

"Why?" Brie asks.

"You do not know this? Do you already not celebrate Saturnalia? Everyone enjoys this merrymaking time, eating and drinking the feast foods and drink sacrificed to god Mithra. We make a feast out of it year after year. It is our grandest celebration. It is a most delicious time of year, especially when the harvest is so plentiful. Saturnalia used to be only one day, on December 17, usually the shortest day of the year. But now the Saturnalia festival lasts from December 17-24. We have always celebrated the return of the sun god, so that the harvest is plentiful next year. What's so wrong with that?" Hannah asks.

"But he makes such convincing points," Hannah sighs. "The part I like about Saturnalia is that we give each other gifts, which makes us all happy. Do you do the gift giving?"

"Yes, we do. We love that!" Brie exclaims.

"I like to make things, so I make gifts to give to my family and friends," Abby shares.

"My family does too. It is easier than trying to meet up with the caravans that come through. We live in the outskirts," Hannah says.

"What else do you like about Saturnalia?" Grammy Rose asks in an attempt to keep the conversion off herself and her family.

"I love the whole thing! I love going out and cutting down the evergreens. They make the house smell wonderful. And it looks so pretty, at least before all the pine needles fall off," Hannah chuckles.

"I know what you mean. Between the garland, wreaths, yule logs and the Christmas tree, the needles can make a mess," Aunt Cher says, trying to add to the conversation.

"Christmas tree? What do you mean Christmas tree?" Hannah asks.

"Oh no," thinks Grammy Rose. "How does Cher explain Christmas? Here is Jesus talking. Cher thinks Christmas and the Christmas tree is about Jesus, celebrating his birth. Why are people cutting down evergreen trees and putting them in their houses if they are not celebrating the birthday of Jesus for two thousand years before Jesus was born? But these are too many questions for my brain right now. What do I say to this woman?"

"Oh, it is just a kind of tree we put in our houses," Grammy Rose stumbles.

"We decorate ours with gold and silver ornaments," Hannah says, gliding right over Grammy Rose's thoughts.

The voice of Jesus cascades down the mountain. A quiet hush comes over the crowd as they listen intently.

"Blessed are the poor in spirit, for theirs is the kingdom of heaven.

"Blessed are those who mourn, for they shall be comforted.

"Blessed are the meek, for they shall inherit the earth.

"Blessed are those who hunger and thirst for righteousness, for they shall be satisfied.

"Blessed are the merciful, for they shall obtain mercy.

"Blessed are the pure of heart, for they shall see God.

"Blessed are the peacemakers, for they shall be called sons of God.

"Blessed are those who are persecuted for righteousness' sake, for theirs is the kingdom of heaven.

"Blessed are you when men revile you and persecute you and utter all kinds of evil against you falsely on my account.

"Rejoice and be glad, for your reward is great in heaven, for so men persecuted the prophets who were before you."

"See what I mean? His words have such comfort," Hannah says.

"Wow," Aunt Cher says. "Jesus just said that people who mourn will be comforted, and people who have a mild spirit, will get to live on the earth."

"Isn't that great? Jesus has been speaking a lot lately about the Kingdom of God in the days to come. He has been saying who gets to be with him in heaven and who gets to live forever on Paradise Earth, as God originally intended. The other day he read Psalm 37 to us. It also says that if we trust in Jehovah and do good, we will dwell in the land and enjoy security. Psalm 37 also says that the wicked will be cut off, but that those who wait on Jehovah shall possess the land. Jesus read all of Psalm 37, which ends by saying the meek will also take delight in abundant prosperity. That is so encouraging." Hannah is happy to share this good news with her new friends.

"I am glad I have a mild spirit," Brie says.

"It sure would be nice to have a break from all the trouble that's around." Aunt Cher admits, still feeling the loss of Andre.

Grammy Rose gives her daughter a hug.

Hannah looks up and says, "I see Jesus is finished speaking with us. He just got up and left with his apostles. Our human traditions go back to Nimrod and Ishtar. She pronounces her name as "Easter." Ishtar called herself, "Semiramis, Night Goddess of the Moon." They are the ones who began the human traditions that Jesus is telling us not to go along with. Jesus said the Jehovah is the first and only, living and true God. He does not want us to worship other gods, and does not want us to participate in the ceremonies that are held in honor of other gods. Jesus said God only wants us to worship him," Hannah says.

"It is going to be hard in a way, doing without all the human traditions we have become accustomed to," Grammy Rose considers.

"It makes sense to me, now that I see where the customs come from," Hannah says.

Aunt Cher shakes her head again thinking, "I do not understand what the big problem is since the Christmas and Easter celebrations in the family have always brought such joy."

"The worst human tradition includes killing the first born child in the family, so I can see how the living God of all creation would not like to have anything to do with celebrating a god like that," Grammy Rose signed.

"Before you got here, Jesus said he did not come so all pagans, Gentiles and Jews could continue worshipping in their own ways, or so that we can combine all our beliefs into one. He said that includes false celebrations that honor false gods. Jesus said he came so that everyone could get back to worshiping his Father in heaven, who is also our Father. Not everyone liked hearing that, but I do see his point. Why would the living God want us to honor other gods when we ought to be honoring him? That's why I say he speaks to my heart. I see my husband calling me to come and meet him. I must go now. It was nice meeting you," Hannah continues, smiling.

With that Hannah scurries down the mountainside.

Bewildered, Brie, Abby, Aunt Cher and Grammy Rose stare at one another and at the landscape around them. In an effort to comfort them, Grammy Rose gives them all a protective hug.

Brie feels for the key and lock from the book in the pocket in her tunic. Once Brie had turned the key in the book, the key and lock had come with her. Now she wonders what will happen as she turns the key back.

Click.

The candle light in the hidden library flickers. Grammy Rose unfolds her hug from her family. They all look at each other in amazement. It had happened again.

"That was Jesus. It was really Jesus," Aunt Cher muses.

"Yes Cher. Jesus was a real historical person," Grammy Rose says.

"But he says he is God's Son," Aunt Cher ponders.

Brie closely observes Aunt Cher, along with Abby.

"Jesus said his Father is in heaven," Aunt Cher says quietly.

CHAPTER 17

KING NEBUCHADNEZZAR'S PROPHETIC DREAM

Abe, Greg, and Sarah leave Santa Claus and his delicious tray of cookie, and opt to walk to the Center Meetinghouse while the Victorian carolers the living manger scene. The tall blonde tenor addresses the guests who are walking about the Village going from workshop to workshop. The bell ringers begin ringing their bells loudly, capturing the attention of everyone. The chiming of the bells subsides as the tenor steps forward.

"I would like to have your attention, ladies and gentlemen. Tonight, for your listening pleasure, we have our most esteemed guest of the here with us as we re-create the first Christmas scene. I proudly introduce to you, Father Joseph Mohr, who is the author of the lyrics to the most beloved Christmas hymn, *Silent Night*," the choir director winks in an exaggerated wink.

"Next we will sing for you a popular song that was only composed twelve years ago. The lyrics are written by Father Joseph Mohr, with the melody written by Frans Xaver Gruber. I invited you all to sing along."

Old Sturbridge Village seems to come to an immediate halt, and joins with the carolers in the most beautiful rendition of *"Silent Night,"* that has ever been sung by hundreds of people at once in the Village.

At the conclusion of the song, Abe, Greg and Sarah enjoy a short horse-drawn ride straight to the Center Meetinghouse for the program on how the Roman Empire affects Old Sturbridge Village in 1830.

The bells become silent as the sleigh stops.

"I will leave you for now to begin another tour of our countryside presentations," Clyde says to Abe, Greg and Sarah, tipping his hat. "If you need more rides around the Town Common to go to the Textile Mill or the Cider Mill, the stagecoach is here to help you."

"Thank you very much Clyde," Greg says, hopping out of the sleigh.

By now, some of the people who have been in other workshops along with them are walking into the Center Meetinghouse ahead of them. Four people in particular are familiar to them; the gruff old man, the older professor couple, and the quiet minister they met at the apple cider mill.

"Come on in everyone," orator of the Roman Empire, Giovanni Vincenzo welcomes in a thick Italian accent. Giovanni is fresh from Sicily, in his 1830 persona having arrived as one of America's newest immigrants through Ellis Island last month, with less than two dollars in cash, the clothes on his back, one pint of olive oil, a half peck of hard bread biscuits, Vesuvian wine from Naples, and grape seeds in his pocket to start new vineyards here in this new country.

"I am so happy to be here with you. I think I am one of your newest immigrants," Giovanni shares with his guests as they are finding their seats. "Sicily has been experiencing much suffering from war these past ten years. Some of us, like myself, need a new start. I am a farmer and intend to have much success growing grapes with the seeds I brought from the Old Country, and making wine and jelly for sale."

"Please excuse my accent. It is good that I give you history on the Roman Empire. I am from Italy!" Giovanni flashes his big toothy infectious smile. "America is land of opportunity. Thank the good Lord!"

This guests give him a rousing applause. "Welcome to America!" the soldier wearing his Army uniform says. Old Sturbridge Village gives service men and women discounts to their programs as a thank you for their service.

The gruff man raises his hand to start things off. "History shows that these empires came to power through a great deal of war and bloodshed. They might have been the ancestors of Noah's sons, and God's people, but there is so much war," he says sighing, shaking his head again.

"People's faith gets tried in all sorts of ways; faith in a nation, faith in their own people, faith in themselves, faith in a cause; and even faith in God. Tonight we are teaching what happened in history. It is documented in encyclopedias. History uncovers human understanding and possibilities as archaeological digs unearth the remains of years gone by. They are well preserved in the earth until they are discovered. These older finds teach us, through radiocarbon dating, usually called carbon dating, but also by other means of dating. Since the time of atmospheric nuclear weapons, carbon dating is not always accurate. Sometimes truth in history lies hidden in the layers of strata of the earth, shining a light on knowledge of history," Giovanni explains calmly.

For emphasis, Giovanni says, "As you know, there continued to be intense persecution within the Roman Empire, especially in early Christian times. Diocletian persecuted the Christians to stop the growth of Christianity from spreading. Churches were burned, Christians were killed, and clergy were imprisoned."

"That didn't work though," the male professor states.

"Correct. Don't forget, Constantine was not only remembered for his conversion to Christianity at the end of his life, giving his stamp of approval on Christianity. He was also called Constantine the Great because he was a great warring leader. His troops called him Caesar in Britain in 312 AD. Constantine began a civil war of succession against potential rivals for the throne. You see, his political interests included religion at the end of his life as a way to further his empire. Does anyone know what Constantine is doing at this point of history?" Giovanni asks his captive and interested audience.

It is the woman professor who answers. "Between the year you mention and 324 AD, Constantine is engaged in a series of battles, culminating in the Battle of Adrianople, which is Turkey today. Constantine was a fearsome opponent and defeated all his rivals. It was only then that Constantine becomes the emperor of Rome."

"Does anyone know what happens the very next year, in 325 AD? Asks Giovanni. His guests are keenly listening to every word.

The male professor smiles, transforming his year-long course into a bite-size paragraph for the group. "Well, let's see, Emperor Constantine personally assures the security of the Danube by defeating the Goths, the Vandals and the Samatians. There is no more combat by gladiators in the Roman Empire. The troops conspiring to defeat Constantine within his own empire in Thessalonica are stopped. The leader of the uprising, Licinius, is executed."

"That is all true. Anything else?" Giovanni questions.

The male professor raises his hand.

"You also have the Council of Nicaea, the great ecumenical gathering of all the churches. They came from all countries where Christianity had reached. This council unified what all churches ought to be teaching, especially about who Jesus was, the Son of God," The male professor sits back down, satisfied with his exposition of the facts as he knows them.

"Who was behind questioning who Jesus really was?" Giovanni asks to further engage his audience.

This time it is the quiet minister they met at the Cider Mill who answers. "That was Arius. He was a leading member in the Church of Alexandria. This thinking was called Arianism. Arians denied the divinity of Jesus, being the son of God. Because of this, the Roman Church Fathers came up with the Nicene Creed. It addressed this issue, of co-essential divinity of the Son of God, applying the term co-substantial. The Nicene Creed also alludes to the trinity, but the trinity is a pagan concept. Not many people know that. I think the important part of the Nicene Creed is that it acknowledged that Jesus is God's Son."

"Thank you for expressing that so clearly. Where is the capital of Rome in 330 AD?" Giovanni asks.

"Rome?" Sarah says, not quite sure of the dates.

"No, that is incorrect. He establishes his capital city in Byzantium. Does anyone know where that is today?"

"Is that Constantinople?" the gruff man asks.

"Yes it is. You will notice by this map," Giovanni says, pointing to the large map on the tripod white board, "that Constantinople is strategically located in the east dominating the Bosphorus Straits. He spent four years building his new capital."

"This next question might be a bit trickier. I might need the help of the professors on this one," Giovanni says, sending his broadest smile directly to them. "From the years 361 to 363 AD, we have the Battle of Argentoratum. Does anyone know what this battle has to do with tonight's program throughout Old Sturbridge Village?"

"Let's see," the older woman professor in the wire rimmed glasses hums. "All of the programs tonight are focusing on the various empires, and their relationship to Noah and God. At this point in Roman history, we have bishops and religious leaders holding councils on what Christians should be teaching and believing."

"We also see non-Christian religions growing. Julian is best known for attempting to reinstitute paganism into Rome," the quiet minister says.

"What else is Julian known for at this time?" Giovanni asks.

The male professor who answers. "That would be the Julian calendar. Time has always been tracked, but at different points in history, calendar accuracy was readdressed. Now we go by the Gregorian calendar. But that was only instituted by Pope Gregory XIII in 1582 AD, one thousand, two hundred, fifty-seven years after the time period you are now covering."

"One of the problems people had using different calendars, is that all of Christendom was holding major religious services, like Easter at different times. Part of what the Council of Nicaea addressed was when exactly to hold the Easter services. They were trying to unify Christian practices. They did not realize that Easter is also built on pagan teachings of Ishtar, pronounced "Easter." What Jesus said to commemorate each year was the Memorial of his death to replace the Passover ritual, not his resurrection. But people had been celebrating Easter with all of its springtime eggs, bunnies and chicks, and May Pole for at least two thousand years before that. They simply did not want to let these pagan ways go, so they combined the two celebrations, just like they did with Christmas. God never said to do that," the quiet minister adds.

"Thank you. Those are correct and concise answers. Another council was held, the Council of Constantinople in 381 AD. It further streamlined the profession of faith noted in the Nicene Creed to pretty much what it is today, although it does go through more revisions through the years. It was at this Council that other well-known scriptures which had been included in many Bibles, especially those along the Nile River and at the churches in Alexandria, were tossed out, or burned as uninspired works. Does anyone know what happened to the books they tossed out?"

"Those would be the Dead Sea Scrolls," the woman profession says.

"And the Nag Hammadi Codices," her husband adds.

"Yes. They were deemed to be uninspired by God. The books allowed to stay in the Bible are considered to be inspired by God. Many Christians say the hidden writings in these discarded books have the influence of Satan on them. They are part of that bad seed that should not be mixed with the good seed planted in the Bible we now have. I think God inspired this Council to eliminate them so that truth about God is revealed. These other writings you talk about introduce pagan ideas back into the Bible," the quiet minister explains.

"Thank you for that explanation. That is what the people at the Center Meetinghouse here in Old Sturbridge Village believed in 1830. As my last thought for the night would you say that the Roman Empire was successful as a worldwide empire?" Giovanni asks.

"I'd have to say it worked. The empire concentrated on religion as a way of ruling over the people as much if not more than it did on political and territorial matters. The Roman Empire expanded through fear, through the Crusades. Today in every country there is the Roman Catholic Church. Everyone may live in their own country, but Roman Catholics in every country belong to this empire, if only religiously," Sarah says.

"That's a good observation. Now let me ask you, what do you think about the dream of Nebuchadnezzar of the statue in the Book of Daniel? Why do you think the people of Sturbridge Village in 1830 would be interested in this?" Giovanni asks, leading his guests to their own conclusions.

"The Roman Empire stands for the legs of iron," deduces the male professor. He takes a breath and continues. "Daniel explained to King Nebuchadnezzar that his Kingdom in Babylon is the head of gold. He said it would be taken over by the Mede and Persian Empire is symbolized by the arms and chest of silver. That in turn is to be taken over by Greece, depicted as the abdomen and thighs of bronze. Now we see that Rome conquers the land, represented by legs of iron. The only thing left is the feet made up of clay and iron which do not mix."

"Well done professor," Giovanni says. "Now this is the exciting part. It is what the people of Sturbridge Village figured out in 1830. It is the focus of our entire evening, helping Old Sturbridge Village to celebrate its 70th Anniversary this year. Daniel explained that each succeeding empire was to be more inferior to the previous one, until the last one, clay mixed with iron, which will be the weakest of all."

The quiet minister explains next.

"Daniel 2:44 foretells that in those last days, symbolized by the political system of clay and iron, God in heaven will establish his Kingdom. It will replace the crumbling governments. God's Kingdom will rule over earth and will never be destroyed. This is good news to a tired, working class, business class, and all people everywhere, rich and poor, man or woman, not only in Sturbridge Village, but in the whole world. The Villagers say this verse promises that the Kingdom of Heaven will never be destroyed. No other earthly government will ever take it over. They are figuring out that the final government will rule from heaven, just as Jesus taught in the Lord's Prayer. Many Christians believe this today."

Giovanni agrees. "Not only that, Daniel promises that all other earthly kingdoms, and governments will be done away with. The people of Sturbridge Village are especially happy about this part since it means no more war, no more nation against nation, no more trouble of any kind."

"Can you just imagine a new world of peace, love, hope and joy?" Sarah muses.

"This is what the Villagers are so happy about. We hope you take these happy thoughts home with you as our present to you this holiday season. We truly wish you all the peace, joy, love and happiness your hearts can hold," Giovanni concludes with his mustache framing his smile.

The guests give him a rousing applause for the last presentation of the evening for Old Sturbridge Village staff's hard work, carriage and sleigh rides, warmth of fireplaces, food, drink and song. They file out of the Center Meetinghouse.

Now, where is the rest of their family?

CHAPTER 18

A MISSIONARY VISIT TO THE SANCTUARY OF THE GREAT GODS

There is panic quickly spreading throughout the city of Rome. Merchants bustling by Brie, Abby, Aunt Cher and Grammy Rose, are sharing their concerns with peasants in the streets looking to buy wheat so they can make bread for their families. Adverse wind conditions at sea have shut down the wheat shipments from Africa and Egypt. Not only are the citizens of Rome not able to buy wheat, the merchants are showing a loss of revenue. Chaos is all around them.

"Did any of you turn the key in one of the library books again?" Grammy Rose asks in exasperation.

"I'm sorry Grammy Rose. It was me," Brie answers in a feeble reply.

Aunt Cher quickly pulls Abby out of the way of a team of oncoming galloping horses pulling an empty cart. The driver is apparently angered at the lack of wheat supplies to take home.

Ships heavily laden with wheat usually take three days to sail the three hundred miles from North Africa, across the Mediterranean Sea, to the Roman port of Ostia. It takes even longer, thirteen days, for the wheat-filled ships sailing over one thousand miles from Alexandria to arrive. But that is when the huge ships are able to sail the seas.

"Each of the vessels expected to arrive are carrying at least one thousand tons of wheat. This city alone consumes over eight thousand tons of wheat per week. How are we ever going to compensate?" the baker complains, waiting by the docks for his overdue delivery.

"We will have to shut our doors until the ships can make it to port," another vendor adds.

"There you are!" a drunk fisherman wails, pointing a crooked finger to Brie, Abby, Aunt Cher and Grammy Rose. "Have you finished mending the fishing nets already?"

"No, not yet," Grammy Rose responds quickly. "You see, one of the nets got caught up in these planks of wood. We are spreading them so we can untangle them."

"Be quick about it. I need the nets mended by sundown today. I will be setting out to sea first thing in the morning," Captain Nostrum orders. Their boss is three sheets to the wind, again.

Sleeping in the bow of the fishing boats makes for an interesting existence. Sometimes the rocking boat lulls their exhausted bodies right off to sleep, but other times when the sea is heaving with the waves, it causes seasickness. On these wind-blown nights, when they are docked, they opt for star filled nights on the solid docks on the far edge of the port. It's quite another story when they are out at sea.

"We haven't had bread in a long time. I didn't realize how much I missed it until it was gone," Brie complains.

"At least we have delicious fish fries," Grammy Rose tries to encourage, glad her family enjoys groupers, slipper lobsters, oysters, squid, clams, snails and vegetables.

"My favorites are the dried figs, dates and plums, and the nuts," Brie admits.

"I like the olives, and the pomegranates," Abby adds.

"I must say, I love the wine from the vineyards around here," Aunt Cher says with a smile.

Days of sunshine make this work enjoyable. Serving as fishing hands, keeping the fishing nets and sails mended is good work, and often leads to interesting ocean adventures from time to time. When they are not mending the torn equipment, they are preparing and cooking food for Captain Nostrum.

Nostrum likes his liquor, is a bit rough around the edges, but is grateful to his newly acquired land-lubber fishermen/cooks, making the women wear pants, and hats to hide their hair. He does not need the aggravation of his competition knowing he has women on board. His last crew abandoned him on his last fishing voyage, taking jobs on a larger Egyptian vessel from Alexandria for better wages. Now, with no time left to find a new crew, Nostrum welcomes the newcomers to his boat before other captains hire them. He dubs them Gabriel, Grabby, Rammy and Chet when others are listening.

"We set off for Samothrace as soon as the wheat ships unload," Captain Nostrum says to his eager fledgling crew.

Two weeks later, the vessels finally arrive from their three hundred mile voyage from North Africa. "More grain shipments are due in from Egypt, but if we can be the first to load up the *Navis*, then we will be the first out of port. Help me load the buckets of grain into the ship."

Brie, Abby, Aunt Cher and Grammy Rose, begin their version of a grain bucket brigade, successfully transporting the grain from shore to ship, greatly impressing their captain. Loading the *Navis*, Captain Nostrum's most sea-worthy ship, took all day.

The *Navis* is a tall ship, with a towering main mast topped by a crow's nest. Numerous shrouds hold the mast in place, with horizontal ratlines strung up like rungs on a ladder. The lower and upper sails on the *Navis* are the most impressive sails of any sailing vessel in the Roman Ostia port.

"Make sure the sails are ready to hoist at sunrise," Captain Nostrum orders before he leaves for the night. "Have all your provisions with you. This will be a longer journey, about twelve days, depending on the weather. Samothrace is a fishing island. They won't buy the fish, but they will buy the wheat, dried fruit, olives and wine on board. If you are hungry before the evening meal, you may eat the wheat kernels raw and dried fruit like you always do."

The calm after the storm that delayed the wheat shipment to Rome, finally made for calm seas. Brie likes the calm seas, but not at the expense of no sailing winds.

Captain Nostrum navigates adeptly out to sea in search of the wind, rather than hug the coastline route. He has brought along a few extra hands to man the sails. Brie, Abby, Aunt Cher and Grammy Rose are ambitious and work very well on the net and sail repairs, and definitely as seasoned cooks.

Captain Nostrum knows how to keep a crew entertained at sea during long voyages. Boredom is never a good mix with men. Nostrum's best time occupier is story-telling. However the drunker he gets, the more he turns to song.

"Samothrace, is an extremely beautiful island in the northern Aegean Sea. It has the second largest mountain of all the islands in this region, Mount Fengari rising five thousand, two hundred, and eighty-five feet from the sea. It is much too mountainous for cultivation. The inhabitants here will buy all the wheat on board. But, I need all deck hands on deck to be on the lookout for rocks as we come in. More than one ship has sunk on this very coast," Captain Nostrum says, stirring the will to be on guard, lest they sink as well.

"Lots of stars out tonight Captain. Looks like clear sailing ahead," the first mate answers.

"Aye! Aye! Right you are! Watch the ship as we get closer to Samothrace. It has no natural harbor. It is always a challenge for expert captains, even myself. I find the best landing spot at a self-made port I call Samothraki."

Nostrum loves his visits to this enchanted island, home to the Sanctuary of the Great Gods. They are the latest version of gods and goddess of which the Greek Empire boasts. Each empire to date prides itself on creating a new pantheon. After all, that is what the Babylonians, and every other empire did. As everyone worth his salt knows, the Greek Empire is the greatest of them all. He always fancies himself at one of their religious ceremonies. His tales continue.

"Imagine yourselves at the Sanctuary of the Great Gods. It has some of the most innovative monuments built to the Greek gods and goddesses. This is what you get for joining the *Navis*. You are going to have one of the greatest religious experiences," Captain Nostrum declares, opening his arms wide up to heaven.

"You are going to be in the real presence of the gods and goddesses. You and I know that these stone statues are not real, yet they represent the reality of the gods and goddess of old that do live through them. They are idolized and immortalized through all of history. You know their stories as passed on to you through your mothers and your fathers,"

Nostrum declares, reminiscing the beloved and famous legends and myths his parents passed on to him.

"Haven't seen any gods or goddess in my lifetime," the second mate smirks.

"Then you are in for a surprise. Many famous people are initiated into the island cult. It is said that Lysander of Sparta, and Philip II of Macedon; and most recently Lucius Calpurnius Piso Caesoninus, the father-in-law of Julius Caesar, whose daughter Julia married Pompey, also was initiated into the Samothracian Mysteries. Mind you, slaves and free men worship here. That is within their bounds to do so. Now, this sanctuary is located on the north coast of the island, and will be the first place we visit after unloading this ship," Captain Nostrum informs his crew.

"Are we allowed to go on the island also?" Brie asks, looking at her wishful family members.

"Aye Gabriel, but keep me in sight, not right by my side mind you. Know where I am at all times. The weather comes up and changes quickly in this part of the north Aegean Sea. Be ready to leave at a moment's notice, just in case. The *Navis* sails with or without you." The captain laughs with a hearty laugh.

"The Persians once occupied this island. It is eleven miles long, and sixty-nine square miles altogether. But that was in 508 BC," Captain Nostrum informs. "Now the Athenians control this great isle. Lately I've seen a lot of Roman ships taking an interest here. Keep your head low and do not cause attention to yourself. Everyone just mingles and gets along," Captain Nostrum cautions.

The days and nights ebb and flow into each other, mimicking the waves of the sea. Brie cannot believe how sailing on this huge ship carried by wind, sails and sun has not bothered her family as she had first feared. She enjoys cooking meals with her family during the days. It is simple work they are all used to, and all very good at. The captain and the sailors are pleased with the expert cooking skills she, Abby, Aunt Cher and Grammy Rose have acquired.

Brie loves the tan she and her family are getting. On off times, she passes the time mending tears in fishing lines or sails as they occur.

"Drop the nets here," the captain bellows to his first, second and third mates. Nostrum knows exactly where the fish in this ocean run. When it is time for a meal, they catch what they need, and move on. The shipmates are quite adept with knives, and waste no time in cleaning the grouper for their dinner.

"Can't get any fresher fish than this!" Captain Nostrum exclaims after eating the fish chowder, one of Grammy Rose's specialties.

"Even the girls like fish chowder," Aunt Cher whispers to Grammy Rose.

Twilight brings out ripped sails, nets to be mended, and all hands on deck, except for one of the mate perched high in the crow's nest, always on alert. Captain Nostrum begins another round of god and goddess mythical stories. Brie wonders if Captain Nostrum knows the real origin of these manmade myths.

The next morning they navigate through the treacherous waters, avoiding sharp sunken rocks on their way to the island. When it is safe, Captain Nostrum orders the shipmates to drop anchor and lower the tender that takes them to shore.

Nostrum was not kidding. Landing on this rocky shore is difficult, even for the small tender carrying the eight of them. The shipmates disembark in waist-high water and pull them to shore.

Brie and Abby assist Aunt Cher and Grammy Rose out of the tender and onto land.

Unloading the grain is going to be a labor intensive day. The men take turns going back and forth to the ship, unloading the wheat off the tall ship and into the smaller boat. Brie and her family work tirelessly on shore, piling the wheat high up on the selling rocks assigned to the merchants. A crowd of people comes down to meet the ships, hoping to buy some of this long-awaited wheat. The panic of lack of bread supplies also affects Samothrace as much as it has in Rome.

"Gabriel, you and your family begin selling the wheat to these people. Do not wait. Sell as much as they want. The mates and I will unload the ship as fast as we can," Captain Nostrum orders, winking at Brie. The secret of her being a girl is safe with him.

The day flies by. It is unbelievable how fast the wheat sells. Word must have gone out, or people simply saw the ship come in. By mid-afternoon, their entire ship is sold out, except for what Captain Nostrum saves for his crew for the journey back to Rome. He promises the people he will return with more.

Deciding to keep his ship anchored where it is, the crew climbs up to the road leading to the Sanctuary of the Great Gods.

"I need to stop and rest a bit under this cedar tree and rock outcrop for a moment," Grammy Rose says, waving her hand to the others. She gets tired, more than she likes to admit these days.

"Wait here and keep an eye on the *Navis*. If there is any trouble, send the boy up to me. The Sanctuary of the Great Gods is right up at the end of this road," the Captain says, without looking back.

Brie and Abby are not used to this kind of work; neither are Aunt Cher and Grammy Rose. They rest in the shade of the fragrant cedar tree, eating dried fruits and nuts they stashed in their pockets earlier in the day.

"Look down there!" Brie points toward the *Navis*. Another ship docks in the harbor, but not too close to their ship.

Men make their way off their smaller boat and onto land. Again crowds of onlookers greet them to the island.

"Welcome to Samothrace," some of the local children say, waving hand-picked flowers to their newest guests.

"Hello my young friends," the stranger returns their greeting. "And hello to you too," one of the two men smiles to Brie and her family.

"Where have you come from?" Brie asks, curious about the newest visitor to the Greek island of Samothrace.

"I am from Jerusalem," the stranger answers. "My name is Paul. This is Timothy, who is traveling with me. What is your name? May we sit and rest a while with you?"

"Sure. I am, Gabriel," Brie stutters over the male version of her name. "This is my cousin, Grabby. Over there is Chet, and next to him is Rammy," Brie introduces, making room on the flat rock for her new friends. Brie knows that the new guests do not know they have been pretending to all be males as the crew of the Navis. Other crew from their ship are within hearing distance, so Brie continues to introduce them by their male names.

The other children and their families flock over to them, seeking some shade and rest for themselves as well.

"We are missionaries and are taking our tour into Macedonia. The truth is, I received a dream last night of a Macedonian man standing up here. He was saying to me, 'Step over into Macedonia and help us. That is why we crossed over the Aegean Sea. We put out at Troas and made a straight run to Samothrace,'" Paul explains.

"Are you here long?" the mother of the girl with the flowers asks.

"No. Tomorrow we plan to visit Neapolis. From there, we are off to Phillipi, Amphipolis, Apollonia, Thessalonica, Beroea, Athens and Corinth, before we head back to Jerusalem. We only stay long enough to share our message of Jesus Christ," Paul answers.

"Aren't you the one we have been warned about, the Jewish man who is persecuting the Christians, and now pretending to be one of them? I heard you were involved with the stoning of a Christian named Stephen, and that was not all that long ago." Captain Nostrum's first mate accuses Paul. He is a big and burley man just arriving to double check on the *Navis*.

Brie watches as Paul gestures and looks at Timothy. Brie is close enough to hear Paul quickly pray to God, in the name of Jesus, to give him the right words to say.

"Yes. That is me. But that was before my conversion. Understand this. People were laying their clocks down at my feet. They thought Stephen was speaking against the faith of Moses. They did not understand what Stephen was telling them, or perhaps they did not like what Stephen was telling them. I certainly did not like what Stephen was saying either, nor did I fully understand until after my conversion," Paul says softly.

"That sounds pretty flimsy to me. How can you be trusted?" the hefty first mate demands.

"It is only after my own experience of the Lord Jesus Christ, when I was riding my horse on the road to Emmaus, that I was suddenly struck blind. I regained my sight through the help of a Christian named Annanias. Both of my eyes and my heart clearly saw and understood. I heard Jesus speaking to me, the risen Jesus Christ, explaining that he called me to this work. This is no easy task I have been given. I have been beaten, left for dead and imprisoned. Do you think I would still be doing this if I wasn't truly called by Jesus to serve him?"

The first mate simply looked down to gather up his thoughts, then says, "Exactly what was Stephen saying that got the people so riled up?"

"That is a good question," Paul agrees. "It began when men from here, Cyrenians and Alexandrians, and men from Cilicia and Asia began disputing with Stephen, and making false accusations against him. It seems that when people do not understand, they strike out and make things up to suit themselves."

"Still, I want to know exactly what was said," the first mate insists, flexing his bulging muscles.

"Alright. Stephen angered people when he recounted exactly what Moses did, how God spoke to him at the burning bush, how he went up to Mount Sinai and came down with the Ten Commandments. Moses told the people not to worship other gods. Stephen was emphasizing that point when the group took exception. Many in the group still enjoyed the other gods, their holidays, feasts and traditions. That is also why we come to this island today," Paul says.

"You have come to the island with the Sanctuary of the Great Gods, and many other temples honoring many gods immortalized in them. I am not so sure you and Timothy will be well-received here either," the first mate says, shaking his head.

"We come in peace. We come in love. We come with the truth of the Good News of Jesus Christ, the son of the God of heaven and Creator of all," Timothy says emphatically.

"I wish you well with that," the first mate smirks again.

"Thank you. There always was, is and will be One God, the Father of Jesus and our Father too. He loves you very much. God is eternal. Stephen began to point out to the people that the gods they idolized through their worship of keeping human customs and traditions offends God, who does not like to share his glory with liars and frauds. It's not all the same, based on the whimsical thoughts of humans, worshipping the oak trees, or the evergreen trees and elves, nor can the corruptible god and goddess icons made by human hands compare to worshipping the incorruptible God of heaven," Paul teaches unapologetically.

"Those are strong words on this island," the first mate challenges.

"But don't you want to know the truth?" Timothy asks. He is Paul's best friend and most recent and youngest traveling companion.

Brie, Abby, Aunt Cher and Grammy Rose share glances, keep quiet, and remember their past, first hand experiences, which would not go over well in this foreign land. They admire Paul and Timothy for their bravery in speaking the truth.

"Yes, but we also have free will. Some of us do not will to give up our most treasured family holiday customs, even if they are based on other gods. People are funny about that," a woman says. She is dressed in a fancy yellow tunic adorned with pearls, just now joining the conversation after buying some figs.

"Free will is very important. Without it, our hearts and minds and voices cannot hope to worship the true God. Our Creator did not want us to be puppets, or he would not have given us free will in the first place. No one *has* to worship God. Everyone has the free will not too. But wouldn't it be better to know accurate history? All along, all nations have had a choice of believing in God or not, or believing in other gods or the One True God who Jesus came to earth to teach us about. We are human and make many mistakes in this area. That is why Jesus came, to help us by telling us the truth. But some people have stubborn hearts. Still, God calls everyone. No one ever calling on the name of Jehovah, God's name, will be forgotten," Paul teaches, more in-depth.

The ever expanding crowd listens in awe, waiting for more heart-stirring information.

"What about Stephen?" the first mate asks, growing impatient.

"The problem Stephen ran into, was that no one wanted to use their free will to listen. Instead, we, I am including myself in this, we chose to use our free will to murder Stephen because our ears, minds and hearts did not want to hear what he was saying. His words bothered our conscience. I have been forgiven by Jesus Christ, as are all people who truly repent of their sins and seek his forgiveness.

"Timothy and I are approved by God and are commissioned to preach the good news, so we speak, not to please men, but God, who reads our hearts. We come to you in all gentleness and genuine love to share this good news of Jesus Christ, whose greatest message, more than any other he preached, is about the forgiveness of sins and the coming Kingdom of God, a Kingdom without end, a kingdom of peace, love and gentleness." Paul pauses to let his words sink in.

"This good news we are preaching today is for your benefit, so you pay more attention to the more important things. Timothy and I pray for all of you, that you may take in accurate knowledge and full discernment. We preach about the living God. I encourage you to behave in a manner worthy of this good news. Stand firm in the faith, and in no way give in to the opposition you have on this island with its manmade gods and goddesses that cannot give life. Yours is a faith in the living God, and in his son, Jesus Christ. He came not only to save you from your sins, but also to light the way for you. Your faithfulness means eternal life for you. We are here today, only stopping for a day on our way to Philippi, for anyone who feels so moved to have their sins forgiven in the name of Jesus Christ who is resurrected. You can be baptized in the name of the Father and the Son by the spirit of God," Paul invites. Timothy is already making his way down to the water.

Unbeknownst to Paul and Timothy, the big burley first mate has slipped away during this last part of Paul's teaching to find his friends. There are many people at the Sanctuary of the Gods now who would love to stone Paul and Timothy for such talk.

"Don't laugh," Aunt Cher says quietly to her family, "but after all these adventures and thinking about God, I do want a new beginning. Something about Paul's preaching is touching my heart. I do want to pay attention to the more important things. I have been fooling myself. I can't fight against it anymore. It is too exhausting to stay mad at God. It is lonely too, spiritually I mean. I can't believe this is all there is in this life, for Andre's sake, and for mine." Tears well up in her eyes.

"I know. It is up to you. God knows your heart and sees your struggle. I do know that if you draw closer to God, he will draw closer to you," Grammy Rose says softly to her daughter.

"If Mom wants to be baptized, so do I," Abby whispers to Brie.

"Let's get baptized as adults too," Brie whispers in Grammy Rose's ear.

Brie, Abby, Grammy Rose and Aunt Cher quickly follow Paul to the bay, and are the first to be baptized here in the name of Jesus by Paul. Their hearts are filled with intense love which no words can describe. It is as if their minds are washed in heavenly waves of faith, hope and love. They each take a moment to bask in this newfound spirit of God. They glance up the mountain towards the Sanctuary of the Gods to see Captain Nostrum on his way back down with his crew.

Captain Nostrum motions for them to follow him to the ship. The good captain feels a notable shift in the wind and feels it is time to leave. This is not a good port, especially when navigating strong winds.

Once on board, Brie spots the locked chest of extra sails for the masts. The family agrees at once by voiceless looks and nods.

Click.

CHAPTER 19

NOAH'S CONNECTION

Over in the Welcome and Educational Center, historical exhibits with large, layered, lit maps have been set up featuring the Babylon, Mede-Persia, Greece, and Rome Empires, as well as Anglo-America superpowers. The time period covers from the beginning of time to the present, with a blue star marking the year 1830 CE, showing Old Sturbridge Village in the historical timeline of the Bible.

Headphones are made available at the entrance to the Educational Center. As Abe, Greg and Sarah stand in front of each exhibit, the maps and automated voice comes alive, telling the history of these four empires. The exhibits cover lands as far west as all of Europe, and as far east as the Middle East and parts of Asia. Lands to the south include parts of Africa and Saudi Arabia along both sides of the Persian Gulf; and as far north as the North Sea. The last map in this series, depicts the Anglo-American rise as a world power in 1914-1918 CE, with a map of the entire earth, bringing viewers to the modern day.

Abe, Greg and Sarah step on the yellow circle in front of the Movie Display. The screen comes to life before their eyes, as soft music swells with intensity as the *Creation of Creation* movie unfolds in the headphones worn by all three of them. Amazing spirals of light, color and sound expand into planets, moons, galaxies and universes. They witness the birth of the Milky Way Galaxy and the birth of earth.

A lush tropical paradise garden is beautifully and artfully portrayed. Microscopic organisms as well as enormous animals animate the scene. The Tree of the Knowledge of good and evil in the middle of the garden and the Tree of Life appear in 3D. A computer generated snake in the Tree Knowledge of good and evil depicts Satan speaking in human logic terms about the common sense of making your own decisions in life, as opposed to listening to the Creator. The law of God is diminished into a power struggle of will and ego.

The family is surprised to see a larger than life, brilliant angel standing at the gate of the Garden of Eden. The angel is guarding the entrance to the Garden of Eden with a spinning, flaming sword. If Adam, Eve or their future children dare to come back in the garden and eat from the Tree of Life, it would allow them to live forever in their corrupt, sinful state.

So many people next populate the scene. The ground is hard to till and work is exhausting. Fruit does not easily grow on trees or in gardens. It takes careful planning to water the ground, to make it fertile, and appears that building houses and cities is also extremely laborious. Crime increases, ever since Cain kills Abel. Public safety outside of the Paradise Garden is an issue. People gravitate to their own villages to try to find peace.

Then right before their very eyes, they see angelic beings float down from the sky, beautiful in the light that emanates from each of them, entering the houses of the humans. Next they see fifteen foot tall giants bullying the humans, and creating even more evil, breaking more laws, with little care of the land or the people. No rules apply to them. The people live in fear.

Generations go by, then Noah appears, building an ark with his three sons. Their wives gather seeds and plants, but it looks like this project takes at least fifty years, by the aging of the people. Building the ark is no easy task. The lawless people taunt and jeer, but Noah and his family continue listening to God, continue praying and try to get people to repent, and save themselves by turning back to God, which they have obviously forsaken. Instead, all of mankind only tells them what fools they are for believing in an invisible God, for building an ark on dry land, and pointing to all the fun they are missing out on.

Next the display shows the animals coming into the ark is a majestic scene. The animals are peaceful. In no time the ark is full of its human and animal cargo, with the huge door closing by the hand of God. The flood waters come. As they watch, they notice that much of the water is also bubbling up from the ground, almost more than the torrential downpour from the heavens above. The Flood is devastating, destroying every living thing, covering every hamlet and village.

The display changes as new captions emerge.

- Still the rains pour down for a very long time.
- *It rains for forty days and forty nights.*
- *Water covers the earth for one hundred and fifty days.*
- *Three months later the waters continue to go down.*
- *After another forty days Noah releases a raven which comes back.*
- *Noah releases a dove, which comes back seven days later with an olive leaf.*
- *Twenty-nine days after that, Noah opens the door to look out.*
- *Eight more weeks later, the earth was dry.*
- *God then tells Noah they may all go out.*

Sarah totals up all the days mentioned. It amounts to four hundred and twenty days; or one year, one month and twenty-five days.

"That is not the forty days and forty nights like I thought it was," Sarah *thinks.*

The upheaval of the torrents of the deep waters of the earth seem to have unleashed a series of volcanic activity. It appears the island of Atlantis off the western coast of Europe is sinking, while enormous volcanoes all over the planet, from Indonesia, South Pacific islands, and every continent on the earth, suffer the effects of unrelenting volcanic explosions. The ocean waters are so hot that a fog bank rises above them, evaporating into the air, which is also filled with volcanic ash and gasses. The sun cannot penetrate through the aerosols, volcanic particles that blanket the earth, as if protecting it from the heat of the sun. The earth is getting colder. The continents cannot recover.

Sarah remembers similar scenes like this in the 1980 eruption of Mount St. Helens in Washington State, when a dark cloud cover, like a dry fog, hid the sun from sight from Washington and Oregon, across Montana and over to the United states east coast. The largest volcano reported in recent times, was in1963, when Agung erupted, an island off the coast of Bali.

The talking display is now showing and telling of the volcano in 1815 in Tambora, Indonesia in the Java Sea, affecting the entire earth for one whole year. It is saying that Sturbridge Village remembers this, since they portray the time 1820-1830, mostly. In Indonesia, in April of 1816, it was called, "the year without a summer," since they had unprecedented cold spells which also froze Old Sturbridge Village as well as the rest of the northeast United States and portions of Canada. It is showing heavy snow falling June 6-8, with the ground freezing solid June 9. The frost not only killed crops that July and August, it also killed animals.

Sarah and the boys are surprised to learn that the volcano that erupted in Tambora shot more than twenty miles high into the atmosphere, and became known as a "stratospheric sulfate aerosol veil." It killed more than ninety-two thousand people.

"Wow. The effects of that volcano did not just stay there. The dry fog they talk about reddened and dimmed the sunlight to such a degree that no wind or rainfall could stop it. It crossed the ocean and came here. I'm glad they are saying that here in Sturbridge Village, they all came together, slaughtered many of the animals so the people did not die as in many other areas. In most other areas, people had to migrate," Sarah thinks. She remembers this was called "The Little Ice Age."

Abe, Greg and Sarah's earphones are saying even Europe experienced the cold that summer. The report is saying that only three years of this type of volcanic activity and weather is enough to start an ice age. It is also saying that without such a worldwide catastrophe such as the global flood, scientists cannot explain through natural causes how the world gets enough heat and aerosols needed to start even one ice age, never mind the many they propose to have happened.

Abe and Greg are enjoying wearing the headsets. They are all progressing through the stations individually, giving them snapshot clips from each era addressed this evening compete with video and sound. As they step up to the yellow tape on the floor before each presentation, the animated video comes to life. Dozens of visitors tonight are enjoying this recap of all the presentations. Some of the older guests attending, with canes and wheelchairs might not have been able to traverse the snow as they had done this wonderful evening, making this last presentation perfect for them. Each workshop of all the empires as well as the one on Santa Claus was included.

The last station highlights Sturbridge Village in 1830. The dramatic scenes of the Underground Railroad are so vivid, they feel as if they are there experiencing the escapes themselves. They see the Panic of 1837, the first banking crisis to hit the area and its effects on the villagers here. And look! There is Abraham Lincoln, before he is president, listening to Daniel Webster and getting inspired. They witness the road repairs that put people to work on the very roads they traveled to get here today. And there is Adin Ballou after he has tried to build his Hopedale commune.

Here comes the Hartford-Worcester Stagecoach system, with a stop right at Stallion Hill Road here at Sturbridge Village. It is mentioned here that Stallion Hill Road used to be called Quinebaug Road, because of the Quinebaug River, and that Old Sturbridge Village used to be called Old Quinebaug Village. But because tourists got so lost, following the river to Connecticut, they changed the street name to Stallion Hill Road, and came up with the name Old Sturbridge Village. John Quincy Adams is in the Stagecoach. Perfect renditions of *"Silent Night"* come to life along with *"The Night Before Christmas."* Not one iota is missing from their glorious night. Even live action video of Southwick's Zoo showing exactly how they got Camille the Bactrian camel and the other animals to Old Sturbridge Village was included. For those missing the apple cider making demonstration, that was included as well.

Hot apple cider complete with a stick of cinnamon, and a slice of orange was then offered to all the guests in the next room. The warm aroma of cinnamon, cloves and hot cider was too much to resist. It seems the perfect place to wait for Brie, Abby, Aunt Cher and Grammy Rose.

Where are they? Abe wonders about the other half of his missing family. He definitely misses his twin when she is not with him.

CHAPTER 20

DOWN THE NILE RIVER

Grammy Rose wakes up in unfamiliar surroundings, finding herself in a hospital bed, surrounded by her family. Brie is taking a turn, reading to her grandmother from one of Grammy Rose's favorite ancient history books.

"Where am I?" Grammy Rose asks suddenly.

"You're awake!" Brie exclaims, with Abby running to her side.

"You're in Harrington Hospital in Southbridge Mom," Brie's Mom says.

"Grammy Rose, can you hear me?" Abby asks excitedly.

"Mom, we are all here. How do you feel? Does your head hurt?" Aunt Cher asks, holding her mother's hand.

"I do have a headache," Grammy Rose replies, feeling the bandage around her head. "What happened?"

"We were at Old Sturbridge Village for the Christmas by Candlelight event they were having. Do you remember?" Brie asks.

Upon hearing all the commotion in her hospital room, the nurse came in, quickly followed by Dr. Shay.

"Well, well, I see you have decided to join us." Dr. Shay smiles warmly. "I have a few questions for you. What is your name?"

"Rose, but my grandchildren call me Grammy Rose," she answers, beaming a broad smile to both of them.

"That's good," Dr. Shay says. "Do you know today's date?"

"That's a bit harder. No, I do not," Grammy Rose replies.

"Let's try this question, how old are you?" the doctor asks.

"A lady is never supposed to tell her age." Grammy Rose winks to her daughters. "But in this case, I'll make an exception. I am sixty-two years old."

"You gave two correct answers out of three questions. That's not altogether bad," Dr. Shay assesses. "You fell and hit your head three days ago. You have some swelling on your left temporal side. We need to run a few tests now that you are awake. You need to stay with us in the hospital a little while longer, at least until the swelling goes down, and you know what day it is. You are mostly out of the woods now."

Dr. Shay holds Grammy Rose's hand in hers, takes her pulse, and observes her breathing, before leaving the room.

"What happened, exactly?" Grammy Rose asks.

"We were at the Gingerbread Contest room at Old Sturbridge Village. We were rushing to the table by the mantle, but somehow you slipped and hit your head on the mantle. We could not wake you up, so they called 911. The ambulance brought you here. Do you remember any of that?" Brie asks.

"No, I don't. The last thing I remember is smelling the wonderful aroma of gingerbread, frosting and orange candies," Grammy Rose reminisces. "And I think I also smelled coffee, but that is it until now."

"I brought your favorite books to read to you. I was hoping that something would sound familiar, and you would wake up," Brie says. Her plan worked.

"I do remember we had a great day together, the day we went to Old Sturbridge Village, and the Christmas by Candlelight Dinner was fun too. Oddly, I also remember some adventures we all had. Brie, you and Abby ate with us. But then Sarah, you, Greg and Abe went on the horse drawn sleigh ride, right?" asks Grammy Rose.

"That's right Mom," Brie's Mom confirms.

"Cher, you, Brie and Abby were with me. We went back in history, I mean, we were really in yesteryear times. We were in the 1830s, and in the Babylonian, Mede-Persian, Greek and Roman Empires. We even went back to the Old Testament time of Jeremiah, King Nebuchadnezzar, and even in Daniel's time. Oh yes! We even went back to Noah's time, and to the time of Nimrod and Ishtar!" Grammy Rose says excitedly.

Brie and her mother look blankly at each other, then back to Grammy Rose. It is Brie who speaks first.

"Grammy Rose, I was reading your Bible to you, the parts that you had book marked. I was also mixing that up with your favorite ancient history books. I was trying to jog your mind on a subconscious level. We all took turns reading to you," Brie says softly, trying not to get her grandmother upset.

"Thank you for all that reading. I think you have helped me figure some things out in the process. It was not like I was asleep. I feel like I was very much awake, but in other times in history. And Brie, Abby and Cher were with me, probably because I knew that Abe, Greg and Sarah were safely all set touring the many presentations by way of Clyde's sleigh ride. Hey! I remembered Clyde's name!" Grammy Rose exclaims.

"We learned a lot too," Brie says. "We all kept reading. I was surprised at how much I didn't know."

"There was a lot of fighting in the history we read, even in the Bible. You and Mom always tell us not to fight," Abe says.

"Grammy Rose, I have a question. Why is it that if God is a God of love, that he destroys cities and people? Doesn't God love everyone? Didn't God create it all, as you say? And what about the "Thou shalt not kill?" commandment," Brie asks. The questions floating in her mind are like puzzle pieces that do not all fit together.

"I used to wonder about the same thing myself. I kept reading and studying the Bible, since this is a God question, to see if I could find an answer. I did," Grammy Rose says.

"What did you find out?" Abe asks, equally interested in this subject, perking up in the hospital setting. Greg is reviving too.

Cher rolls her eyes and sighs out a deep breath, but in the secret of her heart, she has wondered this very same question.

Grammy Rose shares what she has discovered. "For one thing, do you remember how Jesus goes into the desert after he has been baptized by John the Baptist, and is tempted by the devil for forty days and nights?"

"Yes," Brie and the other grandchildren answer in one voice, with the twins red curls bobbing up and down.

"The question is, how could this have been a real temptation to Jesus, if Satan was not real or if Satan did not really have the power to tempt him? The account tells that Jesus had been fasting for forty days and was hungry. Satan tempts him to turn the stones into bread. But Jesus tells Satan that people do not live on bread alone, but on every word of God. Have you ever thought of that before?" Grammy Rose asks.

"Not really," Brie admits, still curious.

"Another interesting point I discovered is that in John's gospel, he says there will be a judging of this world and the ruler of this world will be cast out. Jesus is not saying he will cast himself out, or that Jesus will cast God the Creator out. That means that neither Jesus nor God is the current ruler of this world." Grammy Rose pauses a moment before continuing.

"I never thought of that before," Abby says with wide eyes looking at Brie.

"I think it all goes back to the beginning of Creation, when we first see Satan tempting Adam and Eve. Do you remember what Satan challenged about God?" Grammy Rose knows her grandchildren like deep discussions and enjoy investigating matters in their own minds, rather than merely being talked at.

"Well," Cher says, surprising even herself, "The story is that Satan appealed to their pride. He told them that nothing bad would happen if they ate the fruit of the garden they were told not to eat."

"Yes, and Satan told them they would be like God himself if they ate the fruit of the tree which God told them not to eat," Brie chimes in.

"In effect, Satan is calling God a liar. Satan is also challenging God's right to rule. It is God's sovereignty that has been called into question by Satan. Keep in mind, it is not only humanity at stake with this challenge." Grammy Rose leads them into even deeper theological points to ponder.

"What do you mean?" Greg asks.

"Who else is watching this scene on earth as it unfolds?" Grammy Rose asks.

"The angels! The angels are watching," Brie declares, remembering the choirs of angels in heaven singing at the birth of Jesus in the Bible story her Aunt Cher had read.

"Yes. The challenge has been made by Satan. He says we, all humanity, do not need God to rule us. Satan challenges we have the right to rule ourselves, and that we do not need God, not in our daily lives, not in how the world is run, not ever. So what did God do?" Grammy Rose exchanges glances from Brie and Abby, the boys and her daughters.

Silence.

"Knowing the human mind and the angels' thoughts, God decides to show heaven and earth what it will be like if they use their free will as they wish," Grammy Rose explains.

"I like that God did not take away our free will," Brie says. "I enjoy my freedom."

"So does God. If he wanted puppets, he would have created us without free will. Satan challenged that we do not need God. We have free will to live by God's rule, or by Satan's deceptive rule, and deny God altogether. I think that God is allowing Satan free reign to show all what the world would be like with Satan as ruler," Grammy Rose says.

"Thanks a lot God," Cher mutters in disgust. She has recently been complaining with her neighbors and friends about the state the whole world is in, with global warming, climate change, fracking, terrorism, and the growing concerns of homelessness, world starvation, and especially the obvious increase of earthquakes, floods, tsunamis, record-breaking droughts and out of control wildfires. If that is not enough, she is painfully aware of the political situations in many countries, including the United States of America, with political candidates appearing to be more like heartless and ignorant egomaniacs than competent rulers.

"Why do you say Satan is influencing the earth?" Brie asks, not sure if this makes any sense at all. She also questions the story of Creation, given the information on the science shows on the Discovery and History channels she likes to watch on TV, which she loves. However, now she has real questions. She notices science keeps changing its mind from time to time on "facts." Science has not answered all of his questions. Brie decides to keep an open mind about God, opting for more education in this matter. She feels closing one's mind in any field of study, including religion, is not the way to make intelligent decisions.

"The most exciting book of the Bible I studied is the Book of Revelation," continues Grammy Rose speaking softly to her young and eager, captive audience. "I remember this because it struck my mind so acutely. The part that refers to what we are talking about is found in Revelation, chapter 12, verses 7-9. It says a war broke out in heaven between Michael the archangel and the great dragon, the original serpent, the one called Devil and Satan. In that battle, Satan is cast out of heaven, and hurled down to the earth, and his angels along with him. So the bad angels were also cast out of heaven. From now until the end of time, which Jesus says will come like a thief in the night, Satan is misleading the entire inhabited earth," Grammy Rose concludes, taking a deep breath.

"That sure does explain a lot of things," Cher says.

"God has always warns people of what will happen if they do not follow his directions. He never acts without a warning, like a good parent. Since our first parents sinned, we have this struggle between choosing between good and evil ourselves. I hope that sheds light on your original question Brie," Grammy Rose says.

"I have to say I never thought that deeply about all this before. I certainly never heard it explained that way, either at any Mass I have attended, or at any CCD class I ever took," Sarah says.

"That actually makes a lot of sense to me," Brie says.

Abby nods her head in agreement.

"Brie, there is one more thing I would like to say before I rest. It has something to do with your science questions. As I remember going back to Noah's time, it occurred to me that so many times we humans get caught up in semantics. People use different words to explain the same thing, as if it is different. I think this happens with science, history and religion sometimes. The thought must have come to me as all of you read to me," Grammy Rose pauses for a moment and takes a sip of water before continuing.

"It seems that history reports about the Babylonian, Mede-Persian, Greek and Roman Empires; while the Bible reports about Nimrod, and Noah's sons Shem, Ham, Japheth and Canaan and their descendants. These are not separate times in history. The writings are of the same instances," Grammy Rose says, appearing to be very alert.

"It's very interesting you say that Grammy Rose. I thought of this same thing as we were reading to you," Brie says.

Grammy Rose continues her thoughts out loud. It has been a while since the family has come together, genuinely interested in this subject.

"The same thing goes for the Flood God told Noah that was coming, and the Ice Age that science says killed everything. Genesis 7:11 says that on "that day all the springs of the vast watery deep burst open and the floodgates of the heavens were opened." It does not say that rain only came from the sky. It says that the fountains of the vast watery deep burst open, as in volcanic activity from the oceans," Grammy Rose says.

Her family nods, so she continues.

"I watch the science and history shows on TV and do research myself on these matters too. I've noticed that scientists have tried over forty times to provide an adequate explanation of natural causes that could explain the start of the Ice Age, but they cannot. If you consider what I am saying, and what the Bible is saying, it is clear that these volcanic eruptions could have heated up the water to such a degree that it increased rain and snowfall necessary to start an ice age.

"The continued volcanic eruptions would have put airborne aerosols in the air, in such quantity as to block out the sun, lingering long after the flood that appears in so many histories of people on earth. The lasting effect is that the areas that were once lush tropical gardens became desert. The thing that strikes my mind the most is that without a worldwide catastrophe like the Flood, scientists cannot explain the heat and aerosols needed for even one ice age," Grammy Rose says.

"That's right. We read from the note about this you had in your Bible you were using as a bookmark," Brie says.

"Geology also supports the Flood. There were giant whale fossils found in the middle of the desert, and water deposits found in layers of rock spanning entire continents. The earth is telling on itself, that a huge catastrophic worldwide flood did take place. There are even layers of marine rock, soil and fossils found in the earth's highest mountains, and on elevated continental plateaus." Grammy Rose sinks back into her pillow.

"I never thought to put these two events, the Flood and the ice age, together until now. You've read a lot about this haven't you? Is there any religious question you don't have the answer to?" Brie asks in a flurry of questions.

"I must say, I have always wondered about the point in the Bible where it says that the Israelites were once slaves in Egypt," Grammy Rose answers.

"Why would you question that?" Sarah asks. "Of all things in the Bible, there do not seem to be any questions about that."

"Think of this, do you remember who in Noah's family goes down the Nile River to settle the land?" Grammy Rose's mind seems to be as sharp as ever with this question.

"We read from some of your handwritten notes that it was Ham and his sons, Cush and Mizraim, who go down the Nile River. Your note said Mizraim went down the Nile River and claimed Egypt, and Cush went further down the Nile River and settled Nubia, Egypt. Maybe the Egyptians come from them. We also read that Joseph, Mary and Jesus go to Egypt for a while. The Bible does not say how long they stayed there. Maybe they had more children while they were in Egypt. That would have put more Israelites there," Brie ponders the possibilities.

"Yes. That is my point exactly," Grammy Rose says, reviving a bit. "Maybe the Egyptians are descended from Mizraim, Ham's son. Do you think that is possible?"

"Yes," they all answer in unison.

"Grammy Rose, this is exciting, but you look tired," Brie observes.

"Yes, Mom. Why don't you get some rest now," Aunt Cher says as Dr. Shay comes back in to the room.

"We are all happy she is awake now, but Rose needs to get some rest," Dr. Shay instructs. "We will do some assessments tomorrow.

"Thank you all for reading to me. I feel like I have been on quite an adventure," Grammy Rose says.

"We learned a lot too," Brie says giving her grandmother a hug. "Don't worry, we will take you back to Old Sturbridge Village. They told us to come back. They will give all of us a special tour when you are better. They are leaving the large timeline up for you to see in the Educational Center marking 1830 with a large blue star."

"Sarah and I learned a lot. I don't think either one of us would have taken the time to read all the books that you have if this had not happened to you, giving us the opportunity to read things I would have turned away otherwise. I'm not saying I'm a believer. I still have my doubts," Aunt Cher says, not wanting to tell her mother she feel more like an atheist than anything else at the moment.

"Cher's right Mom," Brie's Mom agrees. "I never would have made those connections on my own. And it was nice to learn it with all of us altogether like this."

"I have some questions of my own," Brie says. "It ties in so much with my recent ancient history class. When you come home, Grammy Rose, can we go over some of it?"

"I'd love to," Grammy Rose says.

"Grammy Rose, when you come home, I'll make a special dinner for all of us. I have discovered I love cooking," Brie says, and gives her grandmother a big hug.

ABOUT THE AUTHOR

The spiritual journey has fascinated Linda Hourihan from childhood to adulthood, affecting every aspect of her working career as holistic health counselor/practitioner, massage therapist, author of The Virtue of Virtues, and former feature writer for *The Milford Daily News* and *Laconia Daily Sun*. She writes a blog, currently highlighting this book, with more than eighty-five thousand, eight hundred worldwide views at **www.lindahourihan.wordpress.com**, and has over 447 followers. Her thirst for Christian knowledge includes the teachings of Jesus in the Bible, and discovering what the Bible really teaches.

Hourihan is the mother of five grown children, and eight grandchildren. While her children were growing up, she was also a foster mother to six additional children, who returned to their homes after their family crises were settled.

She resides with her husband, John Hourihan, author of *Play Fair And Win*, *Beyond the Fence Converging Memoirs*, which he co-authored with Amanda Eppley, and *THE MUSTARD SEED: 2095*.

What about the tradition of Christmas? Ah! There lies the reason for this book.

Printed in the United States
By Bookmasters